To Scott,

I hope you enjoy this story,

and

See the Beetle !

By Steven Sheldon

Best,

[signature]

To Scotti,

I hope you enjoy this story, and !

Best,

For Naomi, a gentle, warm soul whose mindfulness, kindness, and ability to connect endeared her to all.

1

JD strolled into Rosita's Jardin with a natural confidence, smiling and nodding to the restaurant's staff and patrons as if he owned the place. For all I knew, maybe he did. The small iconic establishment would have made a fine addition to his swelling list of other senseless, impulsive purchases over the years.

After removing his designer sunglasses and neatly tucking them into his custom-fit shirt pocket, JD squinted and slowly turned his head like Clint Eastwood sizing up a gunfight. I gave him a few seconds to adjust his vision to the dimly lit room before standing up and waving so he'd spot me at the back-corner table. We greeted one another with the same soulful handshake and brotherly pat on each other's backs that we had given each other since our freshman year in college.

"What's up, Kap?" he said in his familiar upbeat growl.

"Damn, you look nice today . . . even by your standards," I said as I sat back down. "Coming straight from a funeral?"

JD smoothed the front of his gray wool pants that likely cost more than my entire wardrobe.

"Fortunately not. Can you imagine? I'd pay someone not to die while it's this hot." He was joking, but he also meant it. "Good guess, though. I was actually doing my volunteer chaplain work at the hospice."

"You're still doing that?" I said, genuinely impressed. "I thought you were giving that up. Too depressing."

"Nah, it's actually quite enriching work." He sat down across from me. "Marty, nothing's more real and holy than preparing a soul to cross over to the afterlife. You should come with me sometime and experience it for yourself."

I nodded in agreement even though I had little interest in ever doing so. Just because JD had tapped deep into his spiritual side didn't mean I had to follow suit.

He gestured to the table. "What's this bullshit?"

"What? The iced teas or your portfolio statement?"

Before JD arrived, I laid out some financial reports, foolishly thinking that I'd be able to get our lunch off on the serious note we needed.

"Both. Why do you always try to ruin a perfectly good lunch with some pie chart or spreadsheet?"

"Because you pay me to," I snapped. This was a personal record for me, already losing control, and he hadn't been there more than two minutes.

He flagged down the busboy and pointed to his glass. "Let's get some real drinks over here. Talk about a buzzkill! I was having a great day. Let's keep it going!"

Oh God, here it comes.

Our waitress approached from behind JD. He would certainly be distracted by the late twentysomething's big dark eyes, long eyelashes and full lips.

"I see your friend made it." She flashed her bright white teeth. "I'm Bella. I'll be your server today."

I folded my arms on the table, casually obstructing JD's private documents from her view.

JD looked up at her undeniably attractive face and his autopilot charm clicked on just as I expected. "Hi there, Bella." His already deep voice lowered an octave as he locked onto her like a heat-seeking missile.

Years of sitting across a table from clients and prospects made me keenly attuned to body language. Seizing on and reacting to any blink, scratch, twitch, or tilt of the head could mean the difference between a highly satisfied or seriously agitated client. I monitored our waitress for any reaction to JD's appearance and confident demeanor.

"Hi there yourself," she said with a bouncy disposition, already directing the majority of her eye contact toward JD's side of the table. "Are y'all ready to order?"

Boom!

Just like that she was hooked. I'd seen this play out so many times before. JD's charisma, vibe, or whatever you wanted to call it was about to be on full display. Financial business or not, at this point, all I could do was sit back and watch.

JD pushed the tall plastic cups forward. "Bella, my uptight friend here has mistakenly ordered these iced teas. Would you mind bringing us a couple of top-shelf margaritas on the rocks with heavy salt and lime?"

While I rarely, if ever, drank at lunch, JD was always game. His name technically stood for Jacob Daniel, but it was also the nickname he earned in college: JD as in Jack Daniel's.

Any other guy would be at high risk of coming across like a total cheeseball, but not JD. His comfortable demeanor and commanding tone probably had Bella thinking: *Who is this handsome, smooth-talking, margarita-drinking machine with that yarmulke on his head?*

Little did she know, JD was a rabbi at Congregation Beth Am, one of the largest synagogues in Atlanta. As a Jewish clergyman, JD proudly wore a small knitted black kippah that blended into his straight black hair.

Steering JD back once he got moving in another direction was challenging at best, but I had to be agile and play along in order to maintain any semblance of control over our lunch agenda. I'd nurse my margarita and dilute it with copious amounts of iced tea. That way, I'd still be sharp enough to get some work done the remainder of the day. Plus, as assistant coach to my son's basketball team, showing up at that night's practice smelling like alcohol wasn't something I would risk.

Once Bella managed to extract herself from the table, I said, "Jacob, I really want to go over some of this with you today." I pointedly called him out by his given name like I was his mother scolding him for doing something wrong.

"Sure, but before we get into that, can we first agree on how smoking-hot Senorita Bella is?" He rolled the "r"s in "Senorita" and shook his head as if to break himself out of her mesmerizing trance.

It didn't matter that at forty-one, JD was at least ten to fifteen years her senior and a rabbi; he wouldn't see her as off-limits.

I affirmed with a tight smile and a nod. "She's certainly attractive."

"Whoa! The man married for a thousand years can admit it."

"Fifteen."

"Still impressive! You're lucky you found your soul mate the first time around. Anyway, how many times do I have to tell you? I trust you." He waved at the papers on the table like they were meaningless rubbish. "Just make me a lot of fucking money."

His signature line. Whenever I attempted to get into the details of his personal finances, it was always, *"Just make me a lot of fucking money."* He made it sound so easy. He had no interest in what we were buying or selling, our view on the markets, or how his portfolio was allocated. While I generally appreciated the trust he had in me and our financial advisory firm, I actually had an important agenda.

Bella delivered our margaritas and began to take our food order, giving me a little time to figure out the best course of action while JD flirted some more.

After she left, I took my best shot. "Aren't you at all interested in how much money you have left and what we're doing with it?"

He took a huge sip of his margarita, simultaneously dipping a freshly baked tortilla chip into the red-hot salsa.

Of his many talents, peeling back the onion on "the numbers" wasn't JD's strong suit. He was never one to get bogged down in the weeds of anything, especially his deteriorating personal financial position. I had to push harder, even if I risked irking him again.

"Come on, JD, you need to take this stuff more seriously."

"You know what? You're right."

I am?

I stayed silent, not wanting to veer JD off course as he brushed aside the small chip fragments that had collected on the papers and began to study the first page of my presentation. "Let's see," he said, actually sounding serious. "According to this *lovely* pie chart, fifty percent of my portfolio is in US stocks, ten percent in international stocks, thirty-five percent in bonds, and five percent in cash. And the grand total is . . ." He furiously flipped to the last page of the report. "Two million, two hundred and forty-six thousand, two hundred and two dollars. Yep, that sounds about right."

"Sounds about right? Aren't you bothered by the fact that you came out of your divorce with almost five million dollars? And now, less than five years later you're clinging to only two million. All that money you made from that buyout is almost gone, JD. I don't want you to go broke. At least not on my watch."

I hoped my emotional plea might register with him, but I could tell by his shifting eyes that his mind was already moving on.

By most people's standards, Jacob Daniel Aron was still wealthy. However, the multimillions he made from the buyout of the tech company he used to work for had been ravaged by his divorce and years of living large. Now, his nest egg was evaporating at an alarming pace. Sports cars, women, fancy clothes, upscale home, gambling, travel—and that was just part of it. He was also a very charitable guy, finding it hard to turn away anyone asking for financial help. Money just didn't seem to mean all that much to JD, and he never minded parting with it. Nice enough trait for those asking, but as his financial advisor, watching him drain his resources was incredibly frustrating.

"How about we take another shot at putting a budget in place?" I asked, wanting to strike while the window of opportunity was still partially open, knowing full well the suggestion would likely be met with disinterest or worse. The last time I brought up the "B" word, he immediately dismissed the idea. The hatchet I took to his supersized travel and entertainment expenses was a clear nonstarter for him. "Sorry, giving up my Falcons and Hawks season tickets isn't an option." But less spending was exactly what he needed or else he could be staring down financial ruin in the not too distant future. I had to try again.

"Budget? Kaplan, I think that's a great idea."

Wait...what?

"In fact," JD continued as my mind started cycling through all the discretionary expenses we'd agree to slash, starting with the exclusive country club he joined earlier that year. "We need to 'budget' for an immediate withdrawal." He gave me a self-satisfied smile as he gathered the papers off the table, stacked them neatly, and handed them back to me.

"Is that a joke?"

"No, I really do need some money. But it's only temporary," he quickly added, reassuring me it wouldn't be a problem. His straight-faced request was almost comical considering he had just seen all those glossy charts showing his rapidly declining wealth.

It was like someone hijacked my birthday cake, blowing out the candles right as I had taken a deep full breath and was prepared to blow.

"Okay . . ." I exhaled slowly. He probably needed the cash for a down payment on a swanky new Buckhead condo or to add another sports car to his small fleet. I could talk him out of it but needed to better assess the situation.

"How much and when do you need it?"

"Five hundred thousand and next week," JD said matter-of-factly.

The statement hit me like a shovel to the face.

"Next week? Are you serious?" My voice broke like a prepubescent thirteen-year-old's.

"I'm dead serious! I'm chairing a community fundraiser. The event we're planning is going to be awesome."

"*Another* charity event?" JD was always working on some goodwill community project that almost always resulted in him writing a big check.

"Yep. Listen to this . . . Feldstein's performing," he said quietly, turning his head to make sure no one was eavesdropping.

"Feldstein? As in *the* Feldstein . . . like *Feldstein and Friends*?" I whispered back in disbelief. Getting a celebrity of Barry Feldstein's caliber would've represented a pretty stunning feat, even for JD.

"Yep. Arguably the most famous stand-up comedian alive. Can you believe it?" JD said, clearly proud of his accomplishment.

"How on earth did you land Feldstein?" I asked, all discussion of budget gone for the moment.

"Kap, Kap, Kap," he said with a self-satisfied vintage JD smile. "Just about everyone is *available*. It's a matter of price and timing. And if your timing is bad, it's *only* about price. In Feldstein's case, I got lucky on both fronts, which really makes me feel like this is destiny. I managed to get in touch with his booking agent, and Feldstein normally charges over a mil for a private show, but since it's for charity, he'll do an hour set for us for five hundred thou. The only catch is we've got to pay up front even though the event isn't until October, right after the High Holy Days." JD leaned forward conspiratorially. "And get this. According to his agent, he's normally booked well over a year in advance and getting him to do private gigs with such little notice is next to impossible. But apparently some old billionaire was going to have him perform at a surprise birthday party for his young wife's fortieth, but she served him with divorce papers before she knew about the party. Event canceled. Her loss, our gain. Talk about divine intervention, right? I know you're a *value* investor, so I figured you'd especially like that part." He winked.

"That does seem like good value," I said sarcastically. "Bad timing on the wife's part, though. Just to be perfectly clear, how much do you have to pay next week?" I had to make sure I fully understood his request, then decide if I was going to roll over and relent to my client's self-sabotaging wishes once again.

"The whole five hundred. The shul doesn't have that kind of cash lying around, so I'll front it. But, and here's the best part, I'll get it all back as sponsorship money and ticket sales come pouring in. In fact, your firm might want to come in on this deal. Great publicity!" He clearly hoped his plan for repayment would make the whole thing sit better with me.

The reimbursement was, indeed, a material factor to consider, but it hardly eliminated risk from his ridiculous gambit. Feldstein was a draw, but bigtime sponsorship commitments and ticket sales were far from guaranteed.

"And Beth Am's board of trustees is okay with that? Aren't they worried the synagogue will be on the hook for the cash?" My risk-and-return-loving brain was already cycling through all possible outcomes.

"Of course they're not okay. I said I'd sign a waiver that I wouldn't sue them if we come up short. They were fine after I told them that." He casually waved his hand.

You crazy fool.

2

Angela Miller slid the wax paper holding her half-eaten tuna salad sandwich to the end of her desk, clearing space for client file number sixty-three. She was pleased with her progress. Only forty-five more files to go and her audit would be complete.

In just a few hours of meticulous inspection that morning, she already uncovered a variety of minor regulatory violations and deficiencies, documenting each one on the yellow legal pad she always kept by her side.

As chief compliance officer of Kaplan Capital Management, it was on Angela to make sure the firm was observing all industry rules and requirements to a satisfactory level. Given her prior work experience as an SEC inspector, she was well-equipped to identify any threats that posed a non-market-related risk to the firm and its affluent clients.

Upon flipping open the manila folder in the file in front of her on her desk, a newspaper clipping from the *Atlanta Journal* fell into her lap. Angela skimmed the short article, which had conveniently summarized the tragic background history of the clients.

Married twenty-four years, Bernard and Betsy Clausky died in a small plane crash on their way back from a vacation in Montana, leaving behind their twin twenty-year-old sons. The accident resulted from mechanical failure during adverse weather conditions.

How horrible.

Angela casually spun her black ballpoint pen over her right thumb as she dug into the couple's estate documents. She quickly determined that Bernard's mother, Josie, would act as the sole trustee of the couple's assets in the event Bernard and his wife both died at the same time. The Clauskys' only two sons, Danny and Freddie, were the trust's equal beneficiaries. All the pertinent information neatly matched up with the account registration information on file with the bank custodian for the trust.

Step one complete, Angela made a note on her legal pad in her sure, perfect cursive and moved on to step two: ensuring that the correct protocols, as outlined in the firm's policies and procedures manual, had been followed with respect to distributions taken from the multimillion-dollar trust account.

She swung her chair around to face her computer and pulled up the account's transaction history. Since the trust was established a couple of years earlier, a handful of periodic distributions had been made for varying amounts, in addition to the set monthly withdrawals. Angela assumed all the money was used to cover the boys' living expenses. Nothing looked unusual, except a $26,000 payment made a couple of months earlier grabbed her attention. Unlike all other distributions that were deposited directly into the boys' bank account, the $26,000 was made to a third party: Hendrick's Automotive. Angela sat up straight in her chair, scratched her forehead, and took a sip from the Diet Coke can on her desk.

She scribbled a note on her pad then proceeded to check that the withdrawal records had been handled correctly. The dates and dollar amounts all matched those in the account transaction history, enabling her to tick off more boxes on her checklist. As a final step before closing the Clausky file and moving on, she needed to validate that the trustee, Josie Clausky, had authorized all distributions. Angela scanned the electronic forms one last time, finding Josie's name and signature on the bottom of each. Except for the very last one.

The last withdrawal form, the one authorizing the $26,000 payment to Hendrick's, was signed not by Josie Clausky but by Angela's coworker and boss's son: Martin Kaplan.

He can't do that.

In big bold printed letters, she wrote the payee's name, dollar amount, and the words "Martin Authorization??" next to it on her pad.

3

The mix of Rosita's spicy salsa and the reality of JD's half-a-million-dollar Feldstein bomb hit me all at once. Droplets of sweat began leaking out of the pores on the top of my head and dripping down the side of my face and forehead. I took a big swig of my margarita to cool down. Before I could react to JD's statement about being solely on the hook for the event should the sponsorships not come through, two women in their early thirties approached our table.

"Hey, JD, doing a little shul business over some margaritas?" one of them asked flirtatiously.

I smiled and nodded to them politely, then took a nice long look at my watch, hoping they'd catch the universal signal for "we don't have extended chitchat time." They were oblivious.

"What? Margs are kosher!" JD laughed as he stood and gave them both friendly hugs.

The women, who JD introduced as Leslie and Debra, hung around, telling us about their upcoming girls' trip to Italy while I stared on, unable to do anything but fume at how my carefully planned meeting agenda had been obliterated. It didn't help my mood that the mention of their European travel plans made me reflect on my parents, who had just embarked on a trip to Europe. Except theirs wasn't for pleasure. The recurrence of my mother's lung cancer had sent her and my father to Germany, where she would be receiving an experimental treatment.

I saw flashes of Leslie and Debra shopping for purses in Milan mixed with images of my frail mother lying in a hospital bed with an IV hooked to her arm, my father at her side. I thought about Jessica and her being upset with me. Given my dad's extended absence from the office and my mother's precarious condition, I'd told my wife that a summer getaway wasn't likely. She'd told me she understood, but her blank stare and disappointed tone said it all.

I reached for my margarita as some high-pitched laughter from one of the girls snapped me back to the table chatter. I stayed quiet during their remaining conversation in the hopes my awkward silence might shorten the encounter. It seemed to work. The girls walked off a couple of minutes later. However, JD made it clear that my agenda for our working lunch was dead in the water.

"Dude," JD said, watching the two women exit the restaurant. "That Leslie . . . I bet she shags like a minx," he continued, doing a competent Austin Powers impression.

I can't believe he's actually a rabbi.

"I'm shocked you didn't invite them to sit down and join us for a drink," I muttered, not bothering to hide the bitterness in my tone. That's all I needed, for Jessica to hear that I was having drinks with JD and a couple of girls at lunch.

"I was going to, but I didn't want to screw up my chances with Bella," he said, which in a warped way actually made perfect sense.

I was able to hold the line at two margaritas, but the damage was already done. I had a good buzz going, and JD didn't want to talk about anything other than our waitress, the Feldstein fundraiser, and yet another "spectacular" woman he was "mesmerized" with at the synagogue. To think that this was the same guy that saved me from almost dying from alcohol poisoning in college. He found me passed out, face down in my own barf after a frat party. While others walked by, JD showed enough concern to bring me to a hospital. I was forever indebted to him.

When JD went in the bathroom, I finally got a chance to get a market update on my CNBC app. The Dow had basically been flat when I'd left the office for lunch, and it looked like it was holding that way. At least it was a typically dull, listless summer day in the markets, and there was nothing pressing going on at work. Thankfully, Bella brought our lunch over during JD's absence; otherwise, he would have been chatting her up the whole time while my tacos al carbon got cold.

"Shit, did I miss Bella?" JD asked when he returned. In a jarring contrast to his normal mode of speech, he bowed his head, closed his eyes, and quietly said a short prayer in Hebrew before digging into his spinach enchiladas that were topped with a thick layer of greasy melted cheese. After a few bites, he picked up right where he left off.

"I'm telling you, Kap, she was easily top five I've seen at the synagogue—ever. You gotta help me figure out who she is. I can't get her out of my mind. I have this good feeling about her."

Since his divorce from his college sweetheart, JD was a serial dater. He loved women and went through many in search of his "*bashert*, a soul mate." Apparently, this incredibly attractive woman he'd seen at the synagogue during last Friday's prayer services had become his latest obsession. "She was sitting about ten rows away from me. I literally fixated on her the entire service."

He rattled the ice in his now empty margarita glass. "She had this aura. I got so distracted that I forgot the words to the Shema—can you believe that?"

"Wow, that's pretty serious. She must've been unbelievable for you to have totally blanked on the most important prayer in all of Judaism," I said sarcastically.

"I'll say this. From the front she was amazing. But I couldn't get a good read on the rest. I figured I'd get to meet her and check out the full package after services."

"And? Why didn't you?"

"When the service ended, I immediately walked down from the bema platform and started toward her, but then I got cock-blocked by a bunch of congregants wishing me *good Shabbos*. She slipped away before I could make contact. I hope she comes back. Otherwise, I'll never know what could've been."

Mentally numb from the drinking and mindless banter, I felt rudderless, our conversation about his budget now a distant memory. Even so, I somehow suggested, "Maybe she left a prayer shawl behind or something you can use to hunt her down. Like a Jewish Cinderella!"

JD looked stunned for a moment, and then I could almost see the gears physically turning in his head. "Not Cinderella . . ." His eyes perked up. "Bathsheba!"

I wasn't following, but JD was already six steps ahead.

"Maybe you're onto something. I know how I can track her down. You're frickin' brilliant, Kaplan! See, that's why you're my trusted advisor and running that firm of yours."

There was no use in clarifying for JD that I wasn't "running the firm." Officially, I was the director of research, and my dad held the titles of founder and president, at least until he returned from Europe when we were slated to talk about giving me some equity in the firm and more leadership responsibility. I had been hinting at that for a while, and Dad told me he'd address the issue upon their return. Nor was it worth pointing out to JD that I was supposed to be his financial advisor, not his private investigator tasked with chasing down his next illusionary life partner. He was too far gone.

"I'll be sure to keep you posted," he told me as I grinned, pretending to care about what twenty years of friendship with JD told me would become of his latest obsessions. His risky pursuit of a congregant and now this fundraiser idea were just distracting mirages for him. As his friend and financial advisor, it was my job and obligation to protect him. I was supposed to be a line of defense between his emotional impulses and his money. I was failing. He'd likely lose money on the fundraiser and could lose his job if a relationship with a congregant blew up.

"And in the meantime, Kaplan, figure out what you need to do to free up that cash for me. I'll need to wire the money to Feldstein's people by next Wednesday or we risk losing him."

God forbid.

4

My head felt like a greasy, oversized bowling ball. It took a couple of tries before I could fully open my eyes and lift my folded arms off the desk. I tugged the yellow sticky note off my face and wiped semidried drool from my chin. I sat straight back in my chair and slapped both cheeks like they were bongos.

I swung around to face the two large monitors on my credenza and shook the wireless mouse to awaken my computer from its own slumber. I fixated on the clock in the lower right corner on the screen to my right: *4:06 p.m.* The market closed six minutes earlier.

I scanned up to see my screen full of blinking red stock symbols. Red meant losses.

Lots of them.

I hadn't checked the market since returning from my unproductive lunch with JD when our positions had still been flat on the day.

Now, every single one of our firm's holdings was down by a couple of percentage points or more, except for one stock: Lockheed Martin Corporation. LMT was flashing green with a 3.2 percent gain.

I pulled up a program I built that tracked our firm's total assets under management. I reviewed it religiously at the end of each trading day. On that particular day, our clients lost almost $8 million. Eight. Million. Our firm's managed assets now stood at $498.2 million, down from over $506 million that very morning. While 1 percent or greater losses happened fairly often throughout the course of a year, this particular drop stung more than usual. Our firm had just crossed the $500 million milestone for the first time three weeks earlier, and my hope was to never drop below that level again. Half a billion had a nice ring to it. A billion sounded even better. That was my goal. To build a $1 billion firm. According to my calculations, on our current trajectory we'd hit a billion in about four and a half years. If the markets cooperated and we brought in a few whale-size clients, maybe we'd reach it a year ahead of schedule. My dad shrugged my chart and projections off saying, "We do our jobs well, and the rest will take care of itself." I, however, was fixated on it, and the dip pissed me off.

"God dammit!" I yelled, louder than I'd meant to.

Angela knocked twice, then nudged her small head through my partially open office door. "Everything okay in here?"

"Yes, everything's fine," I said wearily. "Sorry, rough day in the market; that's all." Since Dad brought Angela on board, our one-on-one interactions had been limited. She worked down the hall and wasn't on the client-facing side of the business like I was. We were still in that awkward, feeling-each-other-out phase. It had been only a couple of months.

"Well, that happens. I'm sure tomorrow will be better," she said, sounding a bit stiff and tentative but pleasant enough.

"Hope so." I pointedly glanced back at my screen to signal that I wasn't in the mood for company. She didn't immediately retreat. She clutched her legal pad and shifted her feet. Then, she stepped deeper into the office and stood straighter.

"So," she said, more assertively, "when you have time, I'd love to sit down and get some clarification on a few items related to the firm's compliance and trading policies."

Aha. An ulterior motive. It was a vague statement on her part, and the conversation could've gone anywhere had I let it. "I'd be happy to. Let's find some time in the next week or so. Send me a calendar invite."

Her cheery expression wilted a bit.

"Will do," she said, getting the message this time and disappearing like a turtle going back into its shell.

I guzzled the remaining water from the half-drunken plastic bottle on my desk, grabbed the mouse, and started scrolling backward on the headline newsfeed.

It didn't take long to find the cause of the market drop.

•

Bizline News Update: Thursday, June 21, 2:32 p.m. ET

President Pruitt tweets: "Our incredible navy pilots intercept Chinese military aircraft flying off California coast near LA. Dumb move by smart X-Man!! Do you feel lucky? MAKE MY DAY!!!"

Major indexes drop 2 percent. No other comment from White House at this point.

•

Chinese military jets buzzing LA? That would explain a lot. Markets get spooked by geopolitical flare-ups all the time, and Pruitt had been on another one of his tweeting rampages about China. He had an on-again, off-again friendship with China's highly calculating President Xin Yang, who Pruitt nicknamed the "X-Man," a play on the first letter of the president's name as well as his nearly superhero status in China resulting from his Olympic gold medal win in wrestling in his twenties. The relationship had been on shaky ground since the two failed to reach an economic accord at their last summit a couple of months earlier. Plus, there was the market's continual fear that the ever-strained relationship between the two superpowers might lead to an eventual, and perhaps inadvertent, military conflict. This event could be the spark.

Usually, the markets rebounded quickly when it became clear an incident was isolated and wasn't going to escalate, which was almost always the case. Sometimes the markets didn't react at all, like when Russian bombers and fighter jets were periodically intercepted in Alaskan airspace. Old news. But this information, if true, was totally unprecedented. It hit the wires so close to the end of the trading session that there hadn't been time for more clarity on the story. Traders simply hit the sell button. No one wanted to be held accountable if the situation worsened overnight.

A military conflict was good for one thing and one thing only: making money for defense contractors. And no respectable advisory firm would put their clients' entire portfolios in just a handful of military supply companies. If this situation spiraled, our clients would take their lumps like everyone else. For the time being, that appeared to be a low probability event, and being a couple thousand miles away from the action in California, I didn't feel any immediate physical threat.

Sighing, I closed the browser window and turned to my email. I deleted the junk, pausing at a message from the head coach of Ryan's basketball team.

Parents,

I received word that the air-conditioning system at the gym is not working properly. Rather than cancel practice, let's make sure our kids stay well-hydrated. Bring an extra-large cold drink and dress comfortably!!

See you this evening,

Coach Simmons

Ordinarily, I enjoyed the basketball practices with the kids. But this was only a casual summer league, and I certainly wasn't in the mood to suffocate in an eighty-degree gym with a bunch of rank thirteen- and fourteen-year-old boys.

My next email was from Rabbi Jacob Aron, JD's professional alter ego, with the subject line: *"You Rock!"*

Kaplan . . . another successful review meeting!

Thanks for helping me out with the big event! I'll send you wiring instructions next week for the $500k. Don't forget . . . make me lots of f@#king money, bro!!!

Shalom,

JD

P.S. Let me know about KCM's sponsorship. It's a mitzvah!

Firing JD had been a constant topic since we'd taken him on as a client of Kaplan Capital Management—on my recommendation—six years ago. He'd still been married to Tina, whom he'd been with since our junior year in college. Dad couldn't help but notice the erosion of his account over time despite making him good returns in the market.

JD didn't set out to get rich. Rather, it was a function of doing what he did well and being in the right place at the right time. When the tech company where JD had been an early key employee was bought out, I got the "Kap, I hit the jackpot" call. JD and Tina's thirteen-million-dollar windfall made the Arons one of KCM's largest clients. However, following their divorce, Tina moved her half of their money to the firm where her cousin worked, and JD ramped up his spending beginning with the purchase of an upscale high-rise condo and a self-driving Tesla. Now, a few years later, JD's shrinking assets made up less than 1 percent of our firm's total assets under management. Losing a client of JD's current size simply wouldn't be a material event to our firm anymore. However, we took pride in our extraordinarily high client-retention and satisfaction rate. Carefully screening prospects on the front end to make sure they were a good fit with our culture and investment philosophy helped cut down on client dissatisfaction and turnover. We did what we could within reason to keep the tough clients who had slipped through happy, but we had our limits.

Still, showing a client the door was a rarity at KCM. Unhappy clients usually left on their own. The only client we'd asked to leave in recent years was a young, pompous orthopedic surgeon displeased because a stock in his account went down 20 percent almost immediately after we purchased it. While the timing was admittedly unfortunate on our part, our client decided he'd lecture us about how we needed a "better stock-picking process." Dad calmly explained that "short-term market movements are impossible to anticipate" and that we "invest for the long term." When the doctor finally finished his extended rant, Dad looked directly into his eyes and delivered his verdict: "Having the full trust of our clients is paramount to a long-lasting relationship. Since we clearly don't have yours, you should find another firm to manage your funds."

While it would've been nice to end my anxiety over protecting what remained of JD's personal assets, I could never fire him. Nor would I ask Dad to do the deed. Despite his antics, JD was an old friend, he saved my life, and I cared too much to just let him go. And I still held out hope that I could help change his self-sabotaging, financially destructive behavior.

First though, I had to figure out how to get him the five hundred thousand for his Feldstein fundraiser. If it were anyone other than JD, freeing up cash for a withdrawal would have been a task for a junior associate advisor like Sammy.

Instead, I pulled up JD's account and scanned through his holdings. JD wanted to pay himself back once he sold sponsorships from other wealthy synagogue members, but that could take months—if it even happened at all. I needed a plan that made the most sense in case the funds were gone for a while or never returned at all.

Shit.

JD lost almost $30,000 in the market's afternoon sell-off. There was no time to make that money back. Option one was for him to take a margin loan against his current holdings to avoid selling his investments and paying taxes on the recognized capital gains . . . but then he'd have to pay interest on the margin loan. And if he didn't pay that loan off within a few months, the costs would start piling up. Another alternative was to sell down some investments outright, pay taxes on the gains, and take his cash out. A decent option. We could always utilize some of the funds from his bonds and cash positions, which wouldn't stick him with too much of a tax bill. If he ever put the money back in his account—big if—we could reinvest.

Doing this type of analysis, weighing the pros and cons of various alternatives in my head, was where I excelled. Drilling down on the facts quickly, evaluating the merits of various scenarios, and figuring out which direction made the most sense for the client came naturally to me. Usually that was the alternative that either made or saved our clients the most money. That was why they paid us.

Though my energy was returning, my head was still foggy and my mood sourer than that second margarita. I'd come back to this and make my final decision when I was able to think more clearly. The day had turned into a write-off. I detested wasting workdays almost as much as I hated losing money. Which wasn't near as much as I hated this current situation. Normally I'd have used my dad as a sounding board, but this didn't—yet—reach emergency level, the only reason I'd burden him with a work call while he was away with Mom.

My parents relying on a doctor in Germany to save my mom was ironic considering they still weren't comfortable riding in my BMW. As older generation Jews that lost distant relatives in the Holocaust, they still held modern-day Germany responsible for the horrific crimes committed during World War II. But having exhausted all other conventional medical options, they didn't have much choice. I, along with my two siblings, encouraged them to go. Depending on Mom's condition and how well she tolerated the treatment, they would only have to be in the country for thirty days or so. Dad said he needed to do his best to focus on Mom and not get pulled into working while away. I told him not to worry and that I'd manage everything at the office.

Though it was only half past four, a good two or three hours before the end of my normal office hours, I began shutting down my computer, resigned to starting anew tomorrow. With one last glance at my calendar, my mood sank to a new low.

Unfortunately, I had one more appointment left.

5

"Now, where are you hiding my queen?" JD said, logging on to Beth Am's website still on a high from his lunch with Marty, his financial advisor, a short while earlier. He quickly navigated to the saved videos of prior prayer services. As a practice, all Friday night and Saturday morning prayer services in the synagogue's main sanctuary were live-streamed and then archived. For those unable to attend in person, the ability to replay the service had become quite popular.

The view from the camera was a panoramic shot of the sanctuary, like watching a C-SPAN congressional hearing. Anyone standing and sitting on the bema could be clearly identified, but only the tops of the heads and backs of the congregants sitting in the sanctuary were visible.

JD looked at the calendar hanging on his wall and pulled up the last Friday night's prayer service. Unfortunately, while the video was good quality, there was no zoom feature, and if he paused the feed, the picture only got fuzzier. JD put his left index finger on the monitor and started hovering it over the backs of a few brunettes, all with shoulder-length hair sitting about ten rows away from the bema platform. Like this, from the back, any of them could have been his mystery woman.

"Come on, show yourself," he muttered with frustration. "Turn around and talk to the people sitting behind you like everyone else does."

He hoped to find her quickly. Maybe she loved football and would go with him to the Falcons-Cowboys game the following Sunday.

He was about to give up when, toward the end of the service, a few congregants stood. He held his breath as all those in mourning stood to recite the mourner's kaddish prayer. Among the twenty of the roughly two hundred congregants reciting the prayer was a brunette. She swiveled her head, and JD froze the tape. It might have been her, but he was unsure. It was just a side view. He hit play when Dr. Goldstone, a portly man and long-time congregant, swayed to his side and obstructed JD's view from the camera.

"Come on, doctor," JD grumbled, "move it so I can get a good look."

As if the doctor heard him, the doctor plunked straight back down in his seat, giving JD a clear view of the woman.

She was slender, maybe five-five. He peered closer, wanting it to be her. *Damn, she looks good.* After finishing the prayer, the woman finally looked back over her shoulder before returning to her seat. JD paused the tape, getting a clear shot of her face.

Heat flushed through JD's veins. "Bathsheba!"

Shaul is going to love this story.

He made a mental note to be sure to tell his favorite Israeli tour guide all the details about how he tracked down this lovely woman. He flashed back to his trip to Israel several years earlier. It was the trip that catalyzed his spiritual journey and ignited his religious reawakening.

•

After arriving in Jerusalem, Shaul Lesnik walked JD through the ruins of the ancient City of David, captivating JD with a mix of historical facts, fascinating sites, and biblical context along the way.

"This is where your people came from," Shaul explained with his thick Israeli accent, with every "this" coming out like "dis."

He described how King David had conquered the Jebusites. "Before King David, these people lived in the small town on the southern side of the Temple Mount around 1000 BCE." He showed him the remains of the excavated original stone walls of what was thought to be King David's palace.

JD hung on Shaul's every word.

"How long did the Jebusites live here? Did they worship a god? Were they peaceful people?" JD asked his affable, knowledgeable guide. JD stood on the stone path overlooking the site, pointing to the ruins that were purportedly King David's palace. "How many women do you think King David schtupped in this room?"

Shaul laughed. "Of all the years of doing this, I've never had this question before."

"So, over a hundred?" JD followed up, entirely serious.

"Yes, at least." Shaul smirked in amusement. "You know the story of Bathsheba?"

JD perked up. "Bathsheba? No, I don't think so. She sounds sultry. Who was she?"

"The story goes that King David was standing on the rooftop of this palace right around here." Shaul held both hands up to the sky, projecting what was once a palatial landscape. "David looked down on the city below and saw a very lovely woman bathing on a rooftop nearby. He never saw such a woman...so beautiful. So, David sends his assistant to find out who she is and to bring her to him."

"Damn!" JD clapped. "Strong move, impressive!"

Shaul paused, adjusting his cap to keep the late afternoon sun out of his eyes. "She was a married woman named Bathsheba, but that didn't matter to David. Since he is the king, David is used to getting what he wants. One thing led to another . . . Bathsheba gets pregnant, and David sends her back home. He wants to be with her so badly he arranges for her husband, who is a good soldier, to be sent to the front lines of a battle where he will likely get killed. When her husband later dies in a battle, Bathsheba and David get married, and they have a son named Solomon. The future king."

"No shit, Bathsheba was King Solomon's mom?" JD asked.

"Yes, pretty juicy story, right?" Shaul said.

"For sure! Not very cool of David though."

"God didn't think it was so cool either," Shaul said, mimicking JD's American slang. "As punishment for his sins, God didn't allow David to build the first temple on the Temple Mount. That was his son Solomon's opportunity."

•

Now, in his interior office of the synagogue's small administrative wing, JD's heart pounded like mighty King David's. Even fuzzy on the screen, the mystery woman drove him mad. Early thirties, a darkish complexion. Is she Sephardic? Maybe she's Ashkenazi, but just tans well.

His eyes then moved to her left hand. "No ring!" He fist-pumped. "Yes!"

JD imagined himself before her, one hand clutched around her waist and the other tenderly caressing the soft skin of her strong cheekbone. Since his divorce, he had accepted that he and Tina weren't compatible long-term partners. But in the years since, he'd churned through many unfulfilling relationships, looking for an ideal partner with whom he could connect on a deeper level, someone to join him on his spiritual journey.

A warm feeling stirred in his inner soul. She had a certain aura. Might she be his *bashert*, his soul mate? Was it because he'd seen her in a synagogue rather than out at a bar or on some dating app? Maybe. Nonetheless, he couldn't deny the spark and excitement. He visualized their future together. Would she be open to getting married in Israel at an historic temple in Jerusalem? How many children would they have? Would she keep a good kosher home?

JD continued to watch the final minutes of the video. When the service ended, the woman left her row quickly without stopping to chat with the other congregants. She didn't appear to know anyone, at least not well enough to stop and talk to them. He got one more clear shot of her as she moved into the aisle and headed for the exit, but she then disappeared off the screen and the video ended.

It wasn't a glass slipper, but still, this was a clue. Given that he'd never seen her before, and that she didn't seem to know anyone, JD speculated she attended that Friday for the sole purpose of saying the mourner's kaddish prayer. Traditionally, mourners were required to recite the prayer for their departed family member on the anniversary of their passing—the yahrzeit. Yahrzeits were based on the Hebrew calendar, not the regular calendar. Fortunately, Congregation Beth Am kept track of its congregants' yahrzeit dates and notified members so they could attend services to say the kaddish prayer each year.

JD buzzed as he walked out of his office and straight to his assistant's desk, who was editing the shul's monthly newsletter. A congenial divorcee, Susan was in her late fifties and a part-time worker at the synagogue. She helped out with a variety of functions including serving as the assistant to senior Rabbi Borowitz as well as JD, Borowitz's junior associate.

"Susan," JD said grandly, leaning over her desk. "I'm certain that whatever you're working on is really important, but I need to harness your incredible research skills for a special assignment."

"Sure, Rabbi Aron, what do you need?" she replied, immediately putting her papers aside.

He explained his request, suggesting that he needed information about congregants who were remembering or mourning a loved one during that month so he could reach out and get to know their family's situation all the better.

Susan added the task to her organizer. "That's so nice. A call to offer comfort and support is always appreciated by members. I'll get right on it!"

JD returned to his office smiling, already down on one knee, proposing to his soul mate.

6

I walked into the conference room with the numbing effects of the margaritas morphing into a mild nagging headache. The Clausky twins sat next to each other on the far end of our long conference table. They'd dressed up in khaki pants and matching white button-downs and blazers instead of their usual jeans and slogan T-shirts. Pages were laid out on the glass table in front of them. My goals were clear. Be pleasant. Be firm. And send them on their way without releasing any more money from their trust account than necessary.

Danny caught my eyes first. "Hey, Mr. Kaplan, how's it going?"

Going? Actually, it's going to be shitty. Really shitty.

"Not too bad. You know I've told you guys before that you can call me Marty."

"We call you Money Man," Freddie blurted out, which caused Danny to elbow him in disapproval.

I still had trouble telling the boys apart, and their matching outfits only made it worse. Tall, scrawny with light brown bushy hair and hazel eyes. At one point, I thought I noticed a cowlick on the back of Freddie's head, but it was gone the next time we met. The only way I could distinguish between the two was by their demeanor and attitude. Danny was the more assertive of the two, usually speaking first, in complete sentences, and with confidence, while Freddie tended to break up the flow of conversation with unfiltered commentary. The "Money Man" comment was a dead giveaway.

I leaned over the table, shook both their hands, and then took a seat across from them. "Freddie, how's the new car treating you?"

Freddie recently got a new car after his old one was totaled in a rear fender bender. Fortunately, no one was hurt. I personally authorized the $26,000 payment to the dealership. Getting their grandma Josie to sign anything electronically was a challenge, and procuring her wet signature was an even bigger hassle since the senior care facility she lived in was over half an hour north of the city. Besides, she was fine with the purchase when I called her about it, agreeing the Subaru was a reasonably priced, safe, and age-appropriate choice.

"Oh, it's awesome, thanks," Freddie said, briefly making eye contact with me. "Lately, we've really just been walking."

"Walking?" I asked.

A closed-lip smile and look of contained enthusiasm swept over Freddie's face.

"Pretty hot outside to be doing much of that, isn't it?" Between that smirk and the in-person meeting, a whopper of a request was headed my way.

Freddie was about to let it out, but Danny seized the moment. "Yeah, we've been doing some market research for a new venture. We've got a business plan and everything."

And here we go.

"Great, let's hear it." I glanced at the clock, eager to get home, pop a couple ibuprofen, and kick back for a bit before heading to Ryan's hundred-degree basketball practice.

Danny cleared his throat. "Before we show you our business plan, I just want to make sure that whatever we discuss is confidential, right? Otherwise, we'll need you to sign this confidentiality agreement," Danny said, sliding a legal-looking document over to me.

I stifled a laugh, turning it into what I hoped was a professional sounding "Hmm." I couldn't imagine a Clausky idea that I'd ever want to steal. Upon assuming the role of managing director of the firm from my dad, I'd without a doubt be transitioning the boys' account over to our junior advisor, Sammy. But, that was at best months away. In the meantime, I had no choice but to listen and respond to them.

Danny pushed closer the nondisclosure agreement that was clearly nabbed off the Internet.

"Unless you guys are plotting a murder or something illegal, all personal information we discuss is strictly confidential," I assured them since they seemed to fancy themselves the Winklevoss twins, in danger of losing their own "Facebook" to Mark Zuckerberg. "Of course, if it involves a lot of money, I may have to get permission from your grandmother."

Technically speaking, the Clausky boys weren't my clients. Their grandmother, Josie, was. Bernie and Betsy Clausky, the boys' parents, named Josie, the boys' sole living grandparent, as the contingent trustee for their estate. In what was supposed to be the very unlikely event that both parents died before their twin boys turned thirty, Josie would be the one to determine how much money the boys needed to sustain themselves.

Two years earlier, however, the unthinkable happened when Bernie and Betsy's small private jet crashed. They were on their way back to Atlanta from a ski vacation, killing them, the pilot, and the other couple aboard. The plane suffered an unrecoverable mechanical failure and the pilot almost pulled off a miraculous landing on the I-40 just outside Memphis. *Almost* being the operative word. The jet crashed just off the freeway into a rocky embankment, leaving no survivors. Aside from being personal friends of my parents and clients of our firm, the Clauskys were high-profile Atlantans. Bernie was a self-made man, accumulating wealth and notoriety as a personal injury trial attorney. He won a high-profile lawsuit against a large pharmaceutical company that had concealed some detrimental side effects from medication taken for obsessive-compulsive nervous disorders.

Danny and Freddie were twenty-year-old juniors at the University of Arizona at the time of their parents' death. After graduating with degrees in psychology, they moved back to Atlanta and settled into their parents' affluent Buckhead home. Grandma Josie encouraged them to find work, but the twins were not interested in ordinary jobs. They had eight years to go until reaching age thirty when they'd be entitled to half of their nearly ten-million-dollar trust fund, and Josie was getting worried they'd just wait it out.

The boys received a monthly stipend from their trust to cover their bills and provide a little extra for frivolous items. Larger one-time expenses required more thought, paperwork, and authorizations from Josie before the funds would be released. Over the past couple of years, she had given them the occasional additional distribution for travel, home furnishings, and tuition for additional online coursework. Josie wasn't sure if the classes were cover for not getting real jobs or if they were really interested in furthering their knowledge of computer coding.

Josie had told me that she was inclined to just let them have their money as long as it wasn't for something stupid. And there was the rub. Not wanting to have to make the harder decisions, Josie asked the boys to run their one-off requests through me first. If I thought it was reasonable, I'd recommend Josie approve. Danny and Freddie started coming to me directly with surefire ways to lose money—and often.

Danny added another piece of paper to the pile. "I think you'll really like this idea when we tell you about it."

I looked down at the professional-looking formatted sheet, entitled "Business Plan," and containing only four bullet points.

- **Problem:** *How many times has your day been ruined by stepping in a pile of dog shit?*
- **Opportunity:** *Save millions of people from this awful experience.*
- **Solution:** *A mobile app that alerts you to dog shit and other road hazards on streets, sidewalks, and other public places so you can walk and run confidently in your neighborhood.*
- **Cost:** *$30,000 for prototype and launch.*

"You want to build a dog shit detection system?" I asked as calmly as possible, biting back another laugh. Was I being messed with on some reality show?

"Well, technically speaking…it's an app, and it will detect more than just dog shit, but yes," Danny said.

Unsurprisingly, Danny was taking the lead on the pitch. I raised an eyebrow at Freddie, but he deferred to his more articulate brother.

Danny grinned proudly. "Pretty innovative, right? It's hard to believe it hasn't been done already."

"And you've done research to think that there is demand for such a thing?" I asked, figuring the question would at least delay their pending request.

Freddie jumped in for the first time. "Absolutely, that's where all our walking comes in. Every day for the last month, we've walked around a new neighborhood, at least an hour, counting the dog shit and other nasty road hazards you wouldn't want to step in."

"For example, what other things?"

Danny took the lead back from his brother. "Other than dog shit, we found a lot of dead animals, you know, frogs, squirrels, birds, and a couple armadillos."

Freddie interjected. "Don't forget the bird shit and gum."

"I thought I said bird shit," Danny said, annoyed by Freddie's correction.

"No, you said dead birds," Freddie snapped.

I knew the Clausky boys well enough to know when we were about to go off-track. "Okay, I get it."

Danny slid yet another piece of paper over to me. "In fact, on average we found about 4.5 road hazards for every mile."

I looked down and saw a nicely laid out chart with the heading "Market Research" that had 10 days of their research on it.

Market Research

Day	Distance Walked	Road Hazards	Number Detected
1	1 mile	Dog shit, gum, and dead frogs.	6
2	3/4 mile	Dog shit, bird shit, dead squirrel.	4
3	1.5 miles	Dog shit, bird shit, dead bird	8
..	..	..	..
..	..	..	..
Total	32 miles		145
Average			5.7 hazards per mile

These guys are serious.

I wanted to flush out just how much thought they'd put into this. "And how will your app work to map these items?"

Danny played with a loose button on his sports jacket. "Crowdsourcing. Our app relies on a GPS system. Anyone who has it can mark the location of any hazard they come across, which will be logged on our map for that day. Those walking by afterward will hear a personalized alarm sound on their phone if they are about to step in it. Think of it like geocaching, but instead of marking a treasure, you're marking shit."

Despite their sophomoric descriptions of the road hazards, I was impressed by the fact they had done some legitimate primary research, even if it wasn't statistically significant. On the surface it was better than buying Iraqi currency, investing in a friend's indie horror movie, and collecting vintage 1960s televisions to all of which I said a definitive, "No." Who was I to say if anybody would ever use such an app? After all, who wouldn't want to be warned before stepping in a fresh pile of dog crap? But my mind was still hazy from the day.

I looked back at the business plan. "You need $30,000 to develop and bring this app to market?"

"Yes," Danny said, clearly trying to assert himself as the brains behind this venture. "We've already got a preliminary program designed and have been in contact with some coders in India who can get a beta test up and running for $25,000 pretty quickly."

"So, what's the other $5,000 for?"

Danny said, "Online marketing activities."

"And how will this app make money?"

Danny continued, "We think it's an advertising model, but we want to see if the government will pay because they'll want to send the public works over to clean the hazard up after it's reported."

I nodded to give the idea some credence. Emphasis on some. "So, it's a public service project too?" It still seemed out there to me, but I didn't dismiss it out of hand, at least not aloud.

If it flopped, maybe these guys would benefit by having a real failure involving a meaningful amount of money. Perhaps then they'd give up on all these wacky ideas and get some real careers.

"Listen, guys, I see you've put a lot of work into this one." They both squirmed nervously on the edge of their seats. "I'm going to reflect on it. Given the amount of money, I'll have to discuss it with your grandmother." If my non-margarita brain later deemed this idea totally bonkers, I could always use Josie for cover.

Freddie grimaced. "If you have to talk to Grandma, please don't tell her the specifics, or she'll have to sign a nondisclosure, too."

Talking with an eighty-six-year-old grandmother about mobile apps and dog shit wasn't something I intended to do. The reality was, I'd have to decide what to do about this one on my own since Josie explicitly told me she didn't want to be bothered "with their nonsensical requests." On the surface, Josie would likely find their idea to be borderline absurd if she could even understand what they were talking about. While some seniors made a point of keeping up with the latest technology, Josie wasn't one of them. She wouldn't even use email to review financial matters and getting her to sign anything other than on paper was a nonstarter.

I gathered all their presentation materials off the table, but the boys didn't appear to get the hint our meeting was over, so I added, "Guys, thanks for coming in. Let me have some time to stew on it."

Danny crossed his arms across his chest and straightened in his chair. "How long will you need? We want to be first to market!"

I was a bit taken aback as it was more pushback than usual. While I didn't have any idea when I would get around to their request, given their enthusiasm and effort, I was pretty sure I'd be hearing from them soon enough. I was hoping the threat to talk to Josie would buy me some time.

"I'll see what I can do," I told them, getting up from my chair.

Freddie gave his brother a look, apparently looking for a cue if they should keep on me or let it go. Danny pushed his chair back and Freddie followed suit. We were done.

As I walked the boys out of the office, Freddie exchanged a tentative goodbye wave with our receptionist, Elise, who was absorbed in a phone conversation. I glanced at the flat-screen television on the wall in the reception area, noticing the financial news channel now covering the China incident and the subsequent drop in the market. I opened the glass door to our office for the boys, telling them I'd be in touch as I escorted them to the elevator bank.

"Talk to you soon, Money Man," Freddie blurted out right as the metallic silver elevator doors closed in front of them leaving me to stare at my fuzzy reflection.

7

Back in her office, Angela stewed that she hadn't gotten any additional information from Marty that would clear up the Clausky trust authorization issue she had uncovered earlier in the day. Had she still worked at the SEC would he have pushed her off like that? Of course not. But now that she worked in-house, she had to play by a different set of rules.

With a couple of hours left in her workday, she redirected her energy toward another responsibility—cybersecurity. Since hackers and online fraud posed a significant risk to financial advisory firms, the SEC was cracking down hard on firms lacking a robust firewall and satisfactory defense protocols. As part of that effort, Angela periodically tested the strength of the firm's systems by monitoring employee emails to ensure employees were protecting and safeguarding sensitive client information. Employees were forbidden from providing confidential client personal information in an unsecure, unencrypted email. In addition, employees needed to be careful not to allow a crafty cyber thief to penetrate the firm's network. The firm's policy required employees to report suspicious email activity to compliance so they could be evaluated, contained, and neutralized.

After accessing the firm's server, Angela began combing through random emails that had been sent to and from KCM's employees since the last time she did a check a few weeks earlier. At first, nothing looked too interesting or suspect, though compromised and threatening emails sometimes appeared like they were coming from a client's email address when in fact they weren't. Also, criminals often used catchy subject phrases to grab the attention of the email recipient to increase the odds of the email being opened.

One email sent to one of the firm's employees finally caught Angela's eye. The subject line read the odd "Hello, Introduction." Could be a phishing infiltration attempt. Upon further inspection, she determined that it was a harmless note from someone outside the firm wanting to get connected to another friend in the industry. She resumed her search, opening and closing several more innocuous emails. After about half an hour, she was about to shut down her surveillance operation when one more email got her attention.

It was from someone named Charlie Chadwick and sent to her boss, Leon Kaplan, eight days earlier. The subject line wasn't as suspicious as it was intriguing—"Merger Proposal." Angela hesitated a few moments. Was Mr. Kaplan contemplating taking over another advisory firm? An acquisition would mean more work for her, but integrating compliance systems would be great experience. Maybe she'd even get a raise. She perked up. A quick online search for Charlie Chadwick confirmed he was indeed the CEO of an investment management firm in Atlanta named Southern Capital Management. Would Mr. Kaplan get her involved in the due diligence process to assess any compliance-related risks associated with taking over another firm? Surely, he'd bring it up with her when he returned from his trip. Then, she was blindsided by the phrase "$3 billion of assets under management."

Wait, what??

She leaned forward in her chair scratching her chin. A firm of that size could only mean one thing—KCM would be merging into Southern.

Freaking out, she clicked the mouse to open the email even though she knew it could be construed as an inappropriate abuse of her access.

Leon,

Great catching up at lunch last week. I'm pleased that you're finally open to joining us after all these years. I've spoken to our leadership team, and they're enthused about the prospects of a merger. From what you've said, KCM has had some nice growth and would certainly be a great fit with our firm. We will be working on a draft proposal and should have something to you by the time you are back in town next month.

Best regards,

Charlie Chadwick, Managing Partner, Southern Capital Management

"Oh my God," she said, confirming her worst suspicions.

Angela sat stone-faced staring at the screen growing irritated with herself for ever taking the position and moving to Atlanta earlier in the year. Desperate for more information, she continued to search the server for Charlie Chadwick, finding only one other recent email. It was from Leon Kaplan and was sent to Charlie two days after the initial email. This time she didn't hesitate to read it.

Charlie,

Thanks for the note. It's always a pleasure to talk shop with others in the industry. Looking forward to continuing the conversation when I'm back.

Regards,

Leon

Okay, it was noncommittal. But Leon didn't exactly shut the door on the idea either. Was it his way of negotiating, playing hardball to drive up the price? She scoured the "About Us" section of Southern's website. Their executive management team looked impressive including a compliance officer that had been with the firm for over ten years. Her heart sank. At best, Angela knew she stood to be someone's second in command, and at worst, terminated, if this merger went through.

I'm so stupid.

Was she about to get stabbed in the back again? So much for her fresh start and long-term career opportunity.

Just six months earlier, Angela had been in line to become a lead manager in the SEC's high-profile Office of Compliance Inspections, tasked with protecting the public from fraudsters. The promotion would've meant not only more money, but also the opportunity to advance within the organization. However, after her ninth anniversary on the job, a colleague of Angela's tipped her off that her husband, Andy, was getting rather close with one of his team members, also working at the agency. It turns out, he had been taking a young inexperienced female staff member to several out-of-town business meetings and conferences—a fact Andy conveniently left out of his conversations with Angela. Andy's trips with his subordinate weren't just a problem for Angela. His clear favoritism toward his attractive staff member upset several of the group's more senior associates, who felt they were losing out on a highly desirable work experience.

The young staffer admitted to HR she was having an "inappropriate relationship" with her supervisor. Andy was immediately terminated. Angela was devastated. Despite his affair, Andy pleaded with Angela not to leave him, but she never felt so betrayed and embarrassed in her life. She kicked Andy out, hired an attorney, and filed for divorce from her husband of three years. Sadly, her swift action wasn't enough to stave off further personal damage from the ordeal. The drama and embarrassment proved too scandalous and humiliating for Angela to bear, reaching an emotional head when Angela overheard a coworker in her department talking about her, telling another employee that Angela "couldn't even catch a cheating husband, let alone a Ponzi scheme."

She decided that it was time for her to leave.

With her career and personal life tossed in a blender, Angela put her résumé together and started a job search. Soon she was contacted by a recruiter about a chief compliance officer position with a small, growing firm in Atlanta. Intrigued by the opportunity, after a couple of phone interviews, she flew from DC to Atlanta to meet with Leon Kaplan, the founder and president of Kaplan Capital Management. His no-nonsense, practical style impressed her. He expressed that he wanted an experienced professional with real passion for compliance. Someone who can set the right tone and instill the requisite controls to support the firm's growth. A week later, she received an offer letter from Leon, which included financial incentives tied to the firm's long-term performance. Profit sharing was something she would never get working for the government, and it made the opportunity that much more appealing. Eager for a new beginning, she accepted the position with KCM, resigned from the SEC, and moved to Atlanta.

Angela reread the email a few more times, letting the content and repercussions sink in. Had Leon been planning this for some time, long before he recruited her? Was all that talk about growth and opportunity a load of crap, intending her to clean up the files so the firm would look squeaky clean to an acquirer?

Given the dubious way she uncovered the potential merger, she needed to be careful with the information. But going on with business as usual when this was hanging over her would be challenging. What could she do about it?

She rubbed her closed eyes for several seconds. When she opened them, she said, "I can't believe this is happening!"

She began furiously twirling her pen around her thumb while shifting her attention back to her notepad. Scanning her growing list of compliance deficiencies, she zeroed in on Marty Kaplan's name and the unresolved issue related to the distribution from the Clauskys' trust account. She smirked then opened the firm's email server once again. This time she put a filter in place that would automatically forward copies of any email correspondence between the Clauskys and Marty to her.

"Let's see if Marty steps in it," she said to herself before closing down her email surveillance for the day.

8

Leon glanced over at his wife to make sure her eyes were closed before impatiently flipping through twenty-five channels, finally landing on Bloomberg Financial News. He was aware that the markets had tanked from checking his cell earlier in the day but was careful not to stare too long for fear his wife would call him out on it. Leon had committed to not letting the markets consume him while he was away with Sylvia. Even so, was he missing a good buying opportunity? For now, he'd leave the analysis and decision-making to his son, Marty, and investment team back in the office in Atlanta.

The couple arrived in Berlin a few days earlier, spending their time taking short strolls and bus tours around the city, enabling them to adjust to their new surroundings. According to the schedule provided by Dr. Manfred Schmidt's office, they would need to be in Berlin for a full six weeks, perhaps longer, depending on Sylvia's response to the treatment.

Prior to their arrival in the German capital, they spent a few days in Paris. Sylvia initially resisted taking the side trip, but Leon insisted. He was pleased that his plan to put Sylvia at ease by taking her on a little mini vacation before her experimental treatment began seemed to be working. He detected a bit more clip in her step and a more relaxed tone in her voice than she had had for a long time. Eight months of chemo not only failed to halt the spread of Sylvia's cancer, but also left her emotionally and physically drained.

Now, on the eve before meeting with her new doctor, Leon could sense a shift setting in.

"Please turn the channel. There must be something else to watch," Sylvia snipped at her husband inside their comfortable room at the Westin Grand Berlin, a short taxi ride from the hospital where they'd be spending their ensuing weeks. "Why don't you just put it back to *When Harry Met Sally?*" she asked irritably.

"But it's in German, dear," Leon responded, realizing she hadn't dozed off after all.

Sylvia's eyes opened. "So, we'll read the subtitles."

"Okay, maybe we'll catch the Katz's deli scene. It'll be interesting to see what the subtitles say when Sally does all that moaning," he kidded, trying to get a rise out of his wife. Sylvia rolled her now open eyes. Leon's attempts to get a quick laugh from her were a hallmark of their nearly fifty years together.

He shuffled back through several stations before finding the classic American romantic comedy then put the remote down between them on top of the comforter. Even though Sylvia faced the TV he could sense by her hollow glare that his wife's mind had drifted elsewhere.

"What's wrong, dear?" he asked.

She paused, grabbed the remote, and turned off the TV.

"What are the odds Dr. Schmidt's grandparents were Nazis?" she asked. "Do you think he'll care if he figures out we're Jewish?"

Leon marveled at his wife's ability to jump from comedy to tragedy so quickly.

"I'd be lying if I said that question hadn't crossed my mind. But it's best we don't ask him about that . . . at least not first thing tomorrow morning," he said as they both giggled like schoolchildren.

Sylvia fluffed her pillow and leaned back. "You can turn the TV back to the market news if you want. You've been pretty good so far, even with the market falling."

"You noticed that?"

"Leon, I do pay attention to what's going on in the world. I can't believe you haven't said anything about it all day."

"It's nothing to get too excited about. Just a little correction over this hoopla with China," he said calmly.

Sylvia sat more upright. "Have you been in touch with Marty about it?"

"No. I told you I'm not working while we're here. Do you think I need to call him?"

"Well, he *can* get a little flustered."

Leon looked at Sylvia. "I know...wonder who he got that from?" he said, taking a loving jab at his wife.

Sylvia smiled back. "Very funny.... maybe you should hold off. Give him room to figure things out."

Leon nodded in agreement.

"What about this merger situation? Are you going to talk to him about it?" she asked tentatively.

Leon sighed. "Potential merger, dear. At this point it's just an idea and I don't know if it'll go anywhere. So, I'm not planning on bringing it up. And, frankly, I haven't given it too much thought since we've been here. Right now, you're my main concern."

Leon wasn't being entirely honest. He failed to mention that he had sent an email back to Charlie Chadwick that kept the discussions open rather than a *thanks-but-no-thanks* response to the merger overture. Also, the proposition had also crossed Leon's mind on more than one occasion while he and Sylvia strolled the streets of Paris and Berlin over the past week. Was selling the firm something he could seriously consider? Charlie casually brought up the idea on a few occasions over the years, but Leon was evasive, quickly changing the subject to avoid a serious discussion. Most recently over a friendly lunch between the two industry colleagues Charlie brought up the matter of Leon's succession planning once again. Leon was less guarded this time, telling Charlie he was "beginning to give it some real thought." Leon didn't offer up that he and his younger son, Marty, had some discussions where Marty made it clear he was intent on taking over the firm once Leon was ready to step aside. But Marty wasn't fully ready. And just because it was Marty's long-term vision, it didn't make it Leon's only option. Southern had a good reputation and all the resources to take care of KCM's clients. Leon could wind down his responsibilities quickly, allowing him to spend a lot more time with Sylvia. They'd give Marty a good position and he'd have lots of opportunity for growth with a bigger firm. They'd likely keep the rest of employees. Leon could make that part of any deal, but, of course, no long-term guarantees.

"But isn't Marty expecting you to talk with him about ownership in the firm when we're back?" Sylvia asked.

"Yes, but I'm not certain that's the right course, dear. Marty's a good advisor and analyst, he cares about his clients, but he's *so* fixated on our growth."

"Why is that so bad?"

"Growth is good, but not at the expense of what's going on today. Don't want to lose our edge, get sloppy, and not pay enough attention to the little things."

Sylvia bit her lip before speaking. "Does this have more to do with what happened with Alan than Marty? Just because that didn't go so well, doesn't mean Marty can't handle it. Hasn't he proven himself already?"

Leon lay silently. He knew he was having trouble mentally committing to Marty, putting off his son's numerous overtures to formalize the firm's future ownership. Maybe Sylvia was right. Was he punishing Marty for his own failed attempt to bring his older son into the firm? Or, did Marty lack the skill set and experience to effectively lead after he's gone?

"Look, Sylvia…I've got to think about the clients' and employees' best interests, too."

"You do. All I'm saying is that you're going to have to do something at some point. Marty's put a lot of hard work in…and we won't be around forever," Sylvia said, sounding shaky.

Leon reached over and rested his hand on top of Sylvia's sun-spotted forearm. He chose his words carefully. "I know. I'm thinking that maybe I should take a step back so we can spend more time together. Maybe a merger will make that possible, sooner than later."

Sylvia got very quiet and started sniffling. Leon gave her a reassuring closed-lip smile.

She turned to face her husband. "Leon . . ."

"Yes, dear," he said with trepidation.

She sniffled some more, trying to hold back her tears. She took a deep breath. "You've been a good husband to me, and you're a good father."

Leon was silent. Her confession shook him to his core.

He wiped away her tears with the back of his hand and pulled her close. "I wish you wouldn't say things like that."

"Why not? It's the truth."

"Because, it sounds like something someone who has lost all hope would say."

"No, it's something that someone who loves her husband would say," she said firmly. Sylvia looked directly into his eyes. "I've lived a good life. I'm very lucky to have found you."

"Sylvia," Leon said, hearing his own voice tremble in the face of his wife's controlled steadiness. "That's enough. *Promise* me you'll give this treatment a fair shot. We're not giving up."

Sylvia grabbed a tissue off the nightstand to wipe away her flowing tears, nodding in agreement.

"Okay, I promise," she said, giving him a watery smile.

Leon leaned over and kissed her gently on her cheek.

"Tomorrow is a new day," he said.

9

As soon as I pulled into my garage, I heard my son's strained pleas, possibly throwing a monkey wrench into my plans to bail out on the evening's basketball practice.

"Mom! But it's my phone. *My! Mine!*"

She must have taken his phone away again, which was the only real leverage we had over him. Ryan had plenty of nerve for a fourteen-year-old, often saying things that I would never have dreamed of saying to my parents, even now. Once, when he was eight, he told me in a very matter-of-fact way that he learned the word "fuck" from his older cousin, Brian, while on a family beach trip, and by age ten, he was using it liberally. A parenting book Jessica had read at the time suggested we needed to have punishments for inappropriate behavior, hence the phone privileges.

Jessica could always tell from the moment I walked in if I had made or lost money that day at work, and I, in turn, could tell how well Ryan was behaving based on Jessica's mood. I mentally braced myself before going inside. The cool welcoming air and smell of sweet basil emanating from the spaghetti sauce on the stovetop marked a stark contrast to the conflict on the floor above. When I went upstairs, I found Ryan standing bare-chested in his workout shorts outside our locked bedroom door.

"I want my phone back *now*! Give it back, Mom!"

Instead of directly engaging, Jessica chose to ignore Ryan, which was quite difficult, given his relentless pounding and yelling.

He saw me and stopped mid-bang. "Dad, you've *got* to talk to Mom and tell her to give me back my phone."

"What's the problem now?" I asked calmly even though I didn't really want to deal with the answer.

"She took my phone away for *nothing!*" he yelled.

I folded my arms across my chest. "Nothing?" It was never nothing, and Ryan knew it.

He pulled his mop of black hair back off his forehead. "Well," he huffed dramatically. "She'll *say* I was being rude, but it's not true. If anything, she was rude to me first!"

"Whatever the story, I need you to give me some space so I can talk to Mom about it."

"Fine, but I need you to promise you'll get my phone back."

"I'm not promising anything other than I'll talk to her."

Ryan gave another dramatic sigh and stomped off, grumbling something under his breath about us ruining his life.

I knocked gently, and Jessica cautiously unlocked and nudged the door open. "Thank God you're home. He's driving me insane." She pulled me into the bedroom and quickly locked the door behind us as if there were a homicidal maniac on the loose instead of our hormone-crazed son.

"So, what happened this time?"

She scowled. "I asked him very nicely if he could pick up his clothes off the floor in his room, and do you know what he told me? He told me . . . and I quote, 'to leave him the fuck alone.' So, I took away his phone."

A familiar story with a familiar ending. I'd get him to apologize for his poor behavior, and he'd get his phone back within a day or so.

I changed the subject. "Air-conditioning's busted in the gym. It's going to suck, but Simmons still wants to have practice."

"Did you hear what I just said? I really need him out of the house for a while, so please take him," Jessica said, her naturally warm skin tone looking bright red. "They'll have fans at the gym, I'm sure."

In fans-versus-sweaty-teenage-boys, the fans didn't stand a chance. But I loved my wife, so I changed into a sweat-wicking tee and shorts and gathered my grumpy son.

On the way to the rec center, I lectured Ryan about the virtues of "cooperation and respect," but my words seemed to go right through him like they had so many times before.

The thick air in the gym was stifling, and the wind from the fans felt more like a hairdryer blowing warm air in your face.

"Glad you all made it," Simmons, a highly patient, middle-aged coach-for-hire, said after Bill and I circled up the eight boys at the start of practice.

Bill Fredrington, the other assistant coach and father of another boy on the team, was also a financial advisor, but with Peach State Advisors. A big regional firm, Peach was as well-known for catering to ultra-high-net-worth clients as it was for its intense sales culture. It tended to hire a lot of former collegiate and professional athletes like Bill, who had played college baseball. Bill was a slap-your-back kind of sales guy and spent most of his week entertaining clients and prospects on the golf course rather than following the markets and managing client portfolios in his office.

"I know it's a bit hot," Coach Simmons said, "so everyone needs to drink a lot of water."

The rec center better have a good insurance policy in case someone ends up in the hospital.

"If everybody really hustles, we can end the practice early," Simmons said.

We ran the kids through several drills, then split them up into two groups to practice layups and blocking out. As Bill and I stood under the backboard, Peter Sanders, another one of the kids' dads, put down the phone his eyes had been glued to and picked up a stray rebound. An affable middle-aged marketing executive, Peter liked to shoot the shit about stocks as much as the boys enjoyed shooting baskets.

Peter neared us, ball in hand. "Man, what happened to the market today?"

"I know, a real shitshow," I said, after ensuring I was out of earshot of the boys. "Probably just a short-term blip. We'll likely bounce back quickly when this China thing turns out to be a non-event."

Bill spun the ball on his index finger. "No kidding. Listen to this: I was with one of my top clients at East Lake this afternoon, sweating our balls off. Either of you guys ever golfed there?"

Peter and I both shook our heads and shot each other a "here we go again" look. While amusing a times, Bill was a total bullshitter who loved to drop stories about his high-flying and expensive lifestyle that insinuated his success.

"It's awesome. You guys should really play a round there sometime if you get the opportunity. Anyway, I checked my phone while standing on this insane island green on the fifteenth hole and saw the market carnage. I told my client right before he putted: 'Good news is you've got a great chance at a birdie. Bad news is you just lost two hundred grand in the market!'" Bill cracked himself up.

It didn't seem like Bill cared much if his clients lost money as long as he didn't get the blame and still collected his advisory fees. Though I wasn't jealous of his success, I did envy his ability to emotionally detach from the market's ups and downs, just like JD, except JD wasn't in the business of taking care of other people's finances.

Coach Simmons made good on his promise and ended practice about twenty minutes early. In the car on the way home, I watched Ryan fidget, skipping from radio station to radio station. Basketball helped him tone down his anger, but he was still agitated and defiant.

"Remember," I said, "when we get home, apologize."

"I'll apologize when I get my phone back." He sounded calmer but was still determined to stand his ground.

"I'll see what I can do." They'd get through this just like every other fight over the years.

Ryan's rebellion was an endless cause of friction and tension in our house. Ever since he was a toddler, whatever we asked him to do, he seemed determined do the opposite, interactions becoming more trying and challenging as time went on. Our original plan was to have two or three children, but Jessica was diagnosed with gestational hypertension late in her pregnancy with Ryan, making any future pregnancies fairly high risk. By the time Ryan was three, we decided it wasn't a risk worth taking, and I got a vasectomy. I wondered if Jess's difficult pregnancy or Ryan being an only child might have played a role in his strong-willed character.

When Ryan and I got home from basketball practice, I quietly slipped into the bedroom to feel out the situation with my wife. The lights were off, and Jessica was already asleep. Ryan wouldn't wait till the next morning for resolution. He would insist I wake her so he could get closure to their squabble and retrieve his phone.

There was no chance I was going to wake her and draw out the arguing any further. Rather than dig in and send Ryan straight to bed, I resorted to plan B.

I led him to the playroom, out of earshot from my bedroom. "Listen, in exchange for a sincere-sounding apology to Mom first thing in the morning, I'll get you more decorations for your fish tank."

I knew Jessica would be pissed if she found out about it, but since we were planning on including fish tank improvements as part of his upcoming fourteenth birthday anyway, I was able to rationalize it. Maybe I could convince Jessica to see it the same way.

Our differing parenting styles clashed frequently since Ryan came into our lives. She wanted to win the war. She needed to show Ryan who had the power and control. That meant not only taking his phone away, but also taking his video games, toys, and everything other than his bed out of his room. She told Ryan he could earn it all back when he relented and improved his attitude. I was in favor of trying behavior modification through a positive rewards system.

Things started getting ugly a couple of years ago when we started talking with Ryan about his upcoming bar mitzvah. He told us that he didn't want one, which wasn't so unusual for a teenager. While many Jewish kids might dread the months of study that come along with the ritual, most just whine a bit. When it's all over, most enjoy the experience and special attention, especially the party and gifts that go along with the rite of passage. Not Ryan. He threw a fit from the get-go and didn't let up. When we pressed him for why he was so opposed, his explanation was straightforward. "I don't see the need. I'm not religious."

His initial strategy was to make me and Jessica so miserable that we would simply cave in. He began his psychological warfare with a series of nightly outbursts when we were particularly tired and at our most vulnerable. He'd wait until we were in bed and then come into our bedroom while we were watching a show, stand right in front of the TV, and proclaim, "I'm *not* having a bar mitzvah."

This happened every night. And every night, one of us would calmly respond to Ryan with, "Yes, you are. Now please go to bed."

He didn't go. Instead he'd say repeatedly, "I'm not having a bar mitzvah, I'm not having a bar mitzvah," ad infinitum. It was his version of Chinese water torture and a very painful and disturbing experience. Our own personal *Shining* moment, our son's version of "redrum, redrum, redrum."

At times, I admired his resolve, determination, and relentless pursuit of his objective. Even so, it was doomed to fail. After a while, we'd just turn off the television and let him stand there talking. Eventually, he'd leave only to return the next night, and we'd do it all over again.

When it became clear that his evening antics weren't having their desired effect, Ryan changed his strategy. He decided to redirect his recalcitrance from us toward his bar mitzvah tutor, Leah. Leah, a retired schoolteacher in her mid-sixties, supplemented her social security benefits with bar mitzvah tutoring. If he could get her to quit, Ryan's twelve-year-old brain reasoned, he wouldn't be adequately prepared to do the required reading from the Torah, and we'd have no choice but to cancel the event.

"Don't worry, I've dealt with poor attitudes before," Leah said reassuringly when we warned her about Ryan. "They always come around and do great in the end."

Ryan actually behaved reasonably well for the first couple of lessons. But soon, his nonsense resurfaced. He stopped preparing for the lessons and would just sit stone-faced, silently staring at Leah when asked to repeat a prayer back. She called his bluff and sat quietly with him until he was ready to proceed, but she underestimated his endurance. One night they must've sat at our dining room table for a solid hour without either of them making a peep. Jess and I were sitting around the corner in the next room, listening intently to the silence.

Within a month, Ryan had Leah right where he wanted her. Finally, after another unproductive lesson, Leah raised the white flag. "Maybe Ryan would be better off with another tutor."

Jessica lost it. She was livid with Ryan and took a scorched earth approach. "It's one thing for him to be rude to us, but to disrespect his tutor is totally unacceptable," she argued, ever the competitive one in our relationship.

Without Jessica's knowledge (she went ballistic on me when she found out), the night before she was to empty his room, I approached Ryan. I negotiated a deal with him that included a trip to Disney World in exchange for his cooperation. It worked; Ryan got to work and delivered a solid B bar mitzvah performance. Jessica, however, felt we let our twelve-year-old manipulate us into rewarding him for his disobedience. She was especially irritated that I didn't first discuss with her the terms of the deal I made with Ryan. Since then, there had been numerous blowups with Ryan about many other things of much less significance than his bar mitzvah. How many more of these episodes could we endure? I came to accept his antics as part of his personality and dealt with him like any other obstacle, trying to find an acceptable compromise or workaround. To Jessica, there was no alternative, just victory.

After my latest fish tank bribe and a very long day, I was totally exhausted and ready for sleep. I did a final check on my phone before putting it down on my nightstand. I had one new text message:

JD: Good news. On her HOT trail!

Me: Who?

JD: Bathsheba! He responded within seconds.

Me: Awesome! Can't wait to hear about it.

JD: Any more thought on Feldstein sponsorship?

Me: Not yet. Still need to talk to my dad. He's out of the country.

JD: Don't miss this great opportunity! Ltr

10

Strangely, neither the large swells rocking the boat, nor the unobstructed bright sun seemed to bother me. Ordinarily, I would've already puked from exposure to the combination of the two. I was fishing offshore with Henry McCullough, a former high school classmate. As we trolled off the back of the boat, there wasn't any visible land around us, only large, rolling waves and seagulls squawking above in the clear blue sky. Right after Henry told me about how much Julie Meadows, a girl I had a crush on for most of high school, hated me, there was a firm tug on my line. A huge fish leaped high out of the ocean about fifty yards off the side of the boat before diving back into the water. Given the distance, I couldn't tell for sure, but it looked like a beautiful sailfish.

I immediately started reeling him in, but Henry interrupted my progress. "Turn the boat around!" he demanded.

I ignored him.

"Cut the line...let the fish go!" he said.

"No way!" I said. "Are you crazy?" I wasn't about to let go of my only catch of the day, so I kept reeling in the magnificent fish.

Henry got angry and all red in face. He began shouting, "Cut the line, cut the line!"

When I didn't listen, he started spitting. First, he spit off the side of the boat, then on the floor, and finally, directly at me!

With both hands firmly gripping my rod and reel, I couldn't wipe the giant spit wads off my face. I was totally disgusted. My anger grew, but remained determined to bring the trophy fish in. Henry kept pelting me with his large nasty balls of saliva. I was so obsessed with landing the fish that I didn't stop to give Henry a much-deserved punch in the mouth.

Finally, as the fish thrashed about in the blue water off the back of the boat, I pulled the rod way up in the air to see if I could finally land him onto the deck.

As I yanked the rod high above my head with all my strength—

"Marty! What are you doing?"

The shrill in Jessica's voice woke me. She was sitting up in bed in the center of the bed, incredulous at me having torn the comforter completely off her.

"Sorry, go back to sleep," I said, spreading the comforter back over our king-size bed.

I was hot, sweaty, and dehydrated both from those margaritas and my physically active dream. The clock on my nightstand read: 2:33 a.m. Unwilling to risk a return to my disturbing dream, I got up to get a drink of water. I grabbed my phone to use as a flashlight on my way to the kitchen, where I poured a tall glass of filtered water from the container we kept in the fridge and chugged it down like a college freshman shot-gunning a beer at his first frat party.

I shuddered as an image of Henry McCullough hocking loogies popped back into my head and was at a loss as to why my mind would conjure up such a random disgusting character from my past.

Back upstairs in bed, I lay with my phone in my hand, debating whether I should open my CNBC app and check the status of the Asian markets to get a sense of how Friday's trading was shaping up.

If it were bad, it would piss me off, and I could say goodbye to more sleep. But if it were good, I'd satisfy my curiosity, relieve my anxiety, and hello easy sleep.

Unable to stop myself, I glanced at my sleeping wife, lowered the screen's brightness, and opened the app. I scrolled down the tickers of the major Asian indexes that were still open for trading. Not surprisingly, the Nikkei, Shanghai, and Australian markets were all down sharply, following the lead of the US markets. The US dollar and gold were both high-er, and yields on US Treasury bonds were dropping as investors moved into traditional safe-haven assets. I flipped to another screen to see how the Dow and S&P futures were trading. It would indicate what would happen when US markets opened in about six hours. Both suggested a horrifically lower open. Down 2 percent.

Shit!

Friday was going to suck. I shook my head, turned off my phone, and put it back on the nightstand. I rolled to my side, covered my head with my pillow, and tried to go back to sleep. I faded in and out of consciousness, but at least I didn't have to fish with Henry anymore.

11

The red digital numbers on my alarm clock read 5:47 a.m., which was close enough to my regular 6:00 a.m. wakeup time that I didn't bother trying to go back to sleep. Instead, I grabbed my phone to see if the Dow and S&P Futures had improved from a few hours earlier. Futures contract trading, which took place in the pre-market hours, can be very volatile, so it wouldn't have been too surprising to see a recovery from an overnight sell-off.

Unfortunately, that wasn't the case. Asian markets got slammed overnight, and European markets were down firmly. Barring a major turnaround, the US markets were going to open sharply lower. I scanned my primary market news source to see what was pressuring the markets.

•

Bizline News Update: Friday, June 22, 7:30 a.m. ET

Chinese officials claim their aircraft were in international waters when intercepted by aggressive US fighter jets. They will not be deterred or intimidated from conducting more surveillance missions and military exercises in the area. They stress they can and will exercise and protect their sovereign rights.

•

Next, I checked the president's Twitter feed. He had the power to impact the markets with the dissemination of new information. The latest @IamDennisPruitt tweet was posted at 3:30 a.m. and read: *We have THE MOST incredible military in the world KEEPING AMERICA SAFE! Bring it on X!!!*

While a blustery tweet wasn't out of the ordinary, the president's provocative online taunts certainly weren't going to do much to settle the markets down. And what was with the reference to President Xin Yang as simply "X" rather than his usual "X-Man"? An intentional attempt to have readers substitute a derogatory adjective to describe China's leader or did Pruitt make a mistake in haste? Tweet typos weren't uncommon for him, so it was inconclusive, and therefore left the door open to rampant speculation. Irrespective of how one interpreted the president's message, it was an escalation, rather than a de-escalation, and that was bad news for the markets.

I took a hotter than normal shower, hoping the steam would relieve my stress, but my mind was in overdrive. Which clients should I call first? The few we had who lived in California closest to the incident, or the ones who would likely be most nervous about the markets regardless of location? Should we add to our positions now or wait to see what happened? And it was Friday, so I couldn't forget to take out the garbage. A clanging on the shower door interrupted my spiraling thoughts. Ryan stood on the other side of the fogged, water-beaded glass holding something in his hand.

"Dad. Dad. Dad."

"What?" I asked grumpily, raising my voice loud enough to be heard through the spraying water.

"Dad, the TV remote isn't working. Can you fix it?" He pressed his disgruntled face along with the remote directly against the glass as if I could diagnose the problem right then.

For the love of God.

"I'll look at it later!" I shouted. "Now, let me shower in peace!"

He put the remote on the bathroom counter beside my toothbrush and left. I turned up the heat, trying to reclaim my prior train of thought, formulating a plan for the day that lay ahead of me. This whole ordeal would knock our firm's assets down even further.

"I'll make some calls first," I caught myself saying out loud in response to my internal Q&A session.

Typically, during times of market distress, both Dad and I took to the phones to reassure clients we were monitoring the situation. But he was in Germany and specifically said he was trying to disconnect from work while he was gone, not wanting to be distracted given his preoccupation with my mom's treatment. I needed to handle things myself until his return in a few weeks.

Mom's battle with cancer began fifteen years ago. She was fifty-seven, and what started off as a visit to the doctor for a lingering deep cough and shortness of breath had led to the discovery of a small malignant tumor in her right lung. Her oncologist conjectured that even though she'd quit her pack-a-day habit decades earlier, her tumor was due to heavy smoking during her early twenties. She said she quit right before getting pregnant with my older brother, Alan.

They'd discovered her non-small cell cancer early—before it spread outside of the lungs—so the doctors had been optimistic. Mom had a successful operation to remove the tumor and surrounding tissue, followed by a standard regime of chemotherapy and many weeks of daily radiation. Fortunately, her cancer responded well to the treatment, and she had been in remission and good health ever since. She and my dad continued with their otherwise healthy, active lifestyle, going on long evening walks together almost daily. We had all been relieved that she'd gotten through the ordeal in relatively good condition.

However, last year, during one of her routine semiannual scans, her doctor noticed a concerning spot. He'd ordered a biopsy to make sure it wasn't simply scar tissue, and it confirmed that her cancer was back. It wasn't until two weeks later, once they knew what the treatment course would look like, that Dad called me and my two siblings separately to deliver the bad news.

I knew a recurrence was always a risk but had tucked it away in some corner of my mind. I felt terrible for what she would have to go through and knew it would be a strain on both of them. She was a strong woman who would face it head-on.

Mom had immediately begun the standard recurrence protocol of chemotherapy and radiation to shrink the tumor, but the cancer didn't respond like it had before. Rather, it spread more aggressively, moving into both lungs and lymph nodes. My parents expanded their medical research and began seeking out new breakthrough treatments both inside and outside the United States. Through some social media connections with other cancer patients, they learned of a medical center in Berlin that was having early success with a new immunotherapy drug for treating Stage III and IV lung cancers. Even better, the doctors leading the drug's development were looking for new patients that were good candidates to participate in further testing. Mom sent over her medical records and received word that she qualified for the treatment.

Jessica entered the heavily fogged bathroom where I was now shaving. "What was your problem last night? You got out of bed."

"The markets are selling off hard on this China bullshit," I said, splashing cold water on my face.

I caught her twitching her nose in her reflection in the mirror, her inadvertent telltale sign of frustration with me.

"Oh, I thought it might have been about Ryan's behavior toward me," she said with more than a hint of passive-aggressive sarcasm.

Okay, I guess that was the wrong answer.

"Yes, I was upset, too. I talked to him after basketball practice. You were already asleep when we got home, or he would've apologized," I told her.

"Marty, I'm so sick and tired of his disrespectful, rude behavior," she said. "And then you don't back me up—you even reward him, which continually makes me look like the bad guy."

"Jessica, can we *please* pick this up later?" I hoped Ryan wouldn't tell her about our pet store deal. "We may be on the verge of an international crisis," I added, wanting to move past having yet another conversation about Ryan's poor behavior.

"You always want to talk about him later!" she said with frustration in her voice. "At some point we have to talk about his behavior now."

She was right. The only thing I found more draining and frustrating than discussing Ryan's poor behavior was talking about it with Jessica.

And Jessica constantly wanted to talk about him. Our talking about Ryan almost always turned into an argument. Jessica wanted to tame him and modify his behavior through hardball tactics, whereas I was okay keeping the peace through a little win-win negotiation.

"How about we talk this weekend?" I asked, looking for some empathy from her. "When the markets aren't trying to give me a heart attack?"

"Fine," she agreed reluctantly. "How bad is this China thing?"

"Looks like another couple of percent down on top of yesterday's two percent," I said. "Unpleasant for a Friday, for sure."

"I guess I can take Ryan this morning if you need to get to the office early," she offered, with a small conciliatory smile. For all her tough love toward Ryan, I could still count on her to help me out when I needed it. Jessica worked part-time as a bookkeeper for a small accounting firm and had more flexibility than I did. Even so, we did our best to share our Ryan-related responsibilities, including summer driving, and I was supposed to take Ryan on Thursday and Friday mornings to his summer camp when she worked.

"Thanks, it's going to be one of those days," I said, moving to get dressed. "And let me know how things go with Ryan," I added before scrambling downstairs to eat my usual morning bowl of cereal and tall glass of pulp-free orange juice.

As I wolfed down my bowl of Special K, I checked emails on my phone to get a jump on things before arriving at the office. There was mostly spam, but I did have an email from the Clausky boys with the subject line "*Important Question??*"

> Hi Marty,
> *We forgot to ask what name for our app do you like better—CrapMap or GPShit? Also, have you reached a decision yet about the money? We're ready to roll!*
> Sincerely,
> *Danny and Freddie*

Unbelievable. It hadn't even been twenty-four hours and they were already pestering me. While my hazy brain from the day before didn't completely dismiss their concept as the world's worst idea, I was now seeing it for what it likely was—a money-losing venture. How could I endorse such an off-the-wall project with little chance of success? Burning $30,000 would sting. On the other hand, maybe losing money now on one bad idea could save them from losing a whole lot more on ten bad ideas down the road? Maybe a real-world, hard knock business failure would work their penchant for excessive risk-taking out of their systems. Consulting Josie would be a useless exercise since she'd just defer to me and I certainly wasn't going to bother Dad about it.

I put down my spoon and hammered out a short reply.

Danny and Freddie,

While I'm impressed by your research, creativity, and enthusiasm, I think this is a very risky venture that will likely result in a total loss of capital. Sorry, guys.

Regards,
Marty

Something kept me from hitting send, though, and instead, I let the email sit in my drafts folder. With no other emails of consequence, I cleaned off the kitchen table, grabbed my briefcase, and drove off for the office.

I was halfway down the block when I turned my car around. I'd forgotten the trash, which wouldn't have been such an ordeal had one of the three overstuffed plastic bags not broken open, releasing a trail of soggy leftovers along the pavement. While cleaning up the mess, a torn-up greeting card caught my eye. We'd had no recent holidays or birthdays. Intrigued, I reached carefully between a decomposing banana skin and used coffee grounds to extract the pieces of the card. On the outside was just a smiley face. Inside, however, was a personal note that read, *"Jessica, thanks for listening and being there for me. —Mark."*

Mark? Who the fuck was Mark? We had no friends by that name, and her accounting firm had a Jeffrey, a Steve, a Brian, and a Mike, but no Mark.

And where had Jess been? What had she been listening to? What would have made her rip this up before throwing it out? And hide it from me.

I crumpled the torn pieces in my hand, willing my pulse to ease. It must have been work related. Jess had as many clients as I did, and I didn't know any of their names, same as she didn't know most of mine. I tried to imagine the situation being reversed. If a client sent me a seemingly innocuous smiley face as an innocent thank-you, would I show Jess? Maybe. Then again, if someone sent me a card for something *other* than an innocent thank-you, would I show Jess? Definitely not. I'd hide it. I wouldn't leave any trace.

I breathed deeply, compartmentalizing this into a future problem, as today, I needed to focus on the firm's clients and their shrinking portfolios. I slipped the torn pieces of the card into my briefcase and drove off to work.

12

Not good. Pre-market trading showed that almost all our holdings would open down except for Pepsi, Duke Energy, and Lockheed Martin. Consumer staples like Pepsi and utilities were notorious "safe havens" for investors when an outside event threatened to derail the economic expansion. Consumers would likely still drink soda and eat potato chips in the comfort of their air-conditioned homes if war broke out. I needed to get a handle on our positions and determine if we needed to take any action.

I sent a calendar invite to our two research analysts to arrange an eleven o' clock meeting. Even though we had just had our formal monthly investment committee meeting last week, we held ad hoc meetings when market conditions or unexpected news regarding one of our positions warranted it. A sudden 5 percent drop in the markets over two days qualified as one of those situations.

My eyes homed in on the clock on my computer screen. As the twenty-nine ticked to thirty, I braced myself for the carnage. It was 9:30 a.m. Eastern Standard Time, and the markets were open. Real time quotes on our firm's holdings appeared on the monitor to my left, while information on the markets and news showed on the one to my right. Almost all of our holdings opened in deep negative territory. The major indexes were selling off quickly with the S&P 500 and Dow down 2 percent within the first five minutes of trading. Despite the plunge, I remained cautiously optimistic that the sudden drop would be followed by a snapback and an end to the immediate selling pressure. I was right. The market started to steadily climb and recover the morning's early losses until they were only down 1 percent by 9:56 a.m. Maybe, just maybe, rational-thinking, bargain-shopping traders, and the unemotional computer algorithms viewed the drop as an overreaction. The market's minor loss over the last day would be an unnoticeable blip and by the following week and we'd be back over the $500 million mark in no time.

Antsy for some other perspective, I got caught up reading a newly published market outlook from a market strategist I followed and respected. The market's apparent steadiness coupled with the report's optimistic tone allowed me to feel hopeful for almost a full hour until the market took a decisive nosedive at precisely 10:38 a.m. That pushed the index down to a new low: 2.5 percent below the prior day's close.

•

Bizline News Update: Friday, June 22, 10:38 a.m. ET

Pentagon official confirms US Pacific fleet has been put on high alert.

•

I started to sweat. Would this event really spark a war between the two countries? Unlikely, but the whole thing was starting to seem more serious than a minor international incident. While I didn't fear an imminent ballistic missile attack, the story clearly had more legs than an over-and-done-with-type event. The overhang of uncertainty would undoubtedly linger in the markets, and the weight of making the right decisions in a crisis was upon me. Undoubtedly, Dad would second-guess me if I made a mistake that cost our clients big money. It took him a while to get over my terrible stock pick I made early on after joining the firm. He had been eager to give me a vote of confidence, so he hadn't put up much resistance when I'd recommended adding Colton Breezer to our client portfolios. While he hadn't rubbed my nose in it when the drone manufacturer lost half its value and hadn't recovered after the company's government sales contracts dried up, he'd routinely lectured me over the next year about investing in companies too early in their life cycle.

He was right. We should've followed the company longer before putting it in our client portfolios. Lesson learned. But would he go as far as shelving our overdue succession planning discussions if I made some bad calls when he was out? He all but assured me we'd address the issue when he returned. These discussions were years in the making.

I processed the multitude of investment implications from the market turbulence. Should we use clients' cash on hand to add to some holdings that were falling or trim back positions in favor of cash in the event the incident turned into a full-blown crisis? Did the tumultuous market action warrant a note to our clients?

For those less-detached clients, blasting out a note now would potentially cause unnecessary panic. For other clients, ones dialed in to every fluctuation, some communication might ease their worried minds. Clients like Mrs. Benoit. A sweet old widow who had been one of my dad's clients from before he even founded the firm. She must be freaking out. I put a mental pin in place to call her later. First, I had to deal with JD's short-term withdrawal request. *Damn.* JD's $500,000 withdrawal was coming at a bad time—frustrating to have to free up funds quickly during a sell-off.

When a client had a withdrawal request, the standard routine was for the advisor in charge of the relationship—in JD's case, that was me—to make recommendations on what to sell, but then turn it over to one of the firm's two traders to execute the trades.

JD's portfolio had already taken a hit that morning. It was my responsibility to protect him, and I had to take action. Fast, before things got worse. I would take care of the trades myself. After skimming his stock holdings, I sold $300,000 worth, picking equities that hadn't gone down as much as others and that wouldn't result in a big tax hit. Then, I sold another $100,000 of bond holdings. Since he had a bit more than $100,000 of money market cash holdings, that was all it took to reach his magic number of $500,000. I deplored having to sell into the market mess, but there was no way to know with certainty when things would turn around. And I wasn't going to have him blame me for having to tell Feldstein he couldn't come up with the cash.

Taking care of J.D. gave me a brief sensation of relief, like pulling a friend off a busy street before getting hit by a reckless driver. My mind was free to turn to other clients. I picked up the phone to call Mrs. Benoit, readying myself to sound calm, confident, and reassuring.

"Hello?" said a soft voice in a familiar French accent after just one ring.

"Hi, Mrs. Benoit. It's Marty Kaplan."

"*Marteen*, I'm so glad you called," she said, pronouncing my name like I was a fellow Frenchman. She didn't waste any time. "This news with China is so terrible."

"The news makes everyone anxious," I said, keeping my voice as sturdy as possible. "But we really don't know anything yet, which might be a good reason to not watch so much TV."

"Tell me, Marteen, have I lost a lot of money?"

I swallowed hard. When responding to such a client question, my dad drilled into me the avoidance of certain words. "Loss" was one of them. Mrs. Benoit was one of the firm's oldest clients. While her husband's sudden death a couple of years earlier devasted her emotionally, she was financially secure, even though she did not always feel that way.

In times of market turbulence, nervous clients like Camille Benoit would practically beg us to sell to avoid further losses. The dreaded GMO call. I figured this wouldn't be my only "get-me-out" conversation of the day.

My dad had his own folksy charm, calming clients by asking rhetorical questions like, "Do you want to grow your money and protect it against inflation? Then don't worry about the day-to-day ups and downs. It's all noise in the grand scheme of things, and you'll be happy in the long run."

I never felt comfortable adopting my dad's style and had developed my own more academic approach. I gripped the phone and spoke assuredly: "No, Mrs. Benoit, the value of your account is going to fluctuate with the ups and downs of the markets, but over a longer period of time we expect it to increase in value, offering an attractive long-term rate of return. Plus, we made sure to have enough cash set aside to last you a few years, so we are not forced into selling when the market falls like it has the last couple of days. Please don't lose any sleep over this."

I heard her take a deep breath and sigh. "Okay, Marteen, you know I trust you, *and your father*, to do the right thing." The anxiety in her voice was apparent and the pointed reference to my father stung. Over the years, Mrs. Benoit talked with my dad fairly regularly, and she clearly still viewed him as the authority in the firm even though I was largely responsible for the day-to-day management of her portfolio. Would she now ask to speak with him for more assurance?

"My Simon worked so hard to provide for me, but I'm not rich. Marteen, I have to watch my money. One day, God willing, I can leave something to Jacques, Marianne, and my sweet, beautiful grandchildren. I know you'll think I'm strange, but I still talk to Simon almost every day and tell him about his wonderful family."

"No, that's not strange at all, Mrs. Benoit. Have Jacques and his wife had the baby yet?" I asked, redirecting the conversation away from the market and Dad before she asked if he were available to chat.

"No, but any time now."

"How's the quilt coming along?"

"Oh, it's almost finished. It's turning out very nice."

"That's wonderful, Mrs. Benoit. I'm sure the baby will love it. You do beautiful work!"

She was sounding a little less fearful. "Thanks for calling, Marteen. Please keep me informed what's going on."

I told her that I would and was about to hang up when she asked, "Tell me, Marteen, how are your parents doing?"

Ugh! So close.

A request to talk to Dad was coming. I could feel it. But I didn't know whether Dad had shared the news about my mother's relapse and their plans to seek treatment overseas with her. We discussed sending out a note to clients before he left, but ultimately decided that informing clients Dad would be out for a while wasn't necessary. Now, Camille might lose it if she finds out he's out of the country and will be unavailable for an extended period. She'll also get emotional if she hears my mother's sick again.

"They're doing okay," I said, purposely using vague language. "They're traveling in Europe and even spending some time in your native Paris." I figured she'd like that, and that it would give her and my dad something other than the stock market to talk about upon his return.

"Well, that's very nice. Hopefully they are having a wonderful time. You know, Simon and I were planning to go back to France for a visit, but then he had his heart attack."

"He was a good man, Mrs. Benoit," I said, meaning it. Poor Simon. He'd been a great guy who loved his wife and family dearly. Sadly, he hadn't had the opportunity to say goodbye to them, had simply gone to bed one night and never woken up. Heart attack in his sleep.

"Marteen, please give your parents my best when you speak to them," she added.

She apparently didn't know anything about Mom's treatment, and it wasn't my place to tell her. She also didn't seem spooked by my dad's absence from the office with a potential crisis brewing, so I must have done a decent enough job of putting her at ease.

By the time I hung up, it was 10:25 a.m., and the market was still hovering close to the morning's low. I checked my email to pull myself away from the flashing ticker screen.

There were a couple of personal notes, one was an invite from my brother, Alan, who was inviting us to his annual party, and one from a friend wanting to introduce me to a prospective client. And yet another email from the Clausky boys, the second in less than twenty-four hours.

Hi again, any thoughts on our last email? Have you made a decision yet?
Danny and Freddie

Oops. I had forgotten to send them the email I had written that was still in my drafts folder. I pulled it back up, read it back over, then did something I couldn't see coming. I held down the delete button until my email was fully vaporized from the screen. I replaced it with the following:

Hey guys,
Will send the money for your project. Keep me posted on your progress.
Good luck with the CrapMap!
Best,
Money Man

Yet again, I couldn't pull the trigger and let it sit in the drafts folder. I headed to the boardroom to meet Shelley and Devon. Our firm's two research analysts were sitting side by side at the table with their laptops open in front of them.

I pulled out a chair across from them. "Buy, sell, or hold?"

Devon, a modestly overweight thirty-two-year-old with a round freckled face, leaned back in his chair. "Except for the defense contractors and consumer staple names we own, it's pretty fugly right now. Consumer discretionary and financials are getting whacked hard. Nike and JP Morgan are good value around here, so we might want to add a little."

I turned to Shelley, her back straight and arms placed on the table like a yoga instructor in a resting pose. "What do you think?" Of the two, Shelley was the deeper thinker and didn't jump to conclusions too quickly. Even though Devon was a decade older and more experienced than Shelley, I valued their opinions equally when it came to market and stock research.

Shelley closed the top of her laptop, giving me her full attention. "If we were to do anything, I was thinking we should take advantage of the strength in the military and defense names. Consider selling a bit and taking a profit. When this blows over, those will drop as fast as they ran up. Lockheed and Northrop are both up about five percent since yesterday and trading at twenty times next year's earnings. Getting a bit frothy unless a war really breaks out, and that's not in our base case model."

I stretched and locked my hands behind my head. "But if it does, then they might turn out to be really cheap and we'd wish we'd held on. Let's hold off a bit longer before selling to see if we get more clarity. And, let's keep an eye on Steller Biomedical. We've been wanting to pick that up for a while now and might not get another good opportunity."

In last week's meeting, we'd reviewed each of the forty-two stock holdings we owned and our price targets for each. In addition to the securities we held in our client portfolios, we also maintained a smaller "watch list" of stocks for a potential buy if the price was right. Those companies generally represented great businesses but didn't trade at prices that were attractive enough to justify buying them. Many of those were tech and biotech companies that tended to trade at higher valuations given their stronger long-term growth prospects. When buying higher-growth companies, our investment philosophy emphasized doing so but only if paying a reasonable price.

I stood and pushed in my chair. "We also have a few new clients who don't own any Jateroo yet, so let's pick up a little in those accounts. Otherwise, let's wait and see where this all goes before using more of our dry powder."

Despite the terrible market action, I felt like we were doing the right things, which in the investing world, sometimes meant doing nothing.

Later that morning, I got a text from Jessica.

Jess: *Hope things are better today. Ryan apologized. He'll get the phone tonight after he straightens up his room.*

Me: *Another rough day. Glad it went well with Ryan!*

Rinse and repeat. It was only a matter of time until the next battle broke out. It was definitely the wrong time to bring up the card that was still sitting in my briefcase. I was in denial mode, hoping there was some innocuous misunderstanding at play.

I sat glued to my computer screen for the remainder of the trading day, eating a dried-out chicken sandwich I ordered from the building's café at my desk, watching the market vacillate between mild and severe losses. The final thirty minutes of trading were where it would get dicey. If the market could bounce off its low for the day and have a strong finish, it could bode well for Monday, but the lack of fresh news made me nervous.

When trading stopped at four o' clock, the S&P 500 closed 2.7 percent lower on the day. Not the lowest point of the day, but not good. To make matters worse, the steep two-day drubbing of almost 5 percent answered my internal question from the morning: a message to our clients was in order.

Five percent pullbacks in the market were not out of the ordinary, often happening two to three times a year. But a drop of that magnitude due to the potential for a military conflict with China was an entirely different story. Despite the scary news flow, the market turbulence, and my own brewing unease, as a firm, we needed to project calm, reassurance, and discipline. Typically, communications like this came from my dad, the firm's founder and principal. But he was out. A client-wide note from me would also make a statement about the future leadership of the firm. That I had Dad's endorsement.

I sat at my computer and wrote:

Dear (client name),

You may be aware of the international incident that occurred yesterday involving China and the United States off the coast of California. While an escalation of tensions leading to a more serious military conflict is unlikely, the markets have sold off, given the increased potential for global instability. The mild pullback in the markets as a result of this incident has likely been exacerbated by low summer trading volumes. Keep in mind that occasional market pullbacks and spikes in volatility are inevitable and quite normal. We are confident in the quality of our portfolio positions and maintain ample liquidity in client accounts in the event the turbulence continues. We will continue to monitor the situation and will respond as needed.

Please call or email me with any questions.

Sincerely,

Marty Kaplan

VP—Director of Research—KCM

I was about to blast off the email to Angela for a final compliance review and client distribution, when my phone started ringing. It was JD. As usual, JD was in a great mood. He excitedly shared that he already sold his first $25,000 sponsorship to the Feldstein event and had made progress on tracking down his mystery woman, but still hadn't made a positive ID. Then he slid into the conversation he was going out with our waitress, Bella, on Saturday night (apparently, she reached out to him, wanting to learn more about Judaism).

"Mazel tov!" I told him while saving my client email so I wouldn't lose my work during the distraction of talking to JD.

Before JD could ask, I confirmed I'd wire him the Feldstein deposit money as soon as his trades settled early next week. I put a yellow sticky note reminding me to send him the cash on Monday morning on the bottom of my monitor.

Our colorful ten-minute call was starting to eat into my time to get a message out to clients before the weekend. I still needed Angela to review and distribute it as she controlled the main client list serve. It was getting late on a Friday and the window was closing. There was a small chance she'd approve it without wanting to talk about it and make changes first, further risking slippage into the following week.

I wished JD "good shabbos" and ended our call. Returning to my email, I pulled up the drafts folder where my client communique was waiting. In my haste to hit send, I didn't realize that I was on the wrong email—the one to the Clauskys I had parked there earlier in the day.

Oops!

I released the wrong email, inadvertently informing Danny and Freddie I'd approve their seed money for their venture in the process. I could've called the boys right then or sent a follow-up email, instructing them to disregard, but that would've involved a long painful discussion. Did I subconsciously want to give them the money? There was a reason I had changed the email from a "no" to a "yes." Maybe it was my way of making it go away with the least amount of pain as they weren't going to let this idea go without a fight. I didn't share their conviction for their idea. When they lost the cash, what would I do? What if they asked for more money? These types of ventures never go as well as imagined. I let it be, telling myself the lessons learned from giving them the funds for their dog-crap-mapping system would serve them well in the long run.

I pulled up their trust account and confirmed they had enough cash without having to sell any holdings, then signed the transfer request form. They'd have their money by Monday morning. Best of luck to 'em. I made a mental note to mention it to Josie next time we talked and moved on.

With that out of the way, I sent the draft of the firm-wide client email to Angela. It was just a matter of time until I'd hear from her.

I was right.

•

Like clockwork, at 4:57 p.m. there was a knock on my half-opened door. I turned away from my computer screen to see Angela standing in my doorway for the second day in a row. She was a relatively petite woman and with shoulder-length dirty blonde hair in a stiff bob. Her confident voice, professional appearance, and steady demeanor more than compensated for her lack of physical stature.

I waved her in. Angela sat in one of the two leather upholstered chairs on the other side of my desk.

I straightened some loose papers on my desk into a tidy stack. "Did you get a chance to read my client note?"

"Yes, I read it."

"Do you think it's okay?"

"I think it's fine. I added a little language about not making any guarantees about future performance, but overall, it works."

"Great." I hoped that the litany of legal disclaimers she added hadn't made me sound like an unemotional robot to our clients.

I nodded and hoped she'd leave before delving deeper into the world of compliance. She sat straight-legged and burrowed her yellow legal pad into her lap. "I actually wanted to talk to you about something else."

"Sure," I said slowly. Angela sounded serious, and almost a little nervous. "Is it about the firm's policies you mentioned yesterday? Weren't we going to set up a separate meeting about that?" I was still hoping I could push the talk off as it was my least favorite part of the job. Bringing in Angela to run the compliance department was my dad's doing, and while having her run the department saved me from having to mess with it, I'd still have to deal with her internal oversight on occasion.

"Yes, there are a couple of items that have come to my attention I'd like to go over with you," she said.

I gestured for her to go on, hoping nothing was really wrong.

"So, first," she continued, "I was looking over some trade activity reports, and it looks like you directly entered some trades in Jacob Aron's account this morning. Is that correct?"

Angela had access to the firm's trading platform and could pull up a detailed report of all the firm's real-time and historical trading activity. The fact that she'd reviewed my trades from just that morning was a bit odd. That, combined with her stern tone, made me feel like I was under investigation, and was about to get reprimanded, but I knew where she was going with the cross-examination. So, I launched a preemptive strike.

"Yeah, I know. The firm's policy requires me to pass any orders on to one of our designated traders for proper execution," I said, paraphrasing the firm's policies and procedures manual I helped update a couple of years earlier.

Angela sat poker-faced. "Correct."

"I know," I said, acknowledging that I skirted our rules, figuring that I'd take the hand slap and move on. "My bad. I should've handed it over to a trader, but given the short fuse on it, it was easier to take care of it myself. Don't worry. I won't make a habit of it."

She knew that I was the boss's son and his likely successor, so maybe it was her way of asserting some power over me or trying to earn my respect. It was too soon to tell where she was going with this, and I was okay to play along a bit longer to see if I could figure out her agenda.

"Unfortunately, it's a little more complicated than that," Angela said.

I pushed down a wave of irritation. The conversation should've already been over. "How's that?"

"What you probably don't know is that while you sold some McDonald's stock in Mr. Aron's account, there was another sell order that was submitted for the Harney's account that came in through Sammy. Apparently, Chris Harney called Sammy yesterday and said he needed one hundred thousand dollars for a down payment on a vacation home and wanted to sell some stock from their brokerage account to pay for it."

"Okay . . ."

Angela huffed at my blasé response. "Sammy then submitted several stock and bond sell orders—McDonald's being one of them—to our trader this morning."

Damn.

"The problem is that you sold McDonald's in Jacob Aron's account and then John executed a trade for the Harneys ten minutes later and got a dollar less a share," she said, looking at me expectantly.

"I understand the issue," I said. "Not exactly ideal, but not the end of the world either."

Angela bristled at my "what can you do?" smile. "Now *I* know there wasn't any intent to give preference to JD Aron, but an SEC inspector wouldn't necessarily see it the same way if they went through our trade records. They'd have to check phone and email records to try and confirm all that."

"Okay, well let's hope it doesn't come to that," I said testily. She was correct in her accusation, but it was a small infraction. No harm done.

Her hands clasped comfortably on her legs. "I'm going to have to document that we discovered this breach of our trading protocols and acknowledge how and why it happened. That way, we don't have to worry about the SEC finding it in an inspection and risk some fines or worse."

Document...worse?

I caught myself furiously tapping my left heel against the floor below my desk. Angela was getting a little dramatic here, and it was really starting to rub me the wrong way. "Do you really think that's necessary? Is the SEC really going to care?"

"Don't worry," Angela said. "It's better to have a little blemish on our internal compliance report than risk getting shut down because of some broader procedural failures."

"Little blemish?" That was easy for Angela to say since she wasn't the one getting written up.

Still, I didn't want to get into an argument. The internal compliance reports were only accessible to the SEC inspectors and our firm's senior management, which included me, my dad, and Angela. Dad would be annoyed by it as he prided himself on our firm's squeaky-clean compliance record. He always said: "*Without our impeccable reputation and clients' full trust, we have nothing.*" Even so, I could explain it away to him since I was trying to help JD out. As for the SEC, our firm hadn't had a formal inspection for years. I wasn't even working here the last time they came around. And given the agency's budgetary constraints, they weren't likely going to be digging into our books anytime soon. Besides, I had to respect Angela and the integrity of a sound compliance system.

I shrugged. "Okay, do what you think is right."

Angela grinned. "Anyway, sorry I had to go over that with you, but just doing my job. With that being said, there's some activity involving another client I'd like to ask you about."

My foot started tapping harder. I forced a bright smile, but before Angela could begin, my cell rang.

Phew...saved by the bell.

It was Jessica. Looking at Angela and pointing to the phone, I whispered, "It's my wife."

Angela looked annoyed that I pulled the wife card but nodded deferentially and left.

I answered, and Jess asked, "How's it going over there?"

"Well, the market dropped another couple percent, and I've got Nurse Ratched on my case for a minor compliance issue."

"Ratched? Who's that? Is it serious?"

"It's just Angela," I said, somewhat regretting my harsh characterization. "You know, the compliance officer my dad hired a while back. She's the one that got evasive and borderline rude when I asked her if she was married or dating anyone."

"I do remember. That was weird."

"She's a bit overzealous. She found something that's more of an embarrassment than anything, although my dad could be pissed when he finds out about it."

"Sorry, I'm sure it'll be okay."

"I'm just ready for the weekend. Let's relax and just hang out at the house."

"That's fine, but don't forget, we have dinner Saturday night with the Gillmans."

"Seriously?" I liked the Gillmans, but just didn't have the energy for making small talk. "I was planning on chilling out and watching the NBA Finals. It's game seven this weekend."

"I reminded you about it earlier." Her voice got tense. "We've had it on the calendar for over a month."

Jessica had set up a shared calendar on my phone that I was supposed to check to make sure we were in sync for family plans. The problem was that while I was on top of my hectic work schedule, I didn't always pay attention to my personal one, especially during the summer.

"Sorry," I said. "I've been a bit distracted and must've forgot. Any chance we can get out of it? I'm really not in the mood, and you know Jeff's going to take some shots at me for losing a bunch of his money in the market."

"No, he won't. He knows it's not your fault," she said. "We'll go early, and you can watch the game afterward."

"Fine."

I reluctantly agreed, skeptical that the evening would go as smoothly as she thought.

13

Jeff buried his face in the Long Point Grill's extensive two-page glossy menu. "I *was* going to order the calamari as an appetizer, but since I'm getting killed in the market, I'll pass."

I gave Jessica an *I told you so* look, and she immediately came to my defense. "Go ahead and order it. We'll pay for it."

"Just messing with you, Marty," Jeff said, sheepishly backing off.

I took a large sip of my dry martini. "Yep, we're all a bit poorer to-day." I liked Jeff, but he had a way of purposely pushing people's buttons at times. Like some of my clients, Jeff and Samantha Gillman were also friends. Samantha and Jessica had been close since they were kids, and I inherited Samantha and her penny-wise husband after we got married. For the most part, balancing being friends as well as clients was manageable. More so when everyone was making money.

Samantha closed her menu. "What are you guys even talking about?" Thankfully, she chose to remain blissfully unaware of what the markets were doing.

I liked that about her. After all, that's why people paid us, so they didn't have to follow the day-to-day gyrations.

Jeff, unfortunately, was the opposite. Despite making a good living as a podiatrist, he complained about his profession, often counting the dollars and days until he retired. He was determined to work not a day beyond sixty. It was an ambitious goal, but achievable if they kept their spending under control and invested aggressively, which helped to explain Jeff's hypersensitivity to fluctuations in his brokerage account. In his mind, every decline, no matter how miniscule, jeopardized his retirement timeline. He checked his accounts religiously, sometimes several times a day if he wasn't with a patient.

Jessica gave me an exaggerated eye roll. "They're talking about this thing with China. The stock market has had a bad couple of days, that's all."

"Anything we need to worry about?" Samantha asked.

"No!" Jessica and I answered in unison. Jessica glanced at me, and I gave her a look of pure thanks.

"Okay, let's talk about something else then," Samantha said brightly. "How's Ryan doing?"

I hid my grimace.

"Does wanting to send your kid off to boarding school make you a bad person?" Jessica asked, playing her honesty off like a joke.

"Not at all," Jeff said. "Hey, if it's any consolation, you know we can relate. Todd has been acting like a real turd lately, too. I'd ship his ass off, but boarding school is way too expensive, so we'll deal with it."

"Well, what were the odds you'd get two perfect children?" Jessica smiled. "At least you've got one."

The Gillmans' son, Todd, was the same age as Ryan, and the pair had been in the same playgroup when they were infants. They had drifted in different directions in recent years. Todd had a mischievous streak, but wasn't nearly as defiant as Ryan.

Jeff smiled. "Yes, we do have our little angel." Their younger daughter was pretty much a ten-year-old wonder child who couldn't do anything wrong if she tried. "Jamie's awesome, and smart, and beautiful . . . and did I mention how sweet she is?"

Jessica and I looked at each other, trying not to roll our eyes.

"Hasn't she ever done anything wrong? Must be *something*," Jessica jokingly pleaded.

"Well, now that you mention it, I did find a piece of gum stuck to her nightstand last week," Samantha said.

"Oh, the horror," I said mockingly.

Jeffed feigned surprised. "Wait...are you sure it was hers and that Todd didn't put it there? There's no way my little princess would do such a terrible thing."

"Well, if it was her, thank God, at least she's human," Jessica said.

"Speaking of gum . . ." I said, seizing the opportunity to change the subject. The mention of gum stuck in unexpected places reminded me of the Clausky twins and my unintended approval of their funds the day before. The boys emailed me a thank-you note late Friday evening. "Jeff, do your patients complain about stepping in gum much these days?"

Jeff smirked and raised one eyebrow. "Marty, I examine people's feet, not the bottom of their shoes. And we don't have a question on our patient medical history form asking for that. But now that you mention it, I *did* step in some gum in a parking lot not too long ago." He actually seemed to take the question seriously. "It sucked. You'd think someone would come up with a way to deal with that by now."

Oops. Had I just given away the boys' idea? I guess I was trying to make myself feel better about turning over $30,000 to the boys. Perhaps they wouldn't lose all their money.

"What do you mean, honey?" Samantha asked as I silently willed them to not make the connection.

"Somebody needs to invent a device that can help you easily scrape and remove gum off your shoes," Jeff said.

I jumped in to end the conversation I had just started. "Hate to burst your bubble, but they already have one. It's called a shoe brush."

"You know what's even worse than gum?" Samantha said, a little more enthusiastically than I'd have expected for a conversation about gum on one's shoe. "Dog shit!"

Oh shit!

"Todd stepped in it a few weeks ago and came traipsing into the house. It was disgusting and I almost killed him. I literally threw the pair of shoes away rather clean it off."

Jeff looked shocked. "Wait, what? We just bought him those. You threw away a perfectly good pair of seventy-dollar shoes?"

Samantha rubbed her husband's shoulder. "Relax, honey, they were a few months old. Next time I'll leave it for you to clean."

Maybe the boys were on to something.

Jeff shook his head and took a gulp of his drink.

"A good brush would definitely help do the trick with that," I said.

"Yes, we could call it Dr. Gillman's Shoe Brush!" Samantha proclaimed. "We'll be rich!"

"Dr. Gillman's Shoe Brush," Jessica said, playing along. "I'll be in the infomercial if you want me to."

"Oh, no, no, no," I said melodramatically. "A *brush* isn't going to sell. It's not biting enough given the gravity of that nasty situation. What about Dr. Gillman's Shit Stick?" That made everyone laugh. "And I'll be the testimonial guy who steps in it!"

As their laughter died down, my phone started buzzing in my front pocket. I downed my dry martini, asked Jess to order me the pistachio-crusted chicken with extra chutney sauce, and excused myself to the restroom.

All the texts were from JD. The first was a close-up selfie of JD and Bella. Cheek to cheek, they flashed movie-star smiles. He followed up with: *Bella says hi!* Then, *Pray for a Lakers win!!*

I replied with a simple thumbs-up. Knowing JD, he'd taken our former waitress to some swanky new midtown bar. By now, he had likely befriended the bartender and had some kind of specialty signature cocktail made for them.

JD was like a lute player, and we were all his snakes. Even me. The first time I came under his spell, we were both fraternity pledge brothers at Emory. The pledge trainers had organized a road trip to New Orleans. It was to be a weekend of total debauchery highlighted by a late-night, drunken scavenger hunt in the city's historic French Quarter. To foster brotherhood among the pledges, we were broken into small groups of four, with special consideration given to placing us with other pledges we didn't know very well. Armed with only twenty-five bucks in cash, a Polaroid camera, and a French Quarter walking map with clues and riddles on the back, we set out to find the list of treasures. JD and I, both Atlantans, were assigned to a group with Darren Binwald from Dallas and Sid Lefkowitz from St. Louis. JD quickly assumed our group's leadership position. I'll never forget how he firmly shook my hand and coolly asked, "What's up, pussy Kap?" taking a playful liberty with my last name like we had been buddies for years. I liked him right off the bat. We did well at first, knocking off clues and collecting traditional French Quarter paraphernalia like a Pat O'Brien's matchbook, Mardi Gras beads, and a king cake baby. But then the manager at Café Du Monde almost called the cops on Lefkowitz for pissing off some older patrons by blowing powdered sugar all over them and acting like a drunken lunatic. Then he got spotted with one of the establishment's vintage napkin holders, which was one of the highly coveted scavenger hunt items, stuffed under his shirt. JD shook off his buzz and calmly explained to the manager that we drove all the way from Atlanta just to procure the iconic item, which doubled as a menu, as part of a dumb hazing ritual. He offered to pay ten bucks for the thing. The manager, apparently moved by our absurd objective and JD's plea, not only gave us the napkin holder but threw in a bag of free beignets for our long ride home.

Even young and drunk, I noted JD's ability to charm and connect with people. Which would help us on our last, most serious challenge. We had to get a close-up of one us licking Bourbon Street. *"Bare tongue on pavement!"* the scavenger hunt directive read in big, bold letters. Even inebriated no one wanted to volunteer. While the rest of us argued about who should do it, JD stepped aside to chat up a gaggle of Tulane sorority girls who were partying in the heavily trafficked tourist zone.

At first, I was annoyed, thinking he'd abandoned us to hit on some girls. Instead, he craftily brought them into the fold. They, too, were curious to see which one of us was stupid enough to French kiss the filthy street. JD used his charm and street smarts to convince the prettiest of the girls to agree to kiss the guy who took the plunge. That was enough for Lefkowitz.

A small crowd roared as Lefkowitz and the sorority girl smooched, followed by Lefkowitz dropping to his knees and bending his head down to the pavement. To this day, I still gag when I think about Sid swiping his tongue against the street while I took the Polaroid. Sometimes, JD and I joke about tracking down that photo, tagging Sid's social media accounts with it, and earning a few bucks. We figured that Sid, a successful infectious disease doctor, would pay a substantial sum to keep that pic offline. Hazy as my memory was of that pledge night, one of the last things I remember was JD tucking our last few dollars into the shirt pocket of a sleeping homeless guy.

And now the enigma that was JD was schmoozing Bella in a swanky bar, while I was about to resume a ridiculous conversation about shit on shoes with the Gillmans. On my way back to the table, I noticed an email alert on my phone. It was from the Clauskys. I hadn't heard from them since I delivered the unintentional good news.

Marty,
Thanks so much!! We won't let you down. You won't regret this!
Danny and Freddie

My growing list of rationalizations for releasing their funds now included the argument that the boys weren't going to accept "no" for an answer, and if they did, it was only a matter of time until they came back with the next idea. Eventually I would've had to cave in, so why not get it over with?

Upon my arrival back at the table, the conversation moved to summer plans. As much as I welcomed the shift, it also meant that Jessica would disclose our lack of vacation plans. Fortunately, she didn't sound upset when she explained about my father's absence and my need to be present at the firm; it was more matter of fact.

Like many others in the community, the Gillmans were heading to Colorado—Vail, specifically, for a couple of weeks in August. Thankfully, Jeff and Samantha were sensitive enough not to rub it in with graphic detail about their view of the mountains and the cool mountain air while we hunkered down indoors the rest of the summer. They did offer to give us some guest passes to their country club to use while they were in Vail, but not without Jeff venting that the dues were "way too much" and that they wouldn't allow them to suspend their membership for the month.

Jeff dipped his fried calamari into the marinara on his plate. "When your dad retires, maybe you can set up a satellite office in Colorado?"

His suggestion, aimed at cheering us up, definitely held some allure, and he was right—as long as Dad was working, he would never sign off on me being out of the office for long stretches. He was old-school that way. Face-to-face client meetings, demonstrating good work ethic to employees, and showing up early at the office were important to him. I hesitated before responding to Jeff. Should I tell him what's going on? After all, Dad and I would be formally working our succession plan details in a couple of months' time.

"Not sure Dad will ever retire," I said, deciding to play it cautious and then reveal the big news after the fact.

The rest of our dinner was uneventful. On the way home, Jess and I laughed about Jeff's "losing money" comment and how he made a point of splitting the bill even though we said we'd cover the calamari.

I filled her in on the situation with the Clauskys and my concern about accidentally revealing their idea over dinner.

"That's the last thing I need, getting sued by those boys for giving away their nutty idea," I said.

Turning the radio to her favorite pop station, Jess said, "You know, it's not such a bad idea. Maybe they'll be successful."

"Uh…you don't know these boys. What they really need is to get *real* jobs and put a few years of hard work in. That's how you get somewhere. I just hope their grandma doesn't get upset if they lose some money. But maybe it's better they lose a little now, then a lot more later on some other grand idea," I said, not sure if I was trying to convince myself or Jessica I had made a sound decision.

We almost made it home when I mistakenly pivoted the conversation.

"Why don't you take Ryan on a vacation for a week or two while I stay behind to work?"

"What?"

It sounded like a good idea in my head. Let the two of them get away for a while. Why should they have to suffer because I had to be at work?

"No way you're getting out of a family trip," she said while turning down Katy Perry's "Firework."

"I'm not trying to get out of anything. I just thought—"

Jessica cut me off.

"If you really wanted to take a trip, you could do it. I know your parents are away and your mom is sick, but you have employees that can cover for you."

There was no use trying to explain the situation to her. She would only dig in. I kept my mouth shut, and we spent the last five minutes of our drive with the radio quietly playing.

When we arrived home, the kitchen smelled like burned popcorn and dirty dishes lined the countertops. Jessica huffed, "I'll let you take care of this. I'm going to read in bed."

Jess took off upstairs. I found Ryan in the downstairs TV room watching the NBA Finals. I plunked down to join him.

14

In JD's dimly lit bedroom, the ring of a cell phone was nearly drowned out by the loud, heavy breathing and grunting. With a final liberating groan, JD turned over and lay still next to Bella. "Now that's how I like to end my shabbos," he said.

JD promised himself that he wasn't going to sleep with any other women while in pursuit of the mystery woman. He didn't count on getting a text from Bella, expressing interest in "learning more about Judaism" over a drink. Who was he to say no? Education was part of the job.

Bella stepped out of bed and into JD's closet where she pulled a Guns N' Roses concert tee from his stack of neatly folded shirts. It was one of his favorites.

As she slipped it on, he grabbed his phone still reverberating on his nightstand. The caller ID showed "Ben Friedland," one of his synagogue's congregants and a member of the Board of Trustees. Ben was probably returning JD's call. JD had called earlier that week to get an update on Ben's father's condition.

He set the phone down and watched Bella. She was fun and attractive, but it wouldn't go anywhere. She wasn't Jewish, and even if she converted, the age difference was too large and they were in different stages in life. Bathsheba, on the other hand, looked a few years older than Bella. What shirt would she have picked in his closet? A plain white undershirt, simple yet sexy. Or maybe she'd like his Emory sweatshirt, teasing him with what kind of treasure lay hidden underneath.

Bella faced him and giggled. "I can't believe I just had sex with a rabbi."

"Well, you can check that off your bucket list. Was it the religious experience you had imagined?" JD made the line sound unrehearsed despite having said it a dozen times before with a dozen different women.

Bella laughed before heading into the bathroom. JD looked at his watch: 8:28 p.m. The Sabbath had officially ended. He scrambled to find the remote in his nightstand and turned on the large flat-panel TV hanging on the wall. He quickly found the basketball game and saw that the Celtics were leading the Lakers by four points in game seven of the finals with just under two minutes remaining in the game.

Earlier in the year on a trip to Vegas, JD placed a good-size wager on the Lakers, his favorite team ever since his father had given his ten-year-old self a Magic Johnson jersey. At the time he made the bet that the Lakers would win the NBA Championship, the team had been four-to-one underdogs, which would give JD a nice payoff if the Lakers could come back and win the game. He made the bet despite his general rule of not betting on his favorite teams so as to keep his emotions out of his decision-making, but he simply couldn't help himself.

The Lakers had possession of the ball in their backcourt following a score by the Celtics when their coach called a timeout. The network went to commercial, and JD grabbed his cell and listened to the new voicemail.

"Hello, Rabbi. This is Ben Friedland. I'm at the hospital with my dad. He's taken a serious turn for the worse, and the doctors don't think he has much time left. I was hoping you could come down here again and be with us. Please call when you get this message."

"Oh no!" JD said. When JD visited Ben's eighty-eight-year-old father in the hospital earlier in the week, the doctors were optimistic he was recovering from his moderate flulike symptoms, and with some fluids and antivirals, he'd be out of the hospital within days.

The first commercial ended and another one came on. JD figured he could get a quick call in before the game resumed. JD liked to return congregants' phone calls promptly, especially if it involved a board member's seriously ill parent. He also didn't want to give Rabbi Borowitz any ammunition to come down on him for not being available for a congregant in their time of need. Word had made it back to JD that Borowitz was skeptical of JD's commitment ever since he got boxed into hiring him as his associate rabbi.

The game came back on just after JD dialed Ben's number. The Lakers inbounded the ball to Lebron James, who started dribbling up the court.

"Hello, Rabbi Aron?" came Ben's anxious voice through the phone.

JD grabbed the remote and hit the mute button, multitasking.

"Yes, Ben. Sorry, I had my phone turned off for Shabbat. How's your dad doing?"

"Not good. Hang on a second, Rabbi, the nurse is about to give me an update."

Bella returned with a mischievous look in her eye. She took off the T-shirt and straddled JD, blocking his view of the television in a playful attempt to regain his attention. JD, a bit annoyed, had to overlook her perky breasts to focus on the game, frustrated to see he'd missed a pull-up, three-point jumper by LeBron but elated that he drained the shot. The Lakers were now within one point of tying it up with less than two minutes left on the clock.

Ben returned; his voice distressed. "Rabbi, the nurse says his condition is fading quickly." It seemed the machines that tracked his vital signs showed an erratic, slowing heart rate and dropping body temperature. Ben said his father's eyes were mostly closed and he seemed incoherent. JD knew the near-death signs well from his volunteer work at the hospice. Ben's dad would likely pass very soon, and JD's job now was to comfort Ben and help his father's soul prepare for the next world.

"Any chance you can make it over here?" Ben asked desperately.

"I'm not sure I can get down there in time." JD said as Bella continued to grind away on top of him. He felt guilty about not being there for the Friedlands, but he would likely be too late even if he left for the hospital right then.

JD heard some quiet chatter over the phone.

"Rabbi, the nurse just told me he'll go any time," Ben said.

JD's eyes were still locked on the screen. The crowd in the Staples Center, where JD had personally watched many Laker games while visiting LA, was on its feet. The Lakers, down by one, took their final timeout of the game with twenty-two seconds left on the clock.

An adrenaline rush had JD rocking back and forth against the backboard of his bed. Bella was still on top of him, pinning his torso down. He took a long deep breath and exhaled slowly to reset and settle himself. He was overwhelmed and discombobulated. His love of the Lakers, wish to please Bella, and desire to bring peace to a congregant were all colliding. *Why am I being tortured right now?*

"I tell you what, Ben," JD said, "put the phone up to your dad's ear and I'll recite a prayer to him."

JD locked eyes with Bella and slowly mouthed "You....are....so....hot" as he motioned for her to get off him so he could focus on the prayer for Ben's dad.

"I'd really appreciate that, Rabbi," Ben said. "I'm not sure he can hear you, but it would make me feel better. You're on speaker, Rabbi," he said after a shuffling sound.

JD jumped up and scurried out of his bedroom. "Mr. Friedland...it's Rabbi Aron. I'm going to say a prayer with you. Say the words or think of them with me if you can." He then began chanting slowly in Hebrew, "*Shema Yisrael Hashem Elokeinu . . .*"

"His eyelids are twitching," Ben said excitedly. "He hears you, Rabbi! He hears you!"

JD grinned. He continued with the prayer, briefly poking his head back in the bedroom to see what was happening in the game. Lakers were down by one, and Lebron skipped up the court like a gazelle and dribbled in place at the free-throw line. Only one defender stood between him and another championship. Eight seconds remained on the clock.

"Shake him! Shake him!" JD shouted, forgetting that he was in the middle of a prayer and that Ben had the phone pressed against his dying father's ear.

"What's that, Rabbi?" Ben asked. "Not sure I heard you correctly. You said I should shake him?"

JD mentally regrouped, turned his head back away from the game, and concluded with the final confessional prayer: "*Hashem melech, Hashem malach, Hashem yimloch l'olam va'ed.*" He paused, waiting for an update from Ben.

After a few seconds of quiet, JD finally broke the silence. "Ben, what's going on?"

"Mr. Friedland," a woman's soft voice said on the other end of the call. "Your father has passed."

Ben's muffled voice came. "Rabbi, my dad literally went right as you finished the Shema. That was unbelievable."

"Wow, I'm glad we got that prayer in before he went. He was ready," JD said, thankful he was able to be of service despite having been distracted by Bella and the climactic ending to the game. "I'm really sorry for your loss, Ben. Take comfort knowing that his soul is eternal, and he has moved on to a good place."

"Thank you, Rabbi. That means a lot."

"I'll notify the funeral homes so they can get in touch about making arrangements."

JD hung up the phone, satisfied that he had made an impact. When he popped back to his bedroom, the TV was back on commercial break.

"What happened? What did I miss?" he asked Bella.

"Lakers won!" she said.

"Yes!"

JD sat back on the bed and high-fived Bella, who had watched the end of the game. A cool three-thousand payoff on JD's bet.

She pointed to the cell in JD's hand. "What was that all about? That call sounded pretty intense."

"Very!" JD said, turning to Bella. "The Lakers clinch the championship at *precisely* the same time as the passing of an elderly congregant. What can be the meaning in that?"

"No kidding, that's really weird." Bella nudged him gently on the arm. "Are you okay?"

JD didn't respond. He sat there on the bed, digesting what just transpired in his parallel universes.

"Hey, JD, what's up? You okay?" she asked tenderly while gently rubbing his shoulder.

JD looked at her seriously. "Let me ask you something . . . do you like Barry Feldstein?"

Angela reclined on her Pottery Barn sofa in her sparsely decorated apartment's sitting room, her small golden labradoodle, Becky, snuggled under her arm. She cracked open and bent back the stiff binding of a paperback novel. The Amazon reviews were good with 75 percent giving it five stars. She was looking forward to an inspiring read about a middle-aged woman's journey to find meaning in the death of her terminally ill teenage son. But now, on Sunday evening, Angela was stuck on page six with the prose whizzing by her like a foreign language. The uneasiness that had engulfed and distracted her all weekend was still there. With Monday morning closing in, she'd have to decide soon—what, if anything, to do about her compounding Kaplan conundrum?

She talked through her work-related predicament like she was trying to solve a brain teaser, using Becky as an unresponsive sounding board.

"Becky, follow this...if my boss, Leon...sells the company, I'll lose my job. *And*, if I let Marty...screw up again, it *might* kill the merger, in which case I could keep my job...unless Leon fires me for not catching Marty's screw ups. Did I mention that Marty is my boss' son?"

Angela presumed that a documented track record of repeated compliance violations by Marty could be more than an ugly blemish for the firm, potentially thwarting any merger. Who would want to buy a company where the director of research and senior advisor, and the principal's son no less, had a compliance rap sheet? The irony of her predicament was not lost on her, but totally befuddled her pet.

"Save the son...lose the job," Angela mused to her sleeping pooch.

Of course, there was the possibility she was overthinking the situation. Something she had done her entire life. Just because she thought it was a big deal, didn't necessarily mean others would feel the same way, like the time she alerted her parents that her younger teenage brother was smoking pot with his friends in the storage shed in their backyard. They took the information in stride, admonishing her for trying to do their job, rather than come down on the perpetrator.

Angela tossed the book on the carpeted floor, closed her eyes, and stretched out on the sofa. Her mind raced. Finding another job for the second time in six months. Answering tough questions about what happened. Moving again!

A foul smell disrupted her fretting.

"Ooh, Becky!"

Angela sprung back into a seated position, gently lifted the twenty-pound dog and moved her to the other side of the long sofa. She nabbed her tablet off the sleek wooden coffee table and immediately pulled up Marty's email to the boys. She was as flabbergasted as the first time she read it on Friday afternoon. Who did Marty think he was? *CrapMap* and *Money Man*...had he gone off the rails? Marty's trading protocol error involving the stock sales in Jacob Aron's account paled in comparison to his doubling down on distributions from the Clauskys' trust account without their trustee's prior written consent.

The boys' exuberant response to Marty would make matters worse. Their young spirits will be crushed when he tells them there are no funds coming for their project. She'd have to act quickly if she were to intervene since they expected money the next day. But Marty's testy reaction to her last compliance discussion with him made any further reprimands risky. Their working relationship could be damaged, perhaps permanently, if he took her oversight of the matter badly. Had he not rushed her out of his office she could've brought up the subject in a gentle manner. The two could've worked through the matter together, plotting out a satisfactory resolution. But no, he had to take that call from his wife and shoo her away.

She put away the tablet and snatched the paperback up off the rug. Before taking another crack at the book, she noticed a photo album tucked into the coffee table's bottom shelf. She picked it up and began sifting through her past, trying not to be bothered by the conspicuous blank spots that once contained photos of her and her ex-husband. The album was a time warp—beginning around her college graduation and running through her first couple of years of marriage. She came across several photos of her and coworkers from the SEC. In one shot, she and three other colleagues were holding up drinks in a toast. It was from a celebratory outing following their graduation from their formal training program before the start of their field assignments. She recalled the group oath they took to uphold the integrity of our financial markets during their graduation ceremony.

Angela stared at the picture, wondering what had happened to everyone. As far as she knew, the others still worked there.

She grabbed her tablet and wrote:

Hi Marty,

I hope you're having a nice weekend. I really need to talk to you first thing in the morning. It's important! Please let me know when you have time to talk.

Angela

She reopened the book and turned back to page one. Tomorrow would be tough, but she would find the strength to get through it.

•

Bizline News Update: Sunday, June 24, 8:20 p.m. ET

We continue to follow the developments related to last week's incident involving Chinese military aircraft encroaching on US mainland. President Pruitt did a lot of weekend tweeting, none of which addressed the incident. Given the lack of news flow from the White House, several television networks filled the void with both Meet the Press and Face the Nation hosting international relations scholars and military experts.

Panelists fanned the story's flames, speculating that the brazen move would certainly elicit a U.S. response. Madeleine Bernard, an international affairs professor from Georgetown University and notable China hawk, suggested the United States might consider flexing its own muscles to ward off any further provocations. She speculated "such a response could include aggressive military exercise in close proximity to the Chinese mainland territory, Taiwan or the disputed islands in the South China Sea." China has transformed many man-made islands in the South China Sea into heavily fortified military installations in recent years. The United States has a history of sending its battleships into the disputed area, which has led to a few close military encounters in the past. But sending planes might be an entirely hair-raising experience for the Chinese.

Bernard suggested, "The United States could send in an aircraft carrier and have its jets conduct a flyover mission over those islands if it wanted to send a strong signal to the Chinese, letting them know not to poke the United States in the eye with a stick again. Taiwan might also be a flashpoint, given its controversial relationship to both China and the West."

Another analyst, former US Army General Conner Matthews, speculated that the upcoming US holiday might feed into the US response. "With the Fourth of July approaching, that might start to factor into the equation." When pushed to clarify, he said, "Certainly, the president won't want to appear weak around the country's National Day of Independence."

A short while ago, we received unconfirmed reports that the United States' first official action following the Chinese provocation will be to file a formal complaint with the U.N. Security Council on Monday morning. Given that this report is still unconfirmed, and if true, would represent a mild response, US futures indicate the market will start the week flat to moderately higher.

•

16

I was determined to have a more productive week. First thing Monday morning, after getting caught up on the news, I tugged the sticky note off my monitor, pulled up JD's account, and transferred $500,000 over to his bank. Done.

I texted him.

Me: JD, can you say Feldstein?:) Wire's on the way!

It was nice to have that task off my plate even though I wasn't in favor of the use of the proceeds.

Fortunately, after being frozen in time over the weekend, the market was off to a quiet start with stocks bobbing around the unchanged mark at the open. Not getting an early Monday morning distress call from Mrs. Benoit was a welcoming sign. Maybe she was busy working on her quilt or our client note settled her down over the weekend. I was concerned it might have the opposite effect on her and others, but I had received several favorable email responses from clients, thanking me for the update. I also got a note from Angela that came in on Sunday evening. She wanted to meet with me again. No doubt it involved compliance issues we didn't get to during our last meeting. I told her to stop by around ten after I had a chance to get settled in and situated for the day.

I was deep into an industry research analyst's research report on Pepsi when a news flash popped up on my feed.

•

Bizline News Update: Monday, June 25, 9:56 a.m. ET

Unconfirmed report from an unidentified, high-ranking Russian govern-ment official claims the Russian navy would join the Chinese in a block-ade of Hawaii should the United States launch any aggressive or threaten-ing military actions toward China and its sovereign-protected territories.

•

I swallowed hard to suppress the acid ascending my throat. *Russia and Hawaii? This is going to be a shitshow.* The markets and our clients' portfolios plunged instantly, tacking another 1 percent loss to the prior week's decline. It didn't seem to matter that the news source was un-substantiated and potentially meritless. Even the phrase "unidentified, high-ranking official" seemed like spin from an opportunistic short sell-er wanting to make some money off a market drop. It didn't matter. It was a "shoot first, ask questions later" market. So much for getting the week off to a good start.

Right as I was digesting the unfolding story, there were three short decisive taps on my office door. I looked at my watch...ten on the nose. Five minutes earlier, I could've handled having to deal with Angela. But now, with our portfolio getting whacked again, I was in no mood to suf-fer through another beatdown. But I couldn't put her off again. I called her in but kept my monitors illuminated. Maybe she'd notice all the red on the screen, be respectful of my portfolio management duties, and leave quickly.

"Hello, again. So, what can I help you with, Angela?" I asked, plaster-ing a pleasant smile on my face.

"Good morning. Have a nice weekend?" she inquired as she slid her way into my office, a manila folder firmly in her right hand, looking even more serious than usual.

I smelled trouble in that folder and her contrived small talk during which she shared that she'd be heading back to DC later in the week and staying through the Fourth of July holiday.

"Well, enjoy, I'll be holding down the fort here." I gave a mental fist pump. "Hopefully the world and the market will settle down by then," I said, nodding to my monitor.

She appeared unmoved by my unspoken plea for mercy. "So, I really need to talk to you about something. Do you mind if I take a seat?"

"Sure, sit down. What's on your mind?" I asked, eager to get whatever it was over with already. I glanced back over at my screen. The market slid lower, intensifying my angst.

Angela sat in one of the two black leather chairs facing my desk, opened the manila folder across her lap, and took out two pieces of paper, which she laid in front of me on my desk. "Would you mind explaining this to me?"

I leaned forward in my chair so I could get a good look at her exhibits. She had printouts of email exchanges between me and the Clauskys from the prior week. I wasn't sure where she was going, but it was clear that she had been monitoring me again. First the trading report and now this. What was she up to and why was she targeting me yet again?

I looked her straight in the eye. "Okay, it's an email thread between me and the Clausky boys," I said, pointing out the obvious. "What else would you like to know?"

"Well, this is the second incident I've found where you've authorized a distribution from the Clauskys' trust account. This one, apparently to fund something called a CrapMap, and a previous twenty-six-thousand-dollar payment to a Hendrick's Automotive last month. I suppose that was for a car for one of the trust's beneficiaries."

How did she know about the app? Was she reading my emails?

"That's correct," I said, volunteering no other information, electing to let her clarify her issue and divulge what she knew.

"I can't find any record that Josie Clausky, the trustee named in both Bernard and Betsy Clausky's wills, has amended the trust to add you as a co-trustee, thereby giving you the express authority to authorize such distributions."

She scolded me like I was a sixth grader who didn't correctly cite a source for an essay.

"That's what you're all up in arms about? Some money for Freddie's car after his old one flooded and money for their new venture?" I hoped she wouldn't probe deeper into the CrapMap. That the seed money for the app would likely serve no other purpose than teaching the boys a lesson about risk-taking wasn't something I wanted to get into.

I could understand why she was concerned about the transfers, but I knew what she didn't: that Josie had given me the discretion to make those distributions. I was relieved that I'd be making this whole thing go away with my imminent reveal.

"Martin, this is a very serious matter," she said.

No one called me Martin except for Mrs. Benoit, who made it sound charming given her age and endearing French accent.

"You're acting as the trustee without legal permission to do so. And I don't even know what to say about referring yourself as *Money Man* in official client correspondence. That's highly unprofessional and, frankly, a bit weird. It might be even a violation of SEC rules if that phrase can be interpreted to connote some extraordinary financial acumen on your part . . . no offense."

Angela was really blowing everything out of proportion. The word *violation* pierced my ears like a high-pitched fire alarm, and her pressing, aggressive tone was about to make my head explode. I could not take much more of her scolding me. On top of that, my screen was now a bloody red mess with the market tumbling. Our conversation needed to end. Soon!

"For your information," I said, a little more sharply than I intended, "Josie told me I could authorize discretionary payment requests from the boys because she didn't want to be bothered by it. I was actually doing her a favor and following my client's wishes."

"Oh, really? That's great! But where is that in writing?" Angela said, looking hopeful.

"I probably have a note somewhere about it, but I'll ask her to sign a letter saying she said it is okay if it makes you feel better."

"That's a start but won't cut it for the car payment you already authorized. And *please* hold off on sending those boys money for their Crap project or whatever it is until we get this figured out."

My heart really started pumping at that point.

"Too late. Money went out already," I said confidently like I was within my rights to have done so even though I wasn't so sure anymore.

Angela lowered and shook her head, then let out a long exhale. She was clearly disappointed.

She took a deep breath, raised her head, and went off. "What if the Clauskys' idea is a total flop, and they find out their grandma hadn't ever approved it? They could sue you, your dad, me, and this firm. How could you be so cavalier about this? Hubris and sloppy work have brought down fish much bigger than you and this firm. I'm going to have to add this to my compliance report, and we're going to have to find a way to fix this."

That was it. I stood up and launched my own verbal assault. "Look, Angela, coming in here, throwing this shit in my face, and accusing me of being sloppy and unprofessional isn't okay. I pride myself on having a very high degree of integrity and always putting my clients' needs before my own. I don't know what you're up to, prying around my business, but you need to BACK the HELL OFF!" I angrily pointed my finger at her.

I felt outside myself as I was barking at Angela. It wasn't like me to blow up at someone, especially a coworker.

Angela got very red in the face. I needed to bring the conversation to an end before it cascaded into something much worse.

"So," I said, abruptly, clapping my hands together. "Thanks for bringing this to my attention. Now, why don't you go back to your office so you can continue monitoring me?" I added, taking a dig at her espionage-like actions.

"Okay," she said, her voice shaking as she stood. "I'm going to…I think I'll be leaving for my trip a little earlier, and if I don't come back, you'll know it's because I felt totally disrespected here."

Angela stormed out of my office. I ripped up the papers she left behind, tossing the pieces in the trash under my desk. Suddenly, my office felt like a prison, one I had to escape but couldn't. I needed air and to clear my thoughts, but I had to get back to what was going on in the markets. I'd worry about Angela later.

I swung my chair back around to find the markets still reeling. The major US and global stock markets steadily dropped 2 percent in an across the board sell-off since the market opened. Hopefully Mrs. Benoit and our other predictably nervous clients weren't watching.

With no official clarification or confirmation from the US, Russian, or Chinese officials, the markets would remain under duress. I summoned Devon and Shelley back to the conference room to discuss what, if anything, we should do.

•

"Well, that was an unpleasant start to the day," I said to my research team, trying not to sound panicky even though I was still riled up by my tiff with Angela and the market shellacking.

I turned on the TV in the conference room so the three of us could watch the ugliness unfold in real time on the big screen. The prior week's 5 percent loss quickly turned into seven, with no signs of letting up, and it was only Monday.

"Yep," Devon said, "more of the same. Defense contractors up, everything else down, even consumer staples are rolling over. Not a good sign."

Eager for second opinions, I asked, "So, is *this* a good buying opportunity?"

"It looked that way last week, but not so sure now," Shelley said. "For what it's worth, I did do some research on how the market reacted during other significant geopolitical or military events."

Shelley passed around a few colorized printouts containing historical charts and figures.

"This report shows what happened to the stock market following fifty geopolitical crises since 1900," she said, holding up one piece of paper in the air.

I could see a familiar look of envy and self-dissatisfaction creep onto Devon's face. Shelley was a natural go-getter who went the extra mile while Devon was task-oriented, doing a decent job on anything asked of him, nothing more or less. His ability to simply meet expectations was something we had discussed during his prior performance reviews, but my constructive feedback had yet to bear fruit. Even so, both were smart, loyal, and dependable employees, and KCM was fortunate to have them.

"You can see the Dow's average low following a variety of crises was a drop of about eight percent. The oil embargo of 1973 might be an applicable parallel with this talk of a blockade of Hawaii. That event was real disaster for the market. The market fell almost nineteen percent before starting to recover."

Devon straightened his rimless glass frames. "That's a long way down from here to there."

I dove into the handouts, trying to quickly ascertain the important takeaways before Shelley announced her own conclusions.

"Other than that, it's a pretty mixed bag of results. The market dropped almost five percent leading into the Persian Gulf War in 1991, then rallied within days after it became apparent it wouldn't be a long, drawn-out affair. The invasion of Afghanistan following 9/11 also saw a snapback rally after an initial fall, but that was within the context of the ongoing bear markets from 2000 to 2002. So, even though the market tends to climb once the fighting begins, none of those incidents were on US soil. That's obviously a big unknown until it becomes clearer where and how an armed conflict with China might unfold. With that being said, outside of a recession, the odds are in favor of the market coming back once there is more certainty surrounding the conflict."

"Thanks, Shelley," I said, having reached the same conclusion. "So, basically, at some point the market will come back...it's just a question of how long it will take and how much pain we have to endure first. And will we lose any clients in the process."

"Yep," Shelley replied.

I pointed to the monitor. "The market's already off almost eight per-cent, which is, according to these numbers, about the average decline, so maybe the worst is over. Even so, clients hate losing money more than they like making it, so let's be careful."

Devon cleared his throat. "Investors don't like uncertainty. Hard to see a rally until things settle down."

Including the morning's losses, nearly 4 percent of value had been wiped from our clients' portfolios over the last few trading days, less than the market's decline, but it still left a mark. While it didn't sound so bad in percentage terms, when translated into actual dollars, it started to add up to real money. A client with $5 million, of which we had many, had lost at least $200,000. Of course, unless we sold, the losses were only on paper, but it was enough of a cut to get someone's attention, and not the good kind.

The aggregate value of our clients' assets had fallen by a similar number. The $500 million we managed less than a week earlier now stood at $475 million. My chart tracking our firm assets that had shown a nice smooth ascent over the last few years had turned south. I fretted over how low it would go. It wasn't a good feeling, and it was happening on my watch. The unexpected drop put a dent in my billion-dollar ambitions, and who knew how long it would take to get back to where we were, let alone attain the big B?

"What's your dad think about the situation?" Devon asked, assuming I had been in touch with him about the brewing crisis. As far as he knew, interrupting my dad's vacation for a quick conversation to talk shop wasn't a big deal. He didn't know that he was on a mission to save his dying wife's life and I didn't want to bother him with work matters.

Even so, it was an inevitable question though I bristled that a junior member of my research team insinuated that I didn't have a good handle on the situation. The truth was that I really could've used Dad's sage guidance. Even though I was an educated, experienced investment analyst, it didn't make the situation any less scary. Having Dad in the office right next door to me had been a luxury I'd taken for granted. We usually talked about the markets at least once a day. As confident as I was in my analytical and research skills, I hadn't yet managed our portfolio or the office through a crisis. If I were to prove myself worthy of taking over the helm of the firm, I'd have to do both.

Dad never seemed at a loss for what to do. He had a self-assuredness about him that put everyone at ease. With him out of the office for a while, everyone was going to look to me for direction. I had to project confidence to our troops. They needed to believe I had a good game plan, to view me as a capable leader.

My best guess was that Dad would simply shrug off the market drop with one of his folksy Buffett-like sayings like, "The market doesn't move in a straight line up" or "Falling prices just mean we get a chance to buy some good companies on sale." But that was easier said than done. Even though I knew that temporary setbacks in the market were unavoidable, losing clients' money hurt and rattled me. I felt like I was letting our clients down, like I should've been able to see the drops coming and done something about it ahead of time. I needed to be smarter than everyone else.

Since I'd joined my dad at the firm seven years earlier, we'd endured numerous market pullbacks and corrections, the worst of which was a scary 26 percent market drop associated with a mild global economic recession. The firm was much smaller then, and my dad was still doing all the stock picking himself. I was doing some industry and stock research but not responsible for the day-to-day portfolio management. Prior to that downturn, he'd shrewdly tilted our stock portfolio toward utilities and consumer staples that tended to hold up well in recessionary environments. It wasn't that he had been forecasting a recession, he just found valuations and the risk-return profile of stocks in those sectors to be much more compelling than those in other areas of the market. Turns out, it was a prescient call. When the economy slowed, the higher priced growth stocks we avoided got clobbered, and our portfolio held up reasonably well. We came out of the downturn looking smart, and our strong relative performance during that period helped fuel our next phase of growth. On my chart tracking the firm's assets under management, the entire episode wasn't more than a tiny blip.

If Dad had been in the room with us, he'd probably have been the first to reinforce the notion that recessions, often brought on by some unforeseen external shock like 9/11, were next to impossible to predict with any degree of accuracy. By the time you were already in one, most of the damage to the stock market would have likely already been experienced. Even so, it didn't keep investors, both professional and individuals, from trying to do so.

I could've just called and asked Dad what we should do, but I didn't want to. At least, not yet. He hadn't even been gone two weeks. If he were going to turn over the reins of the firm to me, he needed to know he could trust me to run things effectively without him, especially given my mother's precarious condition. I could handle this speed bump. I already got the letter out to clients, now I could handle the portfolio.

"I haven't talked to my dad about it yet," I said to Devon after a moment. "Given what Shelley reinforced, that the markets tend to come back once the incident clears up, I think we should start buying rather than selling at this point."

There. Decision made.

Devon, always the more impulsive and less thorough of our two analysts, said, "Sounds reasonable. What should we buy?"

"Let's start by upping our exposure to the consumer discretionary names in the portfolio," I suggested.

Shelley adjusted her laptop screen. "Target and Best Buy might be good adds here."

I gathered up the papers in front of me and handed them back to Shelley. "And let's go ahead and get Jateroo in those client accounts we identified and add twenty basis points of exposure to Stellar. We might not get another opportunity."

"Sounds good," Devon said. "I'll get the list together."

It felt good to act and add to those positions in the weakness.

When I got back to my office, the calls and emails started to flow in. Guess clients were paying attention after all. For the most part, I was fielding the communications, reassuring everyone that we were following the news flow and would adjust portfolios as necessary.

I took a call from Mitch Sarit, one of our more sophisticated clients. He was calling in from his summer home in Steamboat Springs. Mitch was a successful mergers and acquisitions attorney, married to an equally successful dermatologist. The two printed money. We didn't even manage most of it. They only gave us the funds his wife earned since most of their vast wealth was tied up in various private partnerships and deals Mitch did in his day job. To Mitch's credit, shaky markets didn't bother him. On the contrary, they excited him as he appreciated the opportunity to put more money to work at lower prices.

"What are we going to buy? What are we going to buy?" were the rapid-fire words out of his mouth.

"Cool your jets. This may be something more than a garden-variety summer pullback," I told him. "But we're doing a little nibbling."

Our investment management and portfolio philosophy did not revolve around trying to time the market. Rather, we stressed bottoms-up fundamental research, which meant buying and holding solid companies with proven business models as well as appealing growth prospects. If we could buy them at attractively priced valuations, our clients would likely enjoy capital appreciation over time while offering a high degree of principle protection.

"Good. I've got more dry powder other than the cash in our account," he said. "Let me know if you need some more if you see some real bargains."

"Will do."

Unfortunately, most clients couldn't match Mitch and his wife's ability to print money, nor their enthusiasm for deploying it when market turmoil struck. We had to measure our reaction against each client's circumstances and how they might respond to losses in their account.

By the end of that first trading day of the week, the cumulative four-day slump reached 7.5 percent. I gave myself a small pat on the back for at least selling down a portion of JD's holdings the week before to which he confirmed the transfer receipt with a one-word text: *Sweet!*

Just after the markets closed, I got an email from Devon.

Devon: *Tomorrow's going to be rough. Futures already down. Should we look to add GLD tomorrow?*

Me: *Looks that way. Interesting thought on GLD but let's hold off for now.*

The futures were indeed indicating another half a percent drop in the morning, but a lot could happen in between now and then. I didn't say more to Devon, not wanting to get into a long exchange about the merits of adding a security—GLD—that tracked the price of gold to our clients' portfolios. Undoubtedly, Devon was trying to make up for being outshined by Shelley during our meeting earlier in the day. But, historically, gold was a terrible investment when compared to stocks and bonds. Gold didn't pay interest, had a far worse track record than stocks over the long run, and required someone else to pay more for it than you did to make any money. However, during times of heightened fear and market turmoil, the yellow precious metal's price could spike higher as investors sought safety. We included small amounts of it in our client portfolios from time to time but never bought it into a price surge. Generally, we liked to sell securities after they popped, not buy them. The discussion with Devon would have to wait until the next day. I was drained from the day. It had started badly with my fallout with Angela, who I hadn't crossed paths with since.

I grabbed a couple of corporate annual reports off my desk and stuffed them into my bulging briefcase. In doing so, the greeting card remnants I rescued from the trash a few days earlier came back into view. Wanting to clear some space, I almost threw the card in the paper shredder in my office but held off. I all but dismissed the finding, giving Jessica the benefit of the doubt about its origin and any meaning tied to the unidentified Mark. However, just for final closure, I decided I'd bring it up when I got home so I could have complete closure before purging the card and moving on.

17

The line I practiced repeatedly on the drive home was "Hey, I meant to ask you about something I found in the trash when it broke open the other day..." It struck the right balance of casualness, curiosity, and concern without sounding too accusatory.

Other than the gentle hum coming from the kitchen oven, the house appeared relatively calm when I walked in. If there had been fighting, it was over with for the time being. I could hear Ryan talking to friends on his headset while playing video games in the playroom on the first floor. On my way out of the kitchen I peeked through the oven's clear glass door. Glazed chicken breasts and assorted vegetables were being kept warm in a Pyrex baking dish.

I popped my head in the playroom around the corner from the kitchen to say hi to Ryan. He barely noticed me, giving me a head nod while using his console to take aim and fire his assault weapon at some villainous-looking character on the screen. I dropped my briefcase at the bottom of the staircase and went to find Jessica, who had retreated to our bedroom on the second floor. When I found her, she was reclining on the chaise longue, deeply absorbed in a book called *Oppositional Defiant Disorder (ODD)—Does My Child Have It and What Can I Do?*

"You're going to have to read this when I'm finished," she said before I even opened my mouth to greet her. "We've got real problems with Ryan.

We're doing things *all* wrong."

After assuring her I would read the book, I looked for an opening to mention the card. Wanting to get her mind off Ryan, I opted to give her a play-by-play of the dreadful scene that unfolded between me and Angela that morning to shake our conversation. Hopefully it would lead to a more natural segue.

"You said *what* to her?" Jess said. "What's wrong with you? Wow. The book says ODD can be genetic. Maybe he got it from you."

I would've pointed out that our son's stubbornness was likely the result of her DNA, not mine, but feared the suggestion wouldn't have been well received.

"Please...this is really serious; you know that snapping at a coworker isn't like me."

Jessica rested the open book on her chest, careful not to lose her page. "You've clearly been on edge more than usual lately."

"Ya think?" I asked crankily.

"Ah, yeah."

She was right. I had been irritable and more easily set off the last couple of weeks since my parents left, and the market started acting up. And I was probably a jerk to Angela.

"Do you think she's really going to quit?" I asked.

If Angela didn't return, my dad would freak out. She was his hire, and he viewed her role as a crucial function for any reputable money management firm. But if she comes back, she'll be writing me up in her internal compliance report and Dad will for sure be pissed about that. Either way I'm screwed.

"She probably won't quit. She just needs some cooling off time. But it does sound like she was just doing her job trying to protect you and the firm, and you chewed her out."

I took a seat on the chair beside Jess. "I realize that, but...I don't know...I have this weird feeling she's coming after me, snooping around my client files, like she's fishing for something."

Jessica raised an eyebrow. "That's weird. Why would she be spying on you? Do you trust her?"

The turn in our conversation toward trust effectively slammed the door shut for me to *casually* bring up *the card*. I either had to clumsily address my own perceptible trust issues with Jessica right then or wait for a better opportunity later.

"I'm not sure. But you're right. I'll give her some time to cool down, then apologize," I said, deciding to punt on the whole Mark conversation for the time being.

Jessica took off her reading glasses and hung them on the front of her white T-shirt. "Are you sure you want to take over for your dad? Managing people may not be your strong suit. Just saying."

I was a little taken aback by her negativity. She knew how badly I wanted to take over for Dad. "I'll manage just fine, thank you very much. Why would you say that?"

"Sorry, it just seems like managing more people is going to stress you out."

"It *can* be a stressful job, but I handle it pretty well," I said.

Jessica bit her lip, clearly not buying it.

Before I had a chance to defend myself, Ryan appeared at our door. Jessica closed the book and turned it facedown on her nightstand.

"I'm starving. What's for dinner?" he asked impatiently.

"Chicken and vegetables," Jessica said, not skipping a beat.

"What else can I have?"

She paused. "That's what we're having. Chicken and vegetables."

Here we go.

"But they gave us chicken for lunch at camp. I want something else."

I could empathize. Personally, I didn't like eating the same back-to-back meals either, but Jessica wasn't feeling sorry for him. I'm sure one of the chapters she just read instructed parents not to let your child dictate dinner plans. Hold the line no matter what kind of tantrum your child could throw.

"Ryan, just eat the chicken. It looks pretty good," I said, trying to help out.

"I'm not eating it. Last time it was all dried out," he said. "I just won't eat."

"Okay," Jessica said, waving him off indifferently.

"Ryan, just try it. If you don't like it, I'll get you a pizza," I said, trying to diffuse another argument with what I thought was a reasonable solution.

Jessica looked at me angrily. She huffed, "You two can fend for yourselves. I'm skipping dinner." She got up, went into the bathroom, and turned on the shower.

18

The door flung open, hitting the wall behind it, as Susan rushed into the shul's small library where JD was studying at a table.

"Whoa, where's the fire?" JD joked.

She wiped the sweat off her brow. "Sorry to disturb you, Rabbi, but I pulled together the list of the families with yahrzeits you requested," Susan said, thrusting a set of stapled pages at him. "Sorry it took me so long. I wanted to make sure it was thorough and complete. Seemed important."

JD grinned and grabbed the papers from her, and his heart pounded his rib cage as he scanned the first couple of pages. "Susan, this is exactly what I needed. You're the best!"

Susan's cheeks flushed pink, and she gave a sheepish nod before heading back to her workstation. JD scurried back down the hall to his office and closed the door. He laid the pages across his desk and snatched a black Sharpie from his desk drawer.

He began skimming through the names of the synagogue members who'd passed away during the Hebrew months of Sivan and Tammuz, which overlapped with the secular calendar month of June. He immediately scratched through names he recognized and could rule out, eliminating a good portion of the list within a minute. Six names remained. Those six deceased had a combined total of eighteen living descendants who were to be alerted each year on the anniversary of their loved one's death. His heart beat even faster. Seven were women. His Bathsheba was here.

She had to be.

"Okay, here we go," he muttered to himself.

He fired up his computer and googled the first of the seven names: Claire Bintman. He clicked on a link to an article about a Holocaust survivor, Mendel Tornofsky, and his descendants. He scanned the article, which mentioned a granddaughter named Claire Bintman along with her husband and two children.

Married. Shit!

But as he scrolled, he sighed with relief. There was a picture of Claire with her family. It wasn't her. He scratched through Claire's name and moved on to the next. Twenty minutes later, he had two names left: Alexa Roseman and Karen Amberg.

His initial Facebook search of Karen's name turned up no connections. On LinkedIn, he found a secondary connection to a corporate attorney who lived a little over an hour away in Athens. From the picture, he could tell it wasn't her, but he couldn't be entirely sure that this was even the same Karen Amberg on the list. He circled her name and added a question mark before typing out an email to his assistant.

Hey Susan,

Can you find out if Mel Amberg, a former synagogue member who died three years ago, has a daughter named Karen who lives in Athens? I've got a friend who's looking for a lawyer there and would be nice to refer to a member of the shul.

Thanks,

Rabbi Jacob

That left Alexa Roseman, whose father, Bruce, had passed away four years earlier, leaving behind his daughter and wife. Not only was JD unfamiliar with the family name, his search on social media turned up no mutual friend connections. The synagogue had lots of congregants he had never met as many were inactive, but still chose to maintain their formal membership. He moved on to a broader search. After typing "Alexa Roseman" into the search bar, he paused before hitting "enter." His last hope. What if it turned up nothing? What if this had been a pathetic grab at something that was never meant to be?

And yet now all he could think was: would she be up for keeping a kosher home?

The first result was an article entitled "Atlanta Teacher Going the Extra Mile." An Atlanta schoolteacher named Alexa Roseman was being honored for her work with special needs children. A real mensch, he thought, and felt validated about his intuition. Unfortunately, a click-through to the actual article showed Alexa as a small, gray-haired woman in her late sixties. Not her.

The second, and last, search result was for an Alexa Roseman, M.D. The website was for a holistic medical doctor located across town in the artsy Little Five Points district. There was no picture of her on the website, but her bio was impressive, listing strong academic credentials and multiple board certifications.

Beautiful and smart.

He wrote down the number listed on the website on a scratch pad on his desk, picked up his phone, and dialed.

"Yes, this is Jacob Aron. I'd like to make an appointment with Dr. Roseman please."

19

•

Bizline News Update: Thursday, June 28, 7:45 a.m. ET

Nicholai Trinsky, Russia's ambassador to the U.N., debunks the blockade story as "wild speculation." S&P futures spiking.

•

Relief rally…here we come! Before the opening bell, I sent buy orders to our trader, Phil, so we could put more of our clients' money to work. Even if we were adding to positions at prices higher than the prior day's close, it still represented a decent discount from where prices stood a week earlier. At least we'd look good to our clients that we took advantage of the buying opportunity.

I directed Phil *not* to buy immediately at the open. I didn't want to buy into the initial spike. Usually, there was a small pullback shortly following the start of trading. We'd wait for it. Half an hour into the trading session, Phil sent me an email confirming that the block buy orders had been filled at our target prices and that the shares would be allocated to the client accounts as outlined on the spreadsheet I sent him. The market blasted even higher, propelling our core positions in Target, Nike, Jateroo, and Stellar Biomed beyond our buy points just minutes earlier. I was relieved we got the trades off.

The green on my screen was exhilarating like jumping into an ice-cold swimming pool after a tranquillizingly hot Jacuzzi. Even though it had been only a week since the last up day for the market, I almost forgot what making money felt like. My anxiety melted away with the market's advance. I pulled up the email from Phil and replied back to him, "Nice execution! Maybe we should've gone deeper. This rally looks like it has legs."

Next, I was eager to share my shrewd portfolio moves with my dad. I drafted an email. It was the first real update I'd provided to him since he and Mom had left town. Other than some brief group texts notifying me and my siblings of their safe arrival in Paris, I hadn't reached out in a more meaningful way. I was determined not to bother them while they were unwinding before Mom's treatments started. And up until now, all I had was bad news. Between my rift with Angela and the market slump, there hadn't been anything positive to report. But now, things were looking up.

Dad,
Hope you and Mom had a nice time in Paris. Would like to get caught up. Maybe this Sunday. I know you're trying not to look at work stuff, but the market has been a real mess the last week. We took advantage of the sell-off and did some buying this morning. I hope everything goes well with Mom's treatment.
Thinking of you both,
Marty

By late morning, the market was ripping higher, by a couple of percent or so. Barring any more negative developments, it might rally all the way back to its previous high by the end of the week, and if not by then, the Fourth of July holiday.

It was a great day. After catching up on some emails and having a congenial call with a client that was celebrating a fiftieth birthday, I was so energized that I texted Jessica to see if she wanted to grab lunch. Jess wasn't working that day, and Ryan was at camp, so if she wasn't meeting some girlfriends, she'd likely be available.

Jess: *Just got back from gym. Can meet u in 20 at Terry's.*
Terry's Deli was a casual sandwich shop about halfway between our house and KCM's office. It was nice to feel at ease for a change and I was excited to be with Jess while I was relaxed. If I caught her in a good mood, maybe we'd even go back to our house for a little fun. It had been years since we spontaneously ended up at home on a workday to make love. There was a time after we first got married that Jess and I had a standing Wednesday lunch date that could end up in bed before heading back to work. I could tell by where we were eating if the odds were good or not. Terry's generally meant I had a good shot. We managed to keep our weekly rendezvous going for about a year before my work obligations got in the way. Making myself available to meet with busy clients and new prospects over lunch was a big part of my job at KCM. Jess was understanding, but slowly our lunches went from the regular Wednesday to the ad hoc where I'd see if she was available the morning of.

When I arrived at Terry's, Jessica was already waiting for me. Her normally shoulder-length wavy brown hair was tied up in a tight bun, exposing her slight neck and fit, tone shoulders. She looked relaxed in her stretch pants, tank top, and flip-flops, compared to her more formal work attire. She gave me a guarded kiss on the cheek and a half smile. "Don't get too close. I didn't have time to shower."

"Nice," I said jokingly.

"Well, you didn't give me much notice," she said. "I guess the market's doing better today." Her instincts picked up on my last-minute lunch invitation and easy temperament. Could she also sense what else I had in mind? At that point, I didn't have a good read if my desires would be reciprocated.

At the counter, waiting to order, I told her about our morning trades, which she seemed happy about. After ordering, we grabbed a small table close to the counter. Jessica opened the plastic top of her iced tea and began her usual process of mixing in just the right amount of sweetener and three gently squeezed lemon slices. Watching her complete the ritual brought me back to our first date when I first witnessed her tea preparation. I was intrigued and imagined what other habits she might harbor that could thwart our potential compatibility.

Jessica took a big sip, put the cup back down, and gave me a serious look. "Maybe we can finally talk about some things now that you're less distracted."

"Let's talk. I'm *all* yours," I said, hoping it wasn't another Ryan situation but knowing that was wishful thinking. My tone was playful and light, like I didn't know what on earth could possibly be weighing on her. Wrong move.

"Have we not been living under the same roof for the last couple years?" she asked, looking seriously put off by my carefree tone.

My apparent lack of seriousness led to an uncomfortable lull in the conversation that felt awkward even for a couple that had been married for fourteen years. I wasn't entirely sure where she was going with this, but it was becoming clear that a romantic interlude at the house after lunch was definitely out.

"Look," I said, when it didn't seem like Jessica was going to say anything more. "I know Ryan's been super difficult, and I'll apologize again for undermining you with my pizza offer the other night. I was only trying to help. But I really do think Ryan will mature with time and get easier to deal with."

"It's not just Ryan," she said. "You've been so absorbed with work that you're not paying attention to what's going on around you."

"Paying attention? Jessica, what are you saying?"

"I'm *saying* you've been so distracted and preoccupied lately that you don't seem to know what's going on."

Instantly I became defensive. "Then tell me, what's going on? What am I missing?"

The card?

Suddenly, the item that was parked in my briefcase and that I almost addressed the night before popped into my head. Could she be talking about Mark? I racked my brain for anything else important that I might have missed. Her birthday was two months ago, and our anniversary wasn't until February. Nothing. It was finally time to clear the air.

"Does all this have something to do with Mark?" I asked.

As soon as I said it, I regretted it. My tone came off more accusatorily than I would have liked. I wasn't trying to pin anything on her. But now—was there something more going on?

Jessica's nose twitched and her eyes grew narrow with confusion.

"Is there something going on that I need to know about?" I said a little more gently.

"First of all, who the hell is Mark?" she said tersely, her frustration building.

"That's what I'd like to know." I sighed and went for it. "I found your card."

"Marty, seriously, what *card* are you talking about?" She seemed genuinely bewildered. Was she serious, or was this a case of playing it coy about her secret relationship?

"The one you threw out in the trash last week . . . from Mark."

She paused. Her eyes went blank as she appeared to be searching her memory banks. "Oh, *that* card!"

I started sweating, and my stomach churned. Was my marriage in deep trouble? And was she right that I'd been too distracted to see it? We fought like any couple, and sure, we disagreed a lot about how to parent Ryan, but that didn't mean we weren't still in love. I was still as attracted to Jessica as the day I walked into our mutual friend's party and noticed the cute girl, laughing with her friends and drinking a pilsner. When I'd finally begged our friend for an introduction, I'd been pleased to find her to be smart, interesting, and funny, too.

She rolled her eyes. "So that card was from my friend Mark Rigkin. Remember him?"

Rigkin? It was familiar but I couldn't immediately place the name. The tension in my gut started to give way to confusion, which at least felt a little better. "Who's that again?"

"My college friend...married to Looney Tunes Lisa for a while—remember? They came to our wedding. She was the one who got sloshed and wiped out on the dance floor in the middle of the hora."

Something about this story did ring a bell.

"Mark sent me that card like what? Five or six years ago after his divorce," she continued. "I found it in the closet when I was cleaning out some old boxes of junk." Her brow wrinkled and tone sharpened.

"Isn't the real question here why you were going through the trash? And jumped to... what conclusion, exactly?"

"I don't know," I said, feeling exhausted. "It's been a really stressful week between the market, Angela getting on my case, and my mom."

While it was a truthful statement, I immediately felt bad about using my mother's poor health as an excuse for behaving like an ass. Fortunately, just then, the young man behind the counter called out our number to let us know our food was ready.

"I'll get it," Jess said, probably to escape my presence, if only momentarily.

As she got up, I instinctively pulled out my phone to get my market fix, hoping the soaring stock market would give me that soothing high I was feeling before I'd left for lunch. Instead of green next to all the stock symbols, I saw red. Lots of it.

"For fuck's sake!" I blurted out loud.

"What's the matter now?" a vexed Jessica asked, suddenly hovering in front of me holding my turkey Reuben.

"I don't know. Everything's rolled over." As I scrolled down the list of securities we owned, instead of the 2 percent gains, I was looking at more than 1 percent losses. That was a huge swing from less than an hour ago. Target and Best Buy were now materially down from when we'd bought them. I couldn't take my eyes back off my phone. "I'm not hungry anymore."

"Marty, I think you may need to get some counseling," Jessica said, but I barely heard her.

"I think I'll take mine to go," she said before dropping my sandwich on the table then making a remark about my work being more important and walking off with her lunch.

•

Bizline News Update: Thursday, June 28, 4:30 p.m. ET

An early day rally failed to hold as gains evaporated along with buyer enthusiasm in the final thirty minutes of trading when a report broke that a Pentagon official suggested US satellites detected a Chinese naval fleet amassing in the South China Sea.

Investors apparently are uneasy about adding to positions ahead of the upcoming shortened holiday week. Lack of buyer interest was also explained by the palpable fear of a further demonstration of power from either the United States or one of its superpower adversaries, stoking the China incident into a full-blown crisis. Trading and liquidity are expected to be light during the week of the Fourth of July making the market susceptible to larger than normal price swings.

If reports are correct, for the time being, the Chinese armada doesn't pose an immediate threat to the United States or its allies, but certainly won't do anything to calm fears of a brewing conflict.

The market did have a few new pieces of economic data that were released this week to chew on. Benign consumer inflation data, improving home sales, and an uptick in first-time unemployment claims painted a mixed picture for the US economy. The US economic expansion is getting long in the tooth, and investors are looking for excuses to call an end to the long bull market.

•

20

Jessica had given me the cold shoulder following our disastrous lunch at the deli, limiting our conversations to the required minimum to keep the household functioning. She was clearly irritated by my greeting card interrogation. And then there was my inability to take a stricter posture toward Ryan, along with her general feeling that I was emotionally detached from the family that were really irking her.

"Do you think Stephanie will be at Alan's party?" I asked as Jessica as I crossed paths with her in our bathroom. My effort to defuse the tension between us before heading off to work landed flat.

"Not if she's smart. Your brother was so douchey last time," she said stoically. "I'm not sure I'm even going. Maybe you'll just take Ryan."

Her passive-aggressive response oozed with disgruntlement. Repairing the damage was going to take more time. I'd give it another try later in the day, before we went to bed.

While we slept in the same room, the last few days she was quick to go read alone in our bedroom and fall asleep early each night. And instead of snuggling up to me, the only thing she was hugging was her down pillow on the other side of our king-size bed. We had gone through similar cold spells following arguments before, but this episode was lasting longer than her typical forty-eight-hour silent treatment.

Despite the tension, I couldn't imagine going to my brother's annual Fourth of July barbecue without her. It was five days away, and I had time to improve the things at home by then.

I put down my hairbrush. "We're not going without you," I said to her reflection in the mirror.

She sat down at her vanity and began filing her nails. "I'll think about it."

Ah, yes. She was coming around like she had so many times before. We'd be cozying up to each other by the end of the evening. I didn't press her anymore, leaving her to thaw out on her own.

The day flew by. Lots of client calls, meetings, and research. Late that Friday afternoon, I phoned Jessica to see if I could pick up dinner as a further peace offering. From the second she answered, it was apparent that she was yet in the midst of another flare-up between her and Ryan.

"So, all I did was ask Ryan if he had started working on his summer reading list. Rather than a simple yes or no, he told me that I'm a totally *worthless* mother. Marty, you're going to have to talk with him when you get home and explain very clearly that his behavior is unacceptable. And by *explaining*, I don't mean promising to buy him pizza, more decorations for his fish tank, or anything else," she said with a stinging rebuke of my parenting style.

Guess that means we're on speaking terms again.

My blood pressure and stress level began to rise.

"Okay, I'll be home in a little while," I said.

We hung up, and I breathed deeply and let it slowly out. I looked through my email before shutting down my computer, wanting to make sure I responded to every client. Fortunately, my inbox was empty except for a message from Coach Simmons.

Hey, Coach Marty,

Any chance you can coach the game for me this Sunday afternoon? I've got a funeral to go to at 2 p.m. If you can't, I'll see if Coach Fredrington is available. Let me know.

Coach Simmons

While I had coached some of the games before, it wasn't lost on me that he asked me over Fredrington despite Bill's advanced basketball knowledge.

It would be a fun distraction from work and a good opportunity to show Jessica that I could be more present with Ryan. I already told Jess I'd take Ryan to do something Saturday. Now I was coaching his team on Sunday. It would be a father and son weekend. How could Jess stay mad at me after putting in that kind of effort? I'd be golden! If all went well, by the Fourth we'd be one happy family. I replied to Simmons that I'd do it.

21

"Hey, Ryan," I said from the driver's seat on the way to the Saturday afternoon matinee.

Ryan sat beside me, staring at his phone.

I addressed him again. Nothing. Finally, after my third "Hey, Ryan," delivered like a drill sergeant, he slowly peeled his eyes away from his phone.

"Have you thought more about what you'd like to do for a living when you grow up?"

Even though the question came out sounding contrived, like something an out of touch parent would ask, I was genuinely curious. It had been a while since the last time I had inquired. At the time, Ryan was determined to be an NBA player. Since then, I'd purposely found many money teaching moments. I was selfishly fishing to see if any of that had rubbed off on him and if he showed any signs of interest in joining me at the family firm one day. And besides, having a *real* conversation with Ryan on something other than basketball might also provide some insight into what was making him so stubborn and defiant.

"Not what you do," Ryan said without skipping a beat.

"That's not fair. Wait. Do you even know what I do?" I laughed off his slight. While expecting a teenager to get excited about a career in finance wasn't realistic, expressing *some* interest and a little curiosity would've been a welcome response.

"You get stressed out making money for rich people."

"It's not stressful *all* the time," I said, oddly unsettled that Ryan seemed to be questioning the merits of my career, but taken that he was observant enough to pick up on my angst. "And, heck, it's pretty rewarding when I get to help people achieve their goals, even if they're already wealthy."

I told him about how great it was that I got to work alongside my father and that I hoped maybe one day he'd want to join me in the firm. I was optimistic that Ryan's childhood defiance would eventually give way to a cooperative adulthood and that an interest in my field would take hold.

"Sorry, Dad, but probably not for me," Ryan said.

Ryan's lack of desire to become my business partner didn't take me by surprise, not that he'd ever really been interested in my job. Whenever I tried to bring up money and investing concepts like the revenues, profitability, and market share of the Xbox, something he used often, he never really took the bait like I did when I was growing up.

My own affinity for saving and investing started when I got my first passbook account at the small corner bank when I was seven years old. I loved seeing the typewritten balance in the passbook rise with each allowance payment or birthday deposit. I particularly got a kick out of earning interest. *They are giving me even more money?* I remember thinking. I found the comfort in having money in the bank more desirable than the rush from making a purchase. I was very fixated on seeing the balance grow. The day it finally topped $100, I was elated!

When I was about ten, my dad started talking about investing. He'd often lecture me and my siblings about the importance of investing and the merits of owning quality "blue chips." He'd speak in awe of famous investors like Benjamin Graham, the father of value investing, and Warren Buffett, an incredibly successful disciple of Graham's. At the dinner table, Dad would often launch into elegiac speeches about things like corporate profits, price-to-earnings ratios, book value, and free cash flow. While I really didn't understand most of what he was talking about, I'd still listen intently. My older brother and younger sister, not so much. They'd giggle, roll their eyes, giving each other a "here we go again" look every time our dad asked us questions like "What products do your friends like these days?" as he tried to gain an edge on changing consumer trends and how they might impact and shape his investment theses.

Dad's questions and insights got me thinking. I started to view companies like Microsoft and Coca-Cola not just as everyday products, but as companies that made or lost money. As my dad explained, "If their products and services are good, those companies will make profits." If they were publicly traded, everyday people like us could own a small piece of them and share in those profits by receiving dividends from the company. Or, Dad had said, if the company didn't pay dividends, they could reinvest the profits to create more value for shareholders. The more profits a company had, and the faster those profits grew, the higher the stock price.

I was amazed that even a kid could be a partial owner of a big business and was hooked on the concept of investing from there on. When I turned thirteen, I took the major step from being a *saver* to an *investor*. I used my bar mitzvah and babysitting money to buy shares of solid name brands like Coke, Pepsi, and Disney, as well as a little Microsoft, given the, at the time, boom in personal computers.

Now here I was, many years later, trying to stoke my own son's career interests, even if it wasn't going to be as a money manager. Ryan liked animals and was good at arguing, but my suggestion that he might pursue a career as a veterinarian or trial attorney fell as flat as working with me, eliciting one-word responses.

"Booooring," he said, his eyes still locked on his phone.

Jeez. "What about a video game programmer? You spend plenty of time doing that."

No response.

Logging too many hours of screen time playing video games was another source of our contention at home, but we were pretty lax about it, largely out of our guilt for not having had another child at home for him to play with. Well, "at least he's interacting with other kids," we'd rationalize.

What would happen if both Jessica and I died in a tragic accident, like the Clauskys' parents? Would Ryan be like Danny and Freddie, spending most of his days and nights mindlessly gaming, lost and searching without parents to steer and push him in the right direction?

As we pulled into the theater parking lot, I turned off the car. "Whatever you do, your mother and I want you to be happy. Just be happy. Do you think you can do that?"

He put his phone down and looked at me. "Okay, fine."

Progress?

22

"Hello," I said, my voice thick with sleep as I answered my blaring cell.

"Marty, it's Dad."

I shot upright. "Dad?" I glanced at the clock. It was midnight. "Is everything all right? What time is it there?" My dad had always been an early riser, but I knew it was early in Berlin even for him.

"It's six a.m," he said. "Everything is fine. Sorry for calling so late. We're leaving for a full day concentration camp tour shortly and wanted to get you before we left."

"Okay, that sounds good," I said awkwardly.

Jessica moved from the edge of the other side of the bed closer to me so she could hear. I held out the phone and put it on speaker. "How's Mom doing? Has she started her treatment yet?"

"No, not yet. We met with Dr. Schmidt yesterday morning. He went over the treatment plan with us, and she'll start with some initial testing on Monday morning then get her first treatment by the end of the week."

"Okay," I said. "Do Alan and Stephanie know?"

"I spoke to them a little while ago. Alan said you'll be seeing him on the Fourth at his house?"

"Yes, I think so," I replied, giving Jessica a hopeful look.

"Sorry we'll miss it this year. Give our regards to Jessica and Ryan.

Your mother wants to say hello. Hold on," he said before hastily handing over the phone to Mom.

Mom sounded groggy. It was hard to tell if it was due to the early morning hour or her weakened condition.

We spoke for a couple of minutes. She said they had a nice time in Paris but avoided mentioning anything to do with her health like she always did. She never wanted to dwell on her cancer because she didn't want to be a downer, always putting on a strong front. Right now, I wasn't going to press her. She sounded well enough.

"Wish Ryan good luck in his basketball game. We miss him," my mom was saying. "Make sure to take some good videos." My first half player substitutions for Sunday's game came to mind. Did I have a solid game plan?

Mom got off the phone and put Dad back on. He said he'd keep us informed and hastily said goodbye. I felt rushed to say something before he hung up, but all that spilled out of me was "Hope you have a nice time at the concentration camp." Jessica slapped my arm for my unintentional insensitivity.

Dad's brevity wasn't like him. He hadn't mentioned the office, the market, or anything else at all, which was definitely out of character. But maybe their tour bus was leaving.

Did I have Dad's total confidence with respect to running the firm? Maybe he was mentally ready to turns things over to me so he could check out. If so, we had come a long way. In fact, joining Dad at the firm was far from a forgone conclusion given the whole ordeal with my brother, Alan, and my less than straight line path to KCM.

Coming out of college with a degree in finance, I was hopeful Dad would offer me a job at the firm, just like he had done with Alan. However, by the spring semester of my senior year, he still hadn't brought it up. I got antsy and finally broached the subject. He didn't exactly respond like I hoped, telling me he was "open to the idea, but only after I got experience elsewhere." He didn't say it, but Alan's time at the firm had clearly frustrated him. But I wasn't Alan. I had the passion for the business that Alan lacked. I wasn't thrilled about having to find another job if my long-term future was with KCM. Alan attempted to explain Dad's thinking to me one day while we were working out at the gym. He said, "The risk to Dad is that you don't like it and leave, just like I did. Having two kids join, then leave, wouldn't look good to clients. And you know with Dad...it's all about the clients." It made decent sense to me. I'd have to demonstrate a commitment to the field first and pay my dues. Then I'd earn my spot as successor to the firm.

Through some on-campus recruiting, I landed a job as an analyst with Cornerstone Asset Management, a large regional mutual fund company. I worked in the consumer goods group where I learned the ins and outs of fifty or so small companies engaged in selling products to the general public. My analysis and recommendations helped the portfolio manager figure out which companies' stocks offered the greatest potential for growth and stability for the firm's clients.

After four years, I left Cornerstone to go to graduate school to get an MBA from The University of Texas at Austin. It was far from home, and there was a risk I wouldn't return to Georgia given the vast career opportunities in Texas. In fact, I accepted an offer from an Austin-based firm and put another four years in before Dad finally opened the door for me. Maybe he knew he might lose me for good if he didn't act soon.

"I'm pleased to see what you've accomplished," he said. "Come back to Atlanta and join the firm."

By then, KCM was managing more than $180 million and had eighty or so clients, and a handful of employees. It was a great time to join, with lots of growth opportunities ahead. I could help shape the firm that I'd one day be running. In the years since, there have been some hiccups, but more good stock picks than bad. I've done a great job with client portfolios and even brought in some clients, other than JD. I'd always assumed Dad would turn over the reins to me. And now it was going to happen, just like I envisioned.

After hanging up the phone with Dad, Jess and I wondered if a concentration camp was the right kind of excursion Mom needed right before she started treatment. Perhaps something more uplifting would have been more appropriate.

"At least she's getting out and doing something," Jessica said with more than a hint of envy.

"Don't forget... I'm coaching Ryan's game tomorrow," I said, trying to earn some bonus points with her. "We'll be going a little earlier than normal so I can get organized."

I was hoping for a little praise.

All I got was, "Great. I've got some errands to do, so I'll see you there." She rolled back over on her side.

I fell back asleep while rejiggering my basketball game plan in my head.

23

I cracked open the door to the rec center, and the rush of air hitting my perspiring face nearly froze my lips in place. I shivered, shook it off.

The team arrived a half hour before game time to review some plays I sketched out and get warmed up. Over the course of the next forty minutes, a clipboard would replace my computer monitor, and eight fourteen-year-old boys of varying degrees of basketball talent were a portfolio that I had to effectively allocate to secure a win. For Ryan, basketball offered an opportunity to do something he enjoyed and put a good effort forward. And he was fairly decent at it so that didn't hurt. We could secure a win working together!

I quickly went over the player rotations I had sketched out late Friday night and assigned starting positions right before the game got underway. Before taking the head coach's seat at the end of our team's bench, I gave a brief wave to Evan Lanter, whose son was playing on the opposing team. Last year, Evan unexpectedly asked me about our firm's services and our approach to managing money. His family had sold a high-priced rental property in Newport Beach that had been in the family for generations, and he was looking to reinvest his share of the proceeds. He became a client, and though we would have the occasional lunch to talk about the performance of his account, I struggled to connect with him on a more personal level. I'd make a point to call him the next week and catch up.

The game started on a good note with our team controlling the tip-off and scoring on our first possession. A few minutes later, Ryan, who was playing shooting guard, launched a long three-pointer. He had a nice release, but the ball bounced off the back of the rim. I scanned the small crowd, hoping Jessica had her phone ready to capture the highlights. She was sitting on the fourth row of the wooden bleachers directly across the court from me. I gestured to her to be ready to snap a picture. She gave me a thumbs-up. There would be hell to pay with Ryan had he made a shot, a three-pointer no less, that we didn't capture on film.

Before returning my eyes to the game, I spotted Evan sitting next to Bill Fredrington in the second row. It looked like Bill was talking my client's ear off about something, and by the expression on Evan's face, it was likely some story about an outing with one of Bill's uber-wealthy pro-golfer clients. Bill loved to name drop.

Suddenly, the three boys on our bench were yelling at me, pointing at the game clock. Apparently, I missed their substitutions at the five-minute mark. I apologized and made the switch at the next out-of-bounds.

Neither team was getting many good shots. Offensively, the game tempo was a choppy, back-and-forth, chaotic scramble. The kids struggled to execute any of my well-designed plays. Even so, at half-time we held a respectable 15–11.

As my players took their seats to rest on the bench, I peeped at the spectators without fear of missing any important game action. Jessica was sitting next to another mother chatting, while Evan and Bill were cracking up about something.

A pang of regret engulfed me. Maybe I should've let someone else coach, so I could've been free to buddy up to my client. I couldn't afford to lose a sizable client like Evan, especially not to an advisor like Fredrington. He'd give me crap about it forever.

Money management was a relationship-oriented business as much as it was about performance. Not being able to establish rapport with a client like Evan could be a frustrating experience. Firms like Peach State Advisors where Bill worked, hired expert salesmen, and not necessarily the best money managers. They were trained to sell at all costs. And Bill was really good at it. He'd find a way to bond with a serial killer if he had a few million to invest.

At halftime, I encouraged the boys to hydrate, gave them a little pep talk, and reviewed the second half substitutions. We started the second half with a full court press, which turned out to be a great move because the other team coughed up the ball on each of their first two possessions. We scored on both turnovers, increasing our lead to 23–15. On their next possession, we pressed yet again, trapping Evan Lanter's son under their basket after the inbounds pass. He managed to get rid of the ball without turning it over, but their coach was fuming that a foul wasn't called as three of our players frantically swatted at the ball. His complaints along with the jeering from the opposing team's family members in the stands added to the increasing noise level in the gym. Evan stood sternly in the bleachers, holding his arms in the air in disbelief at the no call. Would he and the other parents think my call for the repeated press was overkill?

When play resumed, the pace settled down, and the other team's shots began to find their mark. They closed the gap to two points with about three minutes remaining. Our easy win had quickly become a nail biter. Tension and energy built inside the gymnasium. Parents stopped chatting and were now on their feet, clapping and cheering. Would Evan and his kid be sore losers if they lost? Would it impact our professional relationship? How could I even think such a ridiculous thing? I had to get my head back in the game.

With forty-five seconds remaining and still down by two, the other team's coach called timeout.

I was pumped up. In our huddle I commanded, "Do *not* press. Get set into our zone defense. No fouling. Let's execute and win this!" Despite our lead, all our starters had scored except for Ryan. I could tell by the look on his face he was down on himself. A win would be good. A win with him scoring would be great.

I pulled him aside. "Ryan, take a quick shot if you're open."

"But nobody's passing me the ball," he complained.

"Just be ready!"

Evan's son took the inbounds pass and dribbled up the court. Ryan played him tight, contesting his three-pointer. It missed. Our center rebounded the ball and quickly passed to Ryan, who took off dribbling.

Please God, let him score.

He ran the entire length of the floor and released an off-balance right-handed layup that rolled around the rim before finally dropping in the basket. I was jubilant on the inside but kept my composure, not wanting to appear too overjoyed. Evan was probably watching my reaction. While it wasn't a game-winning shot, it was the insurance we needed to hold on for the win. Jessica gave me a thumbs-up and wiggled her phone. I beamed, knowing she'd gotten it on video. Evan was stone-faced.

Oh no.

Ryan, all smiles, high-fived his teammates before lining up to shake hands with the other team. Our boys went to grab their after-game snack, celebrating their 38–34 victory.

I noticed Evan Lanter leave the gym with his arm around his son, consoling him on the loss. I wasn't envious of the situation and was hoping I'd have a chance to say something to him before he left. I'd call him in a couple of days and ask him to lunch.

Fredrington walked up and shook my hand. "Congrats, Coach, nice win! Boys looked good out there."

"Thanks," I said. "They really stepped up their D in the second half."

"Hey, I was talking to Evan Lanter. Good guy. Said he works with you."

I tossed the ball I was holding into a bin with all the others. "Yeah, I like him. Unfortunately, I didn't get a chance to say hello." I chose my words carefully. Technically, I couldn't confirm or deny who my clients were, and I wasn't sure if Bill was fishing.

"Just giving you the heads-up," Bill said in a low voice. "Dude, he is *pissed.*"

"Seriously? Over that missed foul call? It's just a kids' basketball game."

"No, Marty," Bill said, arching an eyebrow. "He doesn't give a shit about that; it's the money he's lost in the market."

"What?" If Evan had issues with how our firm was handling the current state of the market, he should have come to me. "I'm sure you backed me up and told him everybody's down now, right?"

"What do you mean? Dude, no!" Bill laughed. I couldn't tell if he was messing with me or telling the truth. "You should've seen his face when I told him we doubled our clients' cash positions back in May. Sell in May and go away. Everybody knows that."

"Thanks for the heads-up, and helping a fellow advisor out," I said sarcastically before walking off. Was Bill really trying to poach my client by making me look bad? Not cool.

"Hey," he called after me. "I'm just messing with you."

"Oh, okay," I said, with an awkward, half-hearted laugh, letting him know it wasn't funny and wasn't sure if I believed him.

I walked outside the rec center where our team usually huddled up after games for a snack and post-game pep talk. My plan was to give a special shout-out to Ryan for making the lay-up, but the team had already scattered, including Ryan who had apparently gone home with Jessica. The glory of the win faded before we had a chance to celebrate together.

24

KCM's office felt eerily quiet. It was a slow week given the Fourth of July holiday sandwiched in the middle of it. Client calls had slowed to a trickle, and I hadn't heard from Angela since she stormed off on Friday despite my reaching out via email. I had written:

Angela, I'm looking forward to following up with you when you're back regarding the issues you brought to my attention. Have a nice holiday!

My note wasn't so much an apology per se. It was more of an olive branch since my intent was to make amends in person when she came back the following week.

After my repeated requests, Jessica finally relented and agreed to go to Alan's barbecue (though not without declaring, "I'm not staying late"), so we headed over, Ryan in tow, on the afternoon of Wednesday, July Fourth. My hope was the party would exceed her already low expectations and set the tone for a relaxing, family weekend.

We pulled up to Alan's contemporary-styled home around three. He and his wife, Marci, had recently finished renovating the home they bought when they got married. I helped Alan do the math on the project and figure out the best way to finance the total gut job, which he embarked on soon after recently being named partner at his law firm.

There were a handful of imported cars parked in the driveway and along the side of the wide street. Bob Marley blared in the backyard. We let ourselves in and easily made our way through the open floorplan to the kitchen at the back of the house where a bunch of guests had congregated. Ryan took off to find his older first cousins, leaving me and Jessica to chat with a female partner from Alan's firm we had met once before. Jess seemed to like her, so I ventured off to find Alan and procure us some beers.

I slid open the glass door to the backyard oasis where the rest of the thirty or so guests were hanging out. The waterfall behind the infinity pool was pumping full blast, and the palm trees, nicely manicured shrubs, and reggae music made it feel more like a Jamaican resort than a Fourth of July party at a Peachtree Heights home.

Alan was easy to find. At six foot two with a gray spot in the midst of an otherwise full head of black hair, he stood out as he walked around serving cold beer.

"Yo, brother!" Alan shouted from across the patio.

He handed me a bottle of craft beer wrapped in a red, white, and blue striped koozie that read, "*Alan and Marci's 6th Annual 4th of July Fest.*"

"Is Stephanie not coming?" I asked, not seeing our sister among the guests.

"No, she texted yesterday to say she wasn't going to make it. Had other plans or something."

"That sucks. I haven't seen her in a while. I guess it's not too surprising given last year," I said, trying to jog Alan's memory as to his role in keeping our little sister away. At last year's BBQ, Stephanie brought a guy she had just started seeing. He seemed nice enough, but things got weird when he took his shirt off to get in the pool, unveiling a rather large tattoo of the Grim Reaper that spanned his entire chest and lower abdomen. While we were all a bit disturbed by the scythe-wielding monster, Alan was the only one brave, obnoxious, or drunk enough to say anything about it, making comments about loving the Grim Reaper scene in Monty Python's *The Meaning of Life*. The guy didn't seem to be too bothered. I initially felt bad about it but later recall thinking that someone that purposely alters their skin like that and takes off their shirt should be fully prepared for the attention that goes along with it. We later learned Stephanie stopped seeing the guy soon after but had recently started dating someone else.

"Oh yeah. Wonder what ever happened to Reaper Man?" Alan said, cracking himself up.

Alan was not only comfortable with himself, but incredibly relaxed around others. He could give you a compliment, then jokingly take a playful dig at you in the same sentence. It drove our sister crazy, especially when Alan started messing with guys she dated. With that being said, he *was* a great host, never one to be accused of not having enough food or drinks for his guests. There was plenty of burgers, hot dogs, and beer to go around. Alan had a son a couple of years older than Ryan, and a daughter, who was somewhat of a tomboy. They could usually be found in the driveway shooting hoops. And Jessica and my sister-in-law, Marci, got along well together, too.

I returned to Jessica, who appeared content. We hit the food table together and parked ourselves down in a couple of chairs on the outside patio with some other guests. After eating, Jess retreated indoors to chat with Marci while Alan and I put on bathing suits, grabbed a beer, and jumped in the pool to cool off.

"Have you heard anything about Mom's treatment?" Alan asked when the two of us were wading alone in the shallow end.

"Not much other than the late-night call I got last Saturday," I said, frustrated by the limited information flow regarding Mom's treatment protocol. "She was finishing some tests, and I think she should've already started her treatments by now."

"That's the same as what Dad told me," Alan said.

"The whole thing is really strange. I'm so used to seeing Dad every day in the office, and now they're completely out of touch."

Alan shook his head. "Marty, I have no idea how you've worked with him for so long. We drove each other totally crazy when I worked there. Just *thinking* about listening to him quote Warren Buffett all the time is enough to put me to sleep."

Alan, four years my senior, joined the firm a few years after my dad founded it. Alan had come out of college with a degree in political science, and his options at the time were either law school, like most of his friends, or getting a job. My dad thought working for a few years would benefit him rather than jumping straight into graduate school. Alan was up for working but didn't know where to start his search. Instead of leaning on his business contacts to help Alan find gainful employment, Dad offered Alan a job himself. Alan jumped at the opportunity without putting too much thought into it, and despite never having demonstrated any interest toward investments or financial markets like I had, he accepted the position. I was envious when I found out about it at the family dinner table after Alan moved back home. I was still in high school and thought about what it would be like for all of us to work together one day, hoping that Alan wouldn't still be throwing the occasional punch to my arm by then.

In retrospect, the experience with Alan was doomed from the beginning and nearly destroyed my chances to be a part of KCM's future. Whereas I had a similar temperament and mindset to my father, Alan was very different. Alan was impulsive in his decisions. Dad was methodical. Alan was excitable. Dad was reserved. Alan looked at the big picture. Dad dove into the details. Alan exaggerated. Dad understated. Alan created loose ends, and Dad neatly tied them up. In short, Alan was plenty smart and capable, but his temperament resembled that of an impulsive client rather than a financial advisor. He needed more action than a steady-as-she-goes asset management firm had to offer. Predictably, within a year and a half of burying his face in annual reports and securities filings, he got restless.

The frustration on both their parts was evident, and our mother wasn't happy with the tension the new work relationship created between two of the most important people in her life. Alan struggled with the numbers part of being a money manager. For Alan, deciphering a company's SEC security's filing was equivalent to learning some obscure Gaelic dialect. The exercise left him angry and frustrated. Alan redirected his efforts in a last-ditch effort to save their working relationship, taking charge of the firm's marketing initiatives. At the time, the firm did virtually no marketing as new clients had all come from referrals. There were no ads or any cold calling. That was by design. My dad abhorred hard sales and any activity that could be construed as pressuring people, especially if he knew them personally.

Alan pushed to advertise on radio to bring the firm's services to a wider audience. Dad reluctantly agreed at first, but ultimately felt that an advertising campaign would compromise KCM's boutique culture and bring the firm in the direction of the mass market brokerage houses he so despised. So, he pulled the plug after he had already put some money down as a deposit for airtime. It was the beginning of the end. After six months on the job, Alan told my dad he was leaving the firm. He traveled with a buddy around South America for a couple of months. When he returned, he was off to law school the following year. I did feel sorry for Alan throughout all of this since every direction he turned it seemed like he couldn't do anything right in my dad's eyes. But things turned out fine for him in the end. He was a partner with a growing, successful firm, had a loving wife, and two great, easygoing children that he didn't deserve.

I scooped a dead wasp out of the water and tossed it into the shrubs beside the pool. "I actually like that Buffett stuff, and Dad's not my problem. It's Angela the Wonder Compliance Woman he hired that's pushing me over the edge."

"Angela who? I don't think I've met her yet."

"Well, you might not have the opportunity," I said, feeling a little uneasy thinking about my interaction with her.

"Why is that?"

"There's a chance she may have quit last Friday."

"Seriously, what happened?" He couldn't hide a smirk, apparently finding some personal enjoyment out of my run-in with a coworker.

"She's been crawling up my butt about some minor compliance issues, and I kind of went off on her the other day," I confessed. "I feel like a total shithead."

"I love it! And Dad doesn't know about it?"

"Nope."

"Even better! Sucks to be you right now." He slapped my bare shoulder with his wet hand.

"You better not say anything. I don't want Dad to get worked up right now. Besides, I think she'll get over it and come back to work next week."

After our pool time, we had our dessert and sat down to watch the DC fireworks on the TV in Alan's living room. I relaxed into his soft leather sofa, finally starting to feel my perpetual tension lift thanks to all the beer. Jess, however, was getting antsy.

"Let's just watch a little bit of the show," I said, and she nodded, twitched her nose, and walked off to the kitchen.

As she left to give Ryan a fifteen-minute-til-departure warning, I got a text from JD: *Happy 4th! At a synagogue board member's party. House OK, but check out this painting in the bathroom. Think he's got real $$$? Potential gold sponsor for Feldstein show.*

I laughed, wishing I could share the text with everyone in the room as the behind the scenes view into JD's life was really quite entertaining. A few seconds later, a picture of a painting popped up on my screen. Based on my limited art knowledge, it looked like a French impressionist's landscape, but I couldn't make out the artist's name.

Me: *Might be a Monet. I'd hit them up!!*

JD: *Will do!*

I settled back down to watch the fireworks display and was at ease until about ten minutes in when a special news alert appeared on the bottom of the screen: *"Pentagon reports Chinese naval fleet moving northeast toward Taiwan."*

My stomach dropped as Alan tapped me on the back and handed me another beer. "I think you'll need this. Tomorrow's *really* going to suck for you."

It was a fair assessment.

Jessica stared at me from the other side of the room as I guzzled down the bottle. I could tell by her shifting posture and awkward smile she was ready to leave. I made my way over to her and asked if she'd grab Ryan while I said my goodbyes. She returned a few minutes later by herself to find me drinking another beer and talking with one of Alan's partners about the China situation.

"You're having *another* beer? I thought we were leaving?"

"Where's Ryan?"

"He's giving me attitude and doesn't want to leave," she said, clearly frustrated.

"Give me a few minutes and I'll go get him."

"Sure you will. You going to offer him ten bucks if he listens?" she said sarcastically. I exchanged looks with the chap I was talking to. He'd been pretending to watch the TV while I talked to Jess. He excused himself to the restroom in an apparent move to avoid witnessing a family argument.

Jessica raised her voice a notch. "Here's an idea. I'm going to take your car home *now*. You've had too much to drink. So why don't you and Ryan *Uber* home whenever you're ready, okay?"

I agreed, turning over my keychain. In my somewhat inebriated state, I couldn't assess if she was angry or being really cool. The answer became readily apparent when I arrived at home an hour or so later, without Ryan.

25

I ditched my swim bag on the kitchen floor, downed a glass of water and two Tylenol, and headed upstairs. It was 10:20 p.m. and a toss-up as to whether I'd find Jess asleep or not. I was hoping for asleep.

I found her watching TV in bed with the lights off. She acknowledged my presence with a simple "hi."

"Ryan really wanted to sleep over at Alan's, so I left him there," I told her, fearing my unilateral decision wouldn't be well-received. When I went to tell Ryan it was time to leave, he begged me to stay over in front of Alan and his kids. They all ganged up to lobby me. I caved quickly. I probably should've checked with Jess first, but I didn't really see the harm.

"Great, so he'll be up all night," she said. "And you know how he gets when he hasn't had enough sleep."

"Don't worry. He can sleep in over there, and I'll pick him up at lunch tomorrow."

"And miss camp? I'm not happy about that. You could've asked me first." She clicked off the TV and turned over to sleep.

Rather than get into it, I'd wait and talk to her in the morning when I had a clearer head.

I was exhausted and crashed out hard. When I woke around eight, Jessica had already gotten up, presumably to go work out at her gym.

The swelling tension between us and the relentless market drubbing were really sapping my motivation and energy for getting out of bed.

After lying in the dark for a while, I finally flipped on *The Today Show* and caught the middle of an interview with some retired general conjecturing that the Chinese were preparing to launch an invasion of Taiwan and possibly other contested territories in the South Pacific. He said the aggressive aircraft incident off the US coast was either meant to deter the United States from getting involved when the Chinese ultimately made their land grab or was a giant diversion so the United States would defensively position its military assets on its western coast rather than be in position to protect Taiwan.

Lingering in bed meant I arrived at work later than usual, right as the market was about to open. The trading bell rung, and the market immediately plunged before hitting some key resistance levels. On an intraday basis, that initial descent pushed the S&P 500 past the 10 percent decline mark, meeting the technical definition of an official correction. I couldn't meet to discuss with Shelley and Devon as both were out. We were working with a holiday skeleton crew—just me and Elise, the receptionist.

The falling stock prices tempted me to put in sell orders to lighten up our exposure in the event the market kept dropping, but I held my ground. Succumbing to the urge would feel great in the short term, but as soon as things turned, it would hurt to trail the market's inevitable move back up. Instead, I took a time-out from watching the market drop to check emails. Among the holiday sale spam was another message from the Clauskys.

Money Man,
Just letting you know our initial field testing is going great. Will keep you posted!
Danny and Freddie

The boys must've been a bizarre spectacle, sweating in this heat, walking around their neighborhood marking dog shit, but still I wrote back an enthusiastic: *Glad to hear!*

At around ten thirty, my phone rang. My heart had already started beating faster with the market dropping, but when the LED caller ID display on our phone system flashed *SEC,* it raced into overdrive. Rather than pick up myself, I let it roll over to Elise. Maybe it was a robocall from the agency, alerting us to the latest investment scam that was going around. Elise could handle it.

About twenty seconds later, Elise called my extension.

"Marty, there's a Mr. Ingram on the line. He asked for Angela, saying he wanted to talk to the firm's chief compliance officer. I'm not positive, but I think he said he was with the SEC." Her voice betrayed her nerves. "It sounded kind of important, so I figured you might want to take it."

I told her to put him through and let the phone ring three times before finally taking a deep breath answering. I tried to keep my voice as calm and authoritative as possible. "Hello, this is Martin Kaplan."

"Yes, hello, this is Gerald Ingram with the Office of Compliance Inspections and Examinations. How are you today?"

As soon as he identified himself, I did a quick—slightly panicked— Google search to confirm Gerald Ingram did in fact work with the SEC. *Not good.*

"I'm doing okay. What can I help you with today, Gerald?" I said, now speaking with a lighter, more congenial tone.

"This is a courtesy call to let you know that I'll be leading a team for an inspection at your offices on Monday morning. Just wanted to make sure that you'll be open, and that the firm's chief compliance officer will be available."

My face and hands grew clammy. Angela must've called one of her old friends at the SEC. It was a total setup, but that didn't change the fact that we were going to be inspected. Going into defensive mode on the phone would be a mistake, suggesting I had something to hide—and I didn't. Everything we were doing was above board. But I did want to buy some extra time to figure out a plan.

"Well, we're open, but our CCO has been out all week, and Monday will be her first day back in the office. Would it be okay if we rescheduled for a later date?"

There was a pause while he ostensibly checked his calendar.

"I tell you what: I can rearrange a couple of things," he said, and I let out a breath of relief. "How's Tuesday at nine sound?"

"This coming Tuesday?" Tuesday was barely any better than Monday.

"Yes, this Tuesday, July tenth." Then I could've sworn he took on this sarcastic tone when he said, "I imagine your CCO can get settled back in by then. And it says on your filings that Angela Miller is your CCO? Is that *still* correct?"

My brain went into overdrive, quickly piecing together a very disturbing puzzle. This Ingram character knew exactly what was going on. He was trying to flush me out and catch me making some untruthful statement about her employment status, knowing she's gone. Then it hit me hard.

Oh my God. She's a mole!

It that split second, I convinced myself that Angela was an undercover SEC agent and running some covert sting operation.

"As long as she comes back from her vacation," I said, trying to be as honest about the situation without making any misleading statements that could be used against me later. The call was probably being recorded.

I had nothing to hide. My dad certainly wasn't running some Madoff scheme. Was one of our employees doing something illegal right under our noses? Do I call him out and tell him I know about Angela?

"Great, then we'll see you Tuesday morning," he replied.

After mumbling "Have a nice day," I hung up the receiver. Then picked it up again and slammed it back down. I banged my fist so hard on the plastic stapler on my desk that it shattered into a bunch of pieces.

"What the fuck?" I shouted to my empty office. "This is total bullshit!"

I needed answers. And fast.

My hands shook as they hit the keyboard, pulling up our firm's phone directory. My anger boiled over as I punch-dialed Angela's cell phone.

"Hello?" I heard her tentative voice on the other end of the line.

"Angela?"

"Yes."

"It's Marty Kaplan."

"Oh...hi, Martin. This is unexpected." She sounded irritated.

Unexpected? Really? She was probably sitting there with Ingram while he called me, laughing her ass off at how badly he scared the crap out of me.

I glanced at the TV monitor on my wall, which showed some talking head, stock footage of fighter jets taking off from a US aircraft carrier, and the market sinking a couple more percentage points all on one screen.

"What you did," I seethed, "is *so* unprofessional that I'm furious right now."

"What *I* did was unprofessional? What *I* did?" she said, clearly still angry. "*You* told me to back the fuck off. That's *real* professional. All I did was my job!"

She clearly didn't know I was onto the operation she was running with Ingram.

"First of all, I told you to back the *hell* off, not *fuck* off. Second, since when is being a mole for the SEC part of your job description, Angela. You're supposed to be working for us, not against us."

My intensity was building as I stated my case and was almost shouting as I worked toward my crescendo.

"And third, I was planning on apologizing to you when you came back from vacation. But it turns out my hunch was right. You've been up to something this whole time. But *why* are you doing this?"

It felt good to get it all out in the open. I wondered if she would offer me immunity in exchange for cooperation into whoever or whatever crime they were trying to investigate.

There was a long pause on the line.

"Wait, *what* are you talking about?" she asked, sounding, I had to admit, genuinely confused.

"I'm talking about how I just got a call from Ingram with the SEC who will be showing up at our offices on Tuesday morning to conduct an inspection."

Angela didn't immediately respond.

She knows I busted her.

"Are you being serious?" she asked, genuine surprise in her voice.

"Unfortunately, yes! You're still working for them...aren't you?"

"What? Martin...calm down. I'm not working for the SEC. Is that what you think?"

"So, you're saying you're not working undercover?" I wanted the tape-recording of our call to reflect my point-blank questions and her clear yes or no answers.

"No, of course not. That's ridiculous. You probably won't believe me, but I had nothing to do with the SEC contacting you. Nor would I ever do anything like that, well, unless there was some fraud going on, which there isn't," she said.

"Then why would the SEC be calling?" I asked, now equally confused.

"Well, it has been like ten years since the firm's last inspection. You're overdue. I know this is hard to believe, but this is probably totally coincidental." She sounded so serious. Was she telling me the truth?

"So you're saying you had nothing to do with this?" I asked one more time for insurance.

"Correct. I'm not saying you haven't got some compliance issues, and there *are* some other things going on that I'm concerned about, but I can promise you, I didn't call the SEC."

Relief washed over me, and I suddenly felt a wave of remorse for how I'd treated her the other day. She had just been doing her job. It wasn't her fault that everything else in my life wasn't going well.

"I know," I said, my anger dissipating. "I was out of line for how I spoke to you, and I really was going to apologize when you came back to the office, *if* you were even going to come back."

"Look, Martin."

"It's Marty, please call me Marty."

"Yes, Marty, I'm annoyed, but I was going to come back. But what's been really irritating to me is that I was hired to put a real compliance program in place, and you seem to be brushing me, and the rules and regulations, off."

"Fair enough, you're right," I told her.

"Thank you," she said with vindication in her voice.

"Now that I've got that off my chest, does your dad know about the SEC yet?"

"No," I said. "Since I thought you were behind it, I called you straightaway."

"You should probably let him know. They'll want to talk to the firm's principal," she said.

"Let me think about that. Hopefully we can handle it," I said, happy that she would be there to help out.

We talked a little about what to expect. Although she didn't say it, I could tell that in her own disturbed way, she was up for the challenge. Successfully navigating through a full-blown SEC investigation would be a career win for her. I respected that. Before hanging up, she assured me that the work she'd been doing since she joined KCM was a great head start and that we'd have enough time to get prepared. We agreed to meet early Monday morning to come up with our game plan for Tuesday when Ingram and his team arrived at our office.

I hung up with Angela and looked at my screen showing the market having closed down more than 2 percent. Another wretched session. I stood staring blankly out my office window. What kind of trouble could come from the SEC inspection? I'd find out in only five days. How long could I keep this from Dad?

26

Leon sat reading the *Wall Street Journal Europe* while Sylvia rested comfortably in a reclining chair next to him. Her right arm was hooked up to an IV that was administering the immunotherapy treatment.

"How are you feeling, dear?" Leon asked quietly.

"So far, okay. Just a little tired. But you heard what Dr. Schmidt said—I probably won't feel anything one way or another for at least a few treatments. This is only my second dose." She offered a weak smile. "Aren't you getting bored just sitting there watching me?"

"Would you rather I watch one of the other patients?" Leon turned his head away from his frail wife and toward the three other sick people hooked up to IVs.

"Leon," she said, acknowledging his attempt to get a laugh out of her by putting her hand on his arm. "You really don't need to stay here."

"I'm fine, dear. Don't worry about me." He patted her knee. The truth was he was less than fine. Sylvia's uncertain condition, the falling markets, and the future of his firm preoccupied his thoughts. Could he really walk away from the business he had built over the years? Was Marty making any moves during the market turmoil?

"No, you're not." She gave him a knowing look. "You're miserable being away from the office for such a long time."

"What makes you say that?" He feigned surprise.

"Because in the forty-five years we've been together, this is the longest I've seen you not working."

She was right. Even before he founded his namesake firm, Leon had always been working, whether he was in the office or not. He was always thinking about the markets, investments, his clients, and their money. Over his long career, his personal and work identities became intertwined. He put in long hours reading annual reports, deconstructing corporate financial statements, and meeting with clients who appreciated his affable demeanor, aura of trust, and competence. Perhaps his greatest strength, which helped him build his business, was his ability to communicate complicated concepts into simplistic layman's terms. Leon operated under the umbrella of "clients always come first" mantra. "We stand for trust and integrity." He was not a stockbroker. "I am an *advisor*," he would proudly proclaim to the many clients that walked through his office doors.

Leon folded the newspaper spread across his lap and leaned in close to Sylvia's ear. "You're right. I do love my job, but I love you more," he whispered as the supposed miracle drug seeped its way into her bloodstream.

"That's sweet," she said. "But, I still know it's hard for you."

"Okay, it's a little hard." He gave a soft laugh. "The markets have corrected a full ten percent since I left the office, but as long as I know the firm and our clients are in good hands, I'm okay."

"I'm sure Marty has everything under control," Sylvia reassured him.

27

A black linty substance started coming out of the AC vent on the dash of Jessica's SUV. At first, I thought it was just a small hairball, but as it floated toward my face, I tried to grab it. It kept eluding my grasp like an agile mosquito, except it wasn't one. More and more began to emerge from the vents. I shut off the air conditioner, but bits of black fluff kept shooting out. Soon, the car was full of them; they swarmed around me.

I pulled into the nearest service station. No one was there, so I decided to leave the car rather than wait. I saw a subway sign and stairs leading underground.

I descended the stairwell about twenty steps, then walked through a glass door leading to a futuristic-looking subway system. The large cars were sleek with a shiny chrome finish.

Confused, I found an attendant and asked for directions home. He told me I needed to take the number nine train and pointed down a corridor.

At the end, I turned a corner and went down another flight of stairs where I encountered another door. As I walked through, I found myself in a room lined with bright red upholstered walls. It was rich with a velvety texture like you'd expect to see in a room in Graceland. The door closed behind me, and I was all alone. I paced the room, running my hands down the sides of the walls looking for an exit when my right foot suddenly got stuck. I looked down. My shoe was immersed in a huge glob of something sticky like a big wad of dried-up gum. I tried hard to break loose. The up-holstery on one of the walls rose like a theater curtain being drawn at the start a performance. From behind the curtain appeared two sets of human chicken legs standing behind a glass wall. As the curtain rose, two human torsos were unveiled. Finally, with the curtain near the ceiling, the two faces became visible. It was Danny and Freddie Clausky. There they stood, holding notepads and scribbling like mad scientists observing a lab rat.

"Hey, let me out of here!" I shouted as they scribbled furiously on their pads. They ignored my pleas for help. I got angry and directed all my energy toward releasing my foot from the floor.

"Ow!" someone shouted as my leg flailed under the covers. A whack on my arm, and Jessica growled, "You just kicked me!"

"Sorry," I said, trying to catch my breath. "But, God, that was such a fucked-up dream."

"What is it now? The SEC, Angela, or the market?" she asked, irritated.

I rubbed my eyes, trying to erase the image of Danny and Freddie from my mind. I faced Jessica, barely visible in the moonlight shining through shutters. "The SEC, the market, my mother, Angela, you, Ryan, the Clauskys, Mrs. Benoit, among a thousand other things," I let out.

"Okay," she said, softening, knowing I had been under a lot of pressure. "I know you've got a lot on your mind. I don't know how to help you. What can I do?"

I was quiet. I wanted to work this out myself, especially given the way things had been between us.

She swallowed and then said, "Marty, your family needs you to keep it together, and you're coming unglued."

"I know," I confessed. "Everything is really starting to get to me. I just need to get through this week with the SEC and things should get better."

"Marty, you'll get through this, but then the next work-related issue will pop up. You're going to have to find a way to let some of this go and focus on what's really important."

"I'll be fine, really," I said, not really registering what she was telling me. I rolled back over to my side of the bed. I waited until I felt her turn the other way then pulled the covers over my head and checked the markets on my phone. The Nikkei was taking another beating, and the S&P futures indicated another lower open in the morning.

After closing my eyes, my thoughts turned from the tumbling markets to the Clauskys' trust and my discretionary distributions. The more I reflected, the more upset I got with myself. Angela had been right. How could I have been so dumb? Even if Josie gave me a signed statement, unless it was a signed, notarized legal document, it wouldn't be good enough. I was only doing what Josie asked me to do, but that wasn't what Freddie and Danny's parents had wanted or expressed in their will. Had it been, they'd have named me as a successor or co-trustee. To compound matters, I never even talked to my dad about the whole thing.

I curled into a fetal position and thought about what I was going to say to Angela the next morning and how with her help we could fix things.

28

"I really am sorry," were the first words out of my mouth on Monday morning when I entered Angela's office.

"Apology accepted," she replied, not diverting much attention away from her current task of riffling through files. Other than appearing a bit weary-eyed, perhaps since it was before eight, she looked and sounded like she always did: professional, confident, and ready to work. "It would be good if we can move past this and work together. We've got one day to get organized." She only raised her eyes to meet mine once since I sat down across from her.

"I totally agree." And, this time, I meant it. "So, what's the plan?"

She took off her glasses and set them atop the tall stack of papers on her desk. "Marty, the key to a successful SEC inspection is to demonstrate that we not only have effective policies and procedures in place, but that we also follow them."

As much as I cared about the future of the firm, I couldn't help thinking more about myself, personally. I half joked: "Can't you just play the former SEC employee card and finesse our way through those small deficiencies?"

"Unfortunately, it doesn't work like that." Her lips turned down, looking grim. "They don't go easy on former inspectors. If anything, it's the opposite."

I swallowed hard. "Have you heard anything about this guy, Ingram?" Maybe he was a super cool, helpful type instead of a straight-and-narrow rules guy looking for any reason to shutter our doors.

"Not much. I called a friend of mine at the agency who says he's a decent guy, but a real stickler."

Great. I still couldn't tell if Angela believed my apology, and I needed to make sure we were allies.

"Listen, Angela, this is a good firm." I tried a new way of appealing to her. "We do right by our clients. I know I haven't given compliance the attention it deserves, and I screwed up on a couple of things, but I promise you there's a great long-term opportunity for both of us here. We've just got to get through inspection in good shape."

She stared at me like Spock doing his Vulcan mind-reading trick on some alien.

"Okay," she said, after taking an extra moment to collect her thoughts. "I'll do my best, but you're going to have to trust me."

Relief flooded to my fingertips. "Of course!" I quickly answered the questions she'd asked me last week. "I did look back over my notes, and unfortunately, I don't have anything in writing from Josie about the Clauskys. But I'm sure I could ask her for something in writing saying she was okay about the distributions I authorized. Should I call her?"

I was totally fine with telling Josie about the car money; it was the app idea that would be tougher to explain.

Angela shook her head. "We can't provide the SEC with any backdated letters or notes. But having her sign something saying that she asked you to handle these requests would be helpful. It's not a legal document, but at least it would close the loop that there was anything fishy going on other than just not following proper procedures."

"But won't that look like squirrely damage control and draw unnecessary attention to the matter?" I asked.

"It's a tough call, but I think it's better to have it than not. I'll draft up something for you to get her to sign. We have to tell them where we made mistakes and how we intend to fix them going forward," she said assuredly.

"I'm with you. Let's do it."

"Marty, we're going to have to be very forthright, lay our cards on the table, and disclose everything."

The prospect of detailing my violations to the SEC was disconcerting. According to our policies and procedures manual, I could face disciplinary action, which would have to be disclosed on my U4 filing. Every investment advisor has a U4, which amounted to a public record detailing an advisor's personal background and any other relevant information, including any securities rule violations. Having a clean record was tantamount in an industry built on personal integrity and trust.

"Look," Angela said, observing the distress on my face. "Burying our own violations, hoping the SEC doesn't find out about them, is *not* the way to go. There was no intention on your part to do wrong by your client, so hopefully we'll be okay." She paused a moment before speaking again.

She was right. This way we would look contrite. Responsible. We spent the rest of the day organizing records and prepping our staff for the arrival of the SEC team. Looking forward to correcting my most blaring wrong, I called Josie and asked if I could stop by her apartment after work.

•

Josie and I sipped hot tea in the quiet lobby of her senior living center. It was just after six, and a few other residents rested nearby in oversized leather chairs.

"They're showing *Gran Torino* down here tonight," she said. "I just love that Clint Eastwood."

After determining that the maintenance of her house and garden was too much for her, Josie moved to Peachtree Meadows, which catered to those mostly capable of taking care of themselves, like Josie, and those who needed greater assistance. The transition had been challenging at first, but after two years, Josie was now happily ensconced. She particularly liked movie nights. She'd become friends with a few other elderly ladies, and together, they ate meals, played cards, and, most of all, gossiped. Before we spoke about business, she liked to fill me in on some of the juicier news.

"Loose, she is," Josie said, launching into a story about the woman directly next door to her who was seeing two different men. One was a "miserable old man" whose wife only died three months ago, and the other a "real player who hits on all the single women." Josie's own husband had died in his sixties from heart disease. She'd never remarried but had several gentlemen she referred to as "friends" over the years.

She pointed out an elderly man crossing the lobby with the help of his walker. "There goes Dr. Marsh," she said. "It breaks my heart. He was a brilliant, handsome cardiologist, and now he barely knows who he is. Marty, I'm just happy I still have my marbles."

As she paused to reflect on Dr. Marsh's condition, I seized the opening to bring up the boys. I brought the letter Angela wrote for Josie to sign and was going to keep my explanation simple.

"Josie, like we had discussed, I've made a couple of extra distributions for Freddie and Danny in the last few months. One, for a car as Freddie's old one was flooded, and the second, for a project related to the computer programming they've been learning. I didn't want to bother you with it."

My explanation of the app-related money was a bit of a stretch, but would hopefully make Josie feel like the boys were putting the online classes they had taken to good use.

"That's wonderful, Marty. I'm so glad you're handling that for me," she said. "I haven't heard much from them lately. They've got a lot of money, but I'm concerned for those boys. They need a strong male role model in their lives. Their father, God rest his soul, loved them, but he wasn't around too much, busy building his law practice. I know they've got some issues, but they needed more structure and discipline growing up. Young boys need that, or they lose their way."

Her words made me think of Ryan. Was I failing him as a father? Was I being too easy on him, conveniently acquiescing to his defiance while I focused on KCM? And while I was fretting about the breakdown in procedures for authorizing the payments to Danny and Freddie, I still questioned my rationale for letting them have the money for their app development. I needed to stay on track. Ingram was coming the next day, and these were questions for another time.

I cleared my throat. "Well, that's what I wanted to talk to you about.

After discussing the matter over with our firm's chief compliance officer, we agreed that it really wasn't appropriate for me to make any authorizations on your behalf. The trust agreement is very specific about you being the one to approve the requests." She looked quizzical, but I pressed on.

"I can still advise you on their needs and cash requests, but I just can't sign the authorization form unless you give me written approval. I'll be happy to come over and get you to sign anything." I tried to downplay the burden on her.

She shook her head. "Lots of rules in your business, but I appreciate your help."

I pulled out the letter and a pen for Josie to sign, explaining that we needed to have something in our files that she was okay with the two distributions. She signed, no questions asked.

I tucked the letter into my briefcase and told her to enjoy the movie. As I walked to my car, I wondered if I was doing enough to steer her grandsons in the right direction. I was a role model whether I'd wanted to be or not. In some ways I felt I was having more of an impact on Danny and Freddie than my own son.

I pulled out my phone and texted them:

Guys,

Your grandma is pleased you're putting your coding skills to work. Keep up the good work!

—MM

29

The clock hit half past eight on Tuesday, July 10, and Gerald Ingram walked through the front door of our office with his two younger-looking subordinates, a lanky woman named Karen and a stocky man named Lee.

I greeted them with small talk. "So, anyone do anything fun over the holiday weekend?" I hoped to build some rapport before they determined my and the firm's fate.

Lee, who appeared to be in his late twenties, spoke first, "If you consider writing up findings from our last office inspection fun, then yes."

His casual sarcasm gave off the vibe of a substitute high school teacher, trying to be cool enough to connect with the students but stern enough to command the respect of the principal.

Gerald, a more refined-looking Weird Al Yankovic circa 1985, with tight curls and square glasses, shot Lee a mild look of disapproval, perhaps for divulging too much information. Not one in the crew looked a day over thirty-five, which was surprising to me. On the phone, Gerald's controlled, measured voice sounded more like a middle-aged man.

I led them the short distance to the conference room. "We'll put you up in here," I said. Angela was already inside. She introduced herself, everyone shook hands, and I blabbed, "Angela's a former SEC investigator herself."

Angela gave me a gruff look, but it wasn't as if they wouldn't find out. Our firm's public disclosures contained a complete work history for all officers and registered financial advisors.

"No kidding," Gerald said, his tone and expression brightening. "Which office?"

"I had a position in DC," Angela said nonchalantly.

I found it odd that she was downplaying her SEC experience. From what my dad said, she'd been a valuable asset at the SEC.

"Really?" Gerald said. "Home office? Which division?"

"Inspections." Angela looked noticeably bothered.

Karen leaned in. "Angela Miller, you say?"

Angela nodded, looking like she wanted to crawl under the large wooden table.

"Are you related to an Andy Miller by any chance?"

Angela turned a deep shade of red. "Actually," she said in a voice much smaller than usual. "Yes, that's my ex-husband. He worked at the SEC as well."

Karen looked sheepish. "Oh. It's just… he was a speaker at one of the training sessions I went to last year at the home office."

It got quiet.

"Great!" Gerald clapped loudly, snapping everyone back to attention. "Since you used to be one of us, I expect that this should go rather smoothly." He gave a congenial yet disarming Weird Al crooked smile.

We all took a seat around the conference table, and Gerald pulled out a small leather-bound portfolio. He reviewed some notes he had scribbled inside before speaking. "So, you're Marty Kaplan. I take it you're related to Leon Kaplan, the firm's principal. Is he here?"

I stood to take off my sport jacket. "Leon's my father. He's actually been out of the country for the past several weeks. I'm the senior vice president, head of research, and an officer of the firm. I'm in charge of operations in his absence."

"And when do you expect him to return?"

If I told him more, would it do more harm than good? Would he think my dad was some rich guy on vacation in Monaco for the summer, leaving his overprivileged son in charge? Or, even worse, an owner who went on the run when he found out the SEC was coming? Bringing up my mother's illness had its own set of ramifications, especially doing so in front of Angela who didn't know the full extent of my mother's condition. We had told the employees that my parents were on an extended vacation, taking the summer off while she recovered from her last round of chemo.

"Well, he's actually with my mother in Germany. She's getting treated for cancer there."

Angela made eye contact with me; it was new information to her.

Gerald scratched his chin. "Sorry to hear that. Is he aware that we're here?"

"We've been in touch, and I'm providing him with updates," I said with an air of confidence even though I felt anything but. Not giving Ingram a straightforward answer was the last thing I wanted to do. I didn't want to land myself in more hot water than I already was. But while my answer might have been a bit misleading, it was technically true. More importantly, I hoped it would firmly establish me and Angela as his team's contacts for the duration of the inspection.

It worked. Gerald moved on and proceeded to go over what his team intended to accomplish over the next few days. It seemed fairly routine, which I took as a good sign. He handed us each a copy of a two-page document that detailed the information they needed us to provide.

As expected, it was a pretty thorough list.

Angela pointed to the small stacks of files laid out on the glass credenza on the side of the room. "I've already got most of this information here. The rest, we can easily pull together and get to you either electronically or on hard copy."

"Terrific," Gerald said. "At this point, Martin, I think we'd like to spend some time interviewing Angela, if that's all right."

"Sure, I'll be in my office, if you need me," I said, eager to recuse myself.

I got up to leave, looking back at Angela as I walked out of the room. If her eyes could talk, they would've said, *"Don't worry. I've got this."*

Good old Angela.

30

Two days later, I was ten minutes into reading the online transcript of a quarterly conference call with Jateroo's management team when my right hand drifted to the mouse and clicked to open a new browsing window. Looking for support that my compliance issues weren't serious, I typed "SEC compliance violations" into the Google search bar.

Bad idea. The search rendered countless instances of firms and individuals fined and censured for all sorts of things ranging from the seemingly trivial, like not updating a firm's privacy policy statement, to the more severe like selling phony interests in oil and gas properties.

I grew anxious and toggled back to Jateroo's transcript, skipping to the more engaging Q&A section. I got hung up on one research analyst's question about the company's amortization of goodwill following a recent acquisition and switched back to resume my compliance violation search. An article about an advisor that got suspended from working in the industry for concealing risks related to an investment sent me into a tailspin. Did the fact that I knew the Clauskys could lose all their money and let them have it anyway make me responsible? Would the SEC banish me from the industry?

Any outcome now seemed possible even though I had no intent to defraud or mislead anyone. Almost certainly the SEC inspectors wouldn't get into the merits of whether it was in the boys' best interests to use a portion of their trust money to develop an app that was doomed to fail. Weren't they really concerned about finding and stopping the next Madoff?

The thought of having disciplinary action with the SEC on both the firm's and my personal record made me physically nauseous. I hadn't weighed myself in over a month, but my appetite was gone, and my pants were loose around my waist. How could I follow in Dad's footsteps and run the firm with a permanent mark on my record? Would our clients drop us if my name appeared along with other violators in a public notice, thinking I'm unethical? Was there even an SEC rule against having an owner with a record of SEC violations? I entered "SEC violations and firm ownership" into the search bar. Pages chock-full of articles all beginning with "SEC charges firm with…" popped up. I about choked on my own saliva. I jumped from my chair and headed straight down to Angela's office.

"Okay, I'm totally freaking out!" I said, bursting into her office.

"What's the matter now?" Angela asked, pulling her head up from the mounds of open client files on her desk.

"How am I supposed to get any work done with the Feds combing through all of our records down the hall? This is like waiting to find out if the jury's found you guilty of murder."

She laughed. "Not quite, Marty," Angela said. She held the palms of her hands toward me. "Just calm down and take a seat."

"I can't calm down," I said while plopping into the chair in front of her desk. "Gerald, Karen, and Lee are probably sitting in that conference room right now talking about *my* screwups and how they're going to stick it to me and the firm just to teach us a lesson. I'm going to go ask Gerald his thoughts on my infractions."

"No, you're not."

"Why?" I asked, slouching back in the chair.

"Marty, we have to let them do their job," she told me. "I told you. I've already come clean with Ingram about everything. It's all in my report."

Angela had told me that during her initial interview with Ingram he'd grilled her on our firm's policies and procedures manual as well as the firm's testing and monitoring systems. She had provided Ingram with her internal checklist report that detailed all known employee violations—

including mine. Nothing in her report was *good*, per say, but it did show that we had a system to monitor employee activities that safeguarded clients from either intentional or unintentional violations, like my own.

"And I can tell you, that if they *do* find something else or have a problem with what we've disclosed, they aren't going to just walk in here and tell us about it," she said. "They're all about following their audit process, and that means completing their inspection, then detailing their findings at a later date. Only then will we know if we're all in the clear."

What would've happened had Angela not been there when the SEC arrived? It was clearly a positive that she had already been conducting her own internal audit beforehand; otherwise, we would have been in a much worse position. However, she was rushed to get through everything and wasn't able to go through the remaining files as thoroughly as she would have liked.

"Assuming they don't find anything else requiring a lot more information requests, how much longer do you think they'll be here?" I asked Angela.

"Usually, inspections for a firm of this size shouldn't last more than three days max, unless there's some real problems," she said. "They should be wrapping up today."

Checking to see if I had any appointments the next day, I grimaced. "Friday the thirteenth is tomorrow. Shit. What do you think? Bad sign?"

Angela laughed again. It was nice to know she was human. "Let's just say it might not be a positive development if they're still here," she said dryly.

In that moment of levity, I felt the beginnings of a real connection with her and decided to pry a bit into her personal life, intrigued by something Lee had brought up during our introductions earlier in the week. At the very least, getting her to open up might be a sign she was warming up to me.

"So," I said, straightening back up in my seat and trying to look extra friendly, "I didn't know your ex-husband also worked at the SEC. Is he still there?"

Her eyes shifted back down at her desk; she took a deep breath before speaking. "No . . . he left a bit before me."

For Angela, that was progress. She hadn't revealed anything about her personal life to me since she started. I hesitated before pressing on, which prompted her to continue talking.

"Look, Marty," she said, a pained expression on her face. "The truth is, I was perfectly happy at the SEC. Things were going really well. Then I found out my husband was fooling around with his junior staff member. Everybody in my department seemed to know about it except for me. I'm sure even Lee out there knew."

My unfortunate "wow" slipped out loud, but Angela didn't seem deterred by it.

"Andy—that's my ex—he ended up getting fired, and my reputation at the agency was compromised. All the good work I did there became overshadowed by my personal drama."

She threaded her fingers together on her desk on top of her legal pad, and my heart tugged. "Why? It wasn't your fault."

She continued, "Well, people started talking behind my back. If *she's* such a great inspector, why couldn't she bust her own cheating husband?" When she finally met my eyes, I could see embarrassment, but also relief.

I thought back to when I was out of my head about Jessica and the mysterious Mark. I couldn't imagine the anguish Angela must've felt. Would I have handled her situation nearly as well? No way. "Jeez, Angela, sorry to hear all that. That must've been really rough."

"Thanks, but I didn't come to this firm looking for any sympathy. I wanted a fresh start. The opportunity to join KCM came at the right time for me. I thought it was some kind of karma."

"And then I was a real pleasure for you to deal with?" I said, giving her a self-deprecating smile.

She smiled back. "Don't worry about it. Keeps me on my toes."

"Look, we'll get through this and get back on track. Thanks for being here, really." It was nice to feel like Angela and I were on the same team.

"So, I've been wondering," she said, her voice back to normal. "What's with the 'Money Man' thing?"

I laughed. "That's just how the Clausky boys refer to me. They're a bit . . . unusual."

"Got a nice ring to it," she said with a mischievous glint in her eye.

"Maybe I'll start calling you that."

I groaned. "Please don't."

All of a sudden, Angela froze up and looked like she was struggling whether or not to say something. Like she was holding back on me.

"What is it?" I asked.

She held out a few seconds longer. "You don't know, do you?"

"Know what?"

"Look, it's not my place to say anything about this, and you've got to promise that you didn't get this from me, because I'll deny it."

"What is it, Angela...is one of our employees up to something?"

"No, not an employee."

"Huh?"

She paused. "I can't tell you *how* I know, but I have reason to believe your dad is considering merging with another firm...a much bigger firm," she said.

I was at a complete loss.

"Merging the firm? That's ridiculous," I said. "Dad wouldn't do that. He's going to be transitioning ownership to me."

Or was he? Suddenly I recalled a conversation I had with my dad when I was graduating college. He knew I wanted to join him at KCM, but he said I had to get work experience somewhere else first. He told me he was supportive of my pursuing a career in money management, but that I needed to establish myself by working for another firm. His comment, "If you ever need another job, that experience on your résumé will come in handy one day," was now buzzing in my head. Was selling the firm his plan all along and he wanted me to have some experience to fall back on?

Angela could tell she rattled me with the news. "Hey," she said to grab my attention. "I'm not saying it's a done deal. I just know there's been some overtures and discussions are ongoing. I've already said too much, and probably should've kept my mouth shut, but I was kinda hoping you knew something and could tell me it's not happening, 'cause if it does, I'll likely be out of a job."

I was about to press her on what information she could possibly have to make her think such a thing, but we were interrupted by a knock on Angela's half-open door. It was Ingram. Had he been listening to our conversation?

"Sorry to interrupt, but I think we've got everything we need. We're wrapping up and leaving shortly. We'll be sending our formal inspection report in the next few weeks or so."

I jumped out of my chair. And before Angela got the chance to speak, I asked, "Is there anything you can share with us at this point?"

Angela looked at me with disapproval, but I could tell she was interested, too.

Gerald looked at us straight-faced. "Unfortunately, at this point, all I can say is that we appreciate your full cooperation and reserve the right to request more information once we get back to our offices and complete our review."

On the inside I was a disaster. Not only was I not getting any closure to the SEC inspection, but Angela had opened a fresh new wound with her merger revelation. I did my best to project composure.

"Well, let us know if you need anything else," I said. "We'll be anxiously awaiting your report."

"Terrific. Thanks for the hospitality. Oh, and the report will be mailed to the firm's principal, your father," Ingram said as he walked away down the hall.

"Okay, I'll tell him to be on the lookout," I said, concentrating on keeping the fear out of my eyes.

I woke at 4:30 a.m. Could Dad really undermine my dream of succeeding him as the future leader of the firm? Getting slapped by the SEC for my screwups certainly wouldn't help my cause if he were really thinking about selling. But maybe the SEC inspection would turn out okay. They were only in the office three days, not the dreaded four.

I checked the futures needing to get my mind off those distressing matters. Before I went to sleep, they were indicating a higher open for Friday. Seeing green would ease my anxiety, perhaps allowing me to get back to sleep. Unfortunately, they had turned and were now down...big. To the tune of negative 2 percent.

I almost threw my phone across the room.

Scanning various news sites, I wasn't able to ascertain any direct cause. Knowing there must be something, I finally checked President Pruitt's Twitter feed. I found my answer:

2:30 a.m. Sending a couple beautiful aircraft carriers to protect Taiwan. What game is X-Man playing? Yang going to hear a BANG if he's not careful. We will win . . . ALWAYS!!

I closed my eyes and drifted in and out of consciousness for a couple hours before finally waking at 6:30 a.m. I groggily checked the futures again, mentally bracing myself to take the pain that Friday the Thirteenth was surely going to offer. The Dow was set to leap nearly 2 percent higher. Shocked, I rubbed my eyes and refreshed my screen to make sure I was seeing correctly or didn't access some old data screen shot. The numbers remained the same. I checked my news feed to see what could have led to the amazing turn in the last few hours.

•

Bizline Market Update: Friday, July 13, 6:04 a.m. ET

European leaders planning to hold an emergency meeting with the United States regarding a unified response to China.

•

Markets must be extrapolating the latest development to mean that China might think twice before doing anything hostile toward Taiwan or risk facing off against not only the United States, but a coalition with its allies.

I skipped breakfast and headed to the office. The strong market open was welcome, but I knew it wasn't too much to get excited about. The markets were so oversold that it wouldn't take much positive news to get a much-needed rally in play. Maybe we hit bottom yesterday? Or maybe it would prove to be a dead cat bounce. Regardless, it was such a relief to see the Dow and S&P 500 still holding gains by midmorning, almost moving out of correction territory. Now, investors were scrambling to buy the beaten-up market for fear of missing out on the rebound.

I checked our list of positions, which showed the reverse of what had been going on lately. The military and defense contractors were selling off hard and virtually everything else was going up as fear of a painful military entanglement receded.

I quickly assessed the various market scenarios playing out and what it meant for our clients' holdings. The market could continue surging if it were truly an "all clear." In that case we should've taken profits on our Lockheed Martin position back when investors were factoring in a possible war driving the missile and weapons makers' stock higher. Maybe we should add more to our other positions because they could keep going up. Then again, this could be a giant head fake, in which case maybe keep some cash in case this rally fades fast and the market heads south again?

My phone buzzed with text messages. The first from JD: *Think I found Bathsheba. Going to see her in a couple of weeks!*

I smiled and texted him back: *Great! Can't wait to hear about it!*

I checked our firm's positions, which were mostly rising. Stellar Biomedical was cruising and outpacing the market's advance. Despite the jump, it felt like we were missing an opportunity to add more to Stellar at the current discounted levels. Like Disney, Stellar had some China exposure that had weighed on the stock. The biotech giant's stock was off a whopping 22 percent from its fifty-two-week high. The company, which developed drugs for both humans and animals, had been an incredible performer for client portfolios, more than doubling over the past couple of years. However, the Chinese swine and poultry industry represented part of the growth story for the company, and the potential for a military conflict weighed more heavily on their stock.

I got our trader Phil on the phone and asked him to put in a block trade to buy shares across all client accounts. It was a small incremental purchase, but action, nonetheless. Not knowing if the market had indeed bottomed or was registering a small tick up before the next leg down was unnerving. Only time would tell.

•

Bizline Market Update: Friday, July 13, 5:40 p.m. ET

Friday the Thirteenth turned out not too frightening after all, finishing an otherwise dismal week with solid gain. Still this crisis is not over. Chinese naval ships continue to hold their position twelve nautical miles to the south of Taiwan as US aircraft carriers begin their trek to protect Taiwan. Some unnamed sources report that the Chinese navy fleet is expected to turn back south to mainland China after it conducts its military exercises, thereby avoiding a direct conflict.

How this tense situation between the world's two largest economies un-folds will certainly help determine if this market correction, now at -10.6 percent, morphs into a full-blown bear market, marked by a decline of 20 percent.

•

32

A steady tapping on JD's keyboard was the only sound emanating from the otherwise quiet administrative wing of the synagogue. Sunday mornings were his most productive studying and writing times. After fifteen minutes, JD's frenetic typing pace slowed, like the last few intermittent pops of kernels in a bag of microwave popcorn. When he finally stopped, he sat back, staring blankly at the screen before walking over to a bookshelf on the other side of the small room. A sermon with a strong message needs a solid biblical reference. He was determined to write something so profound that could help his congregants find more meaning and joy in their own lives. He had a text in mind that would work perfectly but needed to find his notes.

He turned to his contemporary white wooden shelves that displayed a well-organized mixture of rabbinical texts, framed photos, and a few prized items from JD's vast personal collection of sports memorabilia. Scanning the top shelf, JD reached out to pick up a glass case housing a University of Michigan Wolverines' football signed by his sports hero, Tom Brady. He procured the cherished item at a charity auction a couple of years earlier. He smiled thinking about how he had outmaneuvered another sports fanatic at the event in live-auction face-off.

Where the hell is it?

He pulled a couple of books off the second shelf, quickly flipping through the pages.

He set those books back and bent down to view the bottom shelf where he kept his old rabbinical school textbooks. As his fingers slid over book bindings of varying sizes, shapes, and colors, he uttered "bingo" as he pulled a paisley-patterned text titled *Kohelet: A Modern Commentary on Ecclesiastes* from the middle of the shelf. It was propped up by a four-by-six-inch frame displaying a photo of JD alone in front of the Western Wall in Jerusalem taken six years earlier during an early summer trip to the Holy Land. In the picture, JD faced the only remaining wall from the great Second Temple. His hands were spread widely, with his palms pressed gently against the magnificent cool ancient golden stones. He stood with his head gently bowed, eyes closed, and appeared to be in deep prayer or silently meditating.

JD's mind now drifted back to that moment and day in Jerusalem, recalling the powerful feeling of holiness and belonging that unexpectedly overwhelmed him as he stood at the holy site. His spiritual awakening was a momentous twist on a trip that was supposed to be about chasing some beautiful Israeli girls.

Following the divorce, JD found himself rich, single, and unemployed, a dangerous combination for him. He bought a new condo, a Porsche, and with the help of a personal stylist, an entire new wardrobe. He began dating a lot of girls he met through setups and online dating apps.

In the first months after the divorce, he burned through hundreds of thousands of dollars and was apathetic and bored, a state of being he'd never really experienced before. JD wasn't excited about much of anything. While he didn't need to work, not having *something* to do all day enabled him to waste his days. His family and friends were concerned.

Coincidentally, JD ran into an old frat brother who moved to Israel after college and was visiting the United States. He showed JD some pictures of him with some beautiful Israeli girl he met on the beach in Tel Aviv. It was enough for JD to plan a visit.

Within weeks, JD was on a plane. After his arrival, he checked into a five-star hotel and spent his first few days partying with his buddy at some of Tel Aviv's chic nightclubs. His friend convinced him that he needed to do some touring before heading back home. JD reluctantly agreed.

Rather than joining a large group and traveling on a large bus, JD arranged for a private guide to take him around the country in a comfortable Mercedes rental. It wasn't that JD didn't want to be with other people; rather, he was concerned that he might get bored and would want to be able to hurry things along at a faster pace, which he couldn't do as part of a big tour group.

One morning, JD met up with his guide, Shaul Lesnick, over breakfast at a restaurant in downtown Tel Aviv. His planned five-day tour to some of Israel's most visited attractions turned into a two-week religious and spiritual awakening that set JD in motion on a life-changing journey.

After spending a day on a kibbutz located on the northern border with Lebanon and Syria, they headed south down to the small city of Safed, one of the four holiest cities in Israel. Shaul, an easygoing, knowledgeable thirty-one-year-old made him the perfect traveling companion for JD. At first, JD wondered how a former military commando like Shaul could find a career as a tour guide interesting. But at each stop, Shaul's incredible storytelling that intertwined history, geography, religion, politics, and social relevance brought the country's deep history to light. JD was captivated, finding meaning behind things he'd completely missed as a teenager on a youth group tour bus with forty other kids. The moment he laid his hands on the Wall, he knew his life's journey had changed.

JD returned the picture frame to the bookshelf and snapped back to his task at hand. He flipped through the book about Ecclesiastes he had taken off the shelf, trying to recall a class discussion back in rabbinical school. He found the specific reference he was searching for midway through the book. He read a few pages, sat back down, and resumed typing. After another half hour or so of work, he stopped. He gave a half smile at his work, approving of what he had written. Could he do for others what Shaul had done for him? He needed to have an impact, but was it good enough?

33

Despite the market posting solid gains on Friday, my optimism that one good up day in the market would translate into a sustained trend was nothing more than wishful thinking. When I cracked my eyes open at 5:30 on Monday morning, the futures were already sinking.

Great…another shitty week.

As much as I wanted to hide under the covers, I forced myself to get up. I crept into the closet and pulled on shorts and a tee. Other than a little basketball scrimmaging with the boys during Ryan's practices, I had been lax about exercise. I rummaged through the closet looking for my running shoes as quietly as I could as to not wake Jessica. I pushed aside a pile of dirty dress shirts and paused. I could ask her to join. Run together like we used to in the early mornings before the sun rose, evading the oppressive heat. *Aha!* Under a set of crumpled sheets were my shoes.

I returned to my nightstand to grab my earbuds. I almost touched Jessica's shoulder to wake her. But she cherished her sleep. Maybe more than me, at least right now. Besides, I needed to clear my mind.

I hurried downstairs, turned off the house alarm, and ventured out into the quiet predawn morning.

After bending over and unsuccessfully trying to touch my toes on a few attempts, I gingerly took off on my run. Not surprisingly, my initial strides were rough. My legs felt like there were sandbags strapped to them. My muscles were tight, joints stiff, and my right knee ached and buckled each time the base of my foot planted on the unforgiving pavement. I pressed on, knowing the soreness and early fatigue would fade after I warmed up. I hadn't jogged outdoors in a couple of months. The ellipticals at the air-conditioned gym were far gentler on the body.

My hope was that the exercise would help clear my mind, but right from the get-go I lost all control of my thoughts. As I ran through my quiet Virginia Highlands neighborhood listening to my favorite '80s shuffle, my mind clung to my clients like paperclips clumped to a magnet. How would they respond to the mounting losses in their accounts? Are they going to fire me? Will I lose friends over this?

The Gillmans sitting at their dinner table, Jeff losing his appetite and handing Samantha their brokerage statement over his plate of meat loaf and potatoes angrily telling her, "Disney World is out! We're staying home for winter break this year. My retirement just got pushed back a couple years."

And Evan Lanter. If Bill Fredrington hadn't already poached him from our firm, the additional losses piling up in his account would certainly push him over the edge. Evan still hadn't responded to the email I had sent a few days after the boys' basketball game wanting to set up a lunch. I'm sure he was thinking about that Newport property and how his family would've done better holding on to it than losing the money in the market.

Then there was Mrs. Benoit. She trusted me with Simon's hard-earned lifetime savings.

Marteen, you idiot! Why?

One by one, the shell-shocked faces of our firm's clients passed before my eyes.

"I'm sorry . . . I'm sorry," I confessed loudly, to hear myself over the "Jessie's Girl" pumping in my ears.

I pushed through the pain, literal and figurative, and struggling to match my stride with Rick Springfield's hard-charging beat. I begged the endorphins to kick in, like an addict in search of a moment of peace and tranquility.

Back in grad school, I'd experimented with various methods to calm my rapid-fire, stressed-out mind. Okay, well, maybe less than the bohemian undergrad from northern California I was dating and trying to impress at the time. She took me to a meditation session. The male instructor, a retired physician in his late sixties, had the ten of us sit in a circle, close our eyes, and breathe.

"Slowly inhale," he said, "now exhale." He just kept repeating this along with, "Focus on your breath." This went on for a full half hour, and after the first few minutes of squelching my laughter, I got so relaxed that I almost fell asleep. Not the spiritual enlightenment I'd been aiming for, at least according to my date. The meditation was supposed to help remove all extraneous, harmful thoughts from our heads, relieve stress, and free us to be more present and focused, all things I now desperately needed.

I had no idea if *running meditation* was a thing, but if there was ever a time to try, it was now. Taking stock of my breath, I found myself panting like a dog on a hot summer day with short choppy breaths through my mouth. I reset and began inhaling through my nose. Slowly in through my nose, and then exhaling through my mouth.

In and out.

In and out.

My breaths became increasingly deeper with a smooth, consistent cadence, yielding a cool sensation deep inside my sinus cavity, which was unexpected given my deviated septum. Ever since a trampoline incident in the tenth grade when I broke my own nose with my knee while attempting a flip, I hadn't been able to consistently breath through my nose. Now, it was like the pure, open airway tingly sensation one gets after sucking on a mentholated mint. With each inhale, air filled my lungs and dispersed throughout my body. I visualized the oxygen, rich with vital fuel, sliding through my body's web of veins and tiny ventricles. The blood flow supported my legs and feet as I glided over the pavement. Sure enough, my mind began to break free from the clumps of negative thoughts that were clogging it up.

I wiped the sweat from my forehead and picked up my pace, still paying attention to nothing but my breathing and my feet connecting with the ground. My legs were strong, and the pain in my knee gone. The hard pavement was now a layer of fluffy marshmallows. As I closed in on the intersection of Ponce de Leon and Oakdale, my energy remained surprisingly high. I circled the light pole at the corner of the street, tapping it three times just like Jessica used to do on our morning runs.

Turning back toward home, Duran Duran's "Hungry like the Wolf" pumped me up for the back half of my run. With my shirt completely soaked, I pealed it off, using it as a sponge to sop up the sweat that was stinging my eyes.

Even though the morning sky had already brightened, I was still alone on the eerily quiet streets. I'm not sure if it was the sweat, music, endorphins, or my Zen-like state, but I was incredibly energized and my mind clearer than it had been in a long time.

I skipped over "Do You Really Want to Hurt Me?" on the shuffle, and when "Eye of the Tiger" came on, it felt like fate.

I broke into an all-out sprint that would've made Usain Bolt— well, maybe Rocky Balboa—proud. Crossing our neighbor's driveway, I reached my virtual finish line. Downshifting into a brisk cool-down walk, I held my arms up high and locked my hands behind my head to open up my lungs.

Staring into the glare of the breaking sunrise, I was overwhelmed by an incredible sense of accomplishment, like I had just finished the Boston Marathon. Making it through the run without stopping was one thing, but doing so without checking the market futures the entire thirty minutes was quite another. I wasn't thinking about the market, my clients, or any of the other things that were troubling me. I was aware of the music still playing in my ears, but I couldn't really hear it. I was just simply there.

I pulled out my AirPods and plopped down on our front doorsteps. Jessica hated it when I left a trail of sweat on the hardwood floors. As I sat perspiring profusely, waiting to drip-dry, the neighborhood bird chirp rang sweetly in my ears. The streaky rays of sun broke through the overhanging oak tree branches and began to illuminate my street. I stared blankly ahead, and my mind was totally open, uninhabited by concern and worry. Enjoying my moment of peace, I homed in on a small beetle about the size of a pencil eraser a few feet away on the ground. It was flipped over on its back, and its tiny six legs flailed about madly as it tried to right itself. I stared curiously for a couple of minutes to see if it would succeed in saving itself, knowing that the capsized beetle's efforts were likely futile. Even if one of his fellow beetles were around, it would neither be equipped nor motivated to save him.

Before heading back inside, I did something I had never done before. I kneeled next to the still-thrashing beetle, reached out with my index finger, and gave it a gentle flip. It scrambled back into the flower beds. To me, it was an insignificant gesture. To the beetle, it was literally a lifesaving moment. I reflected on my impact. What if I never noticed it? Laughing to myself...if raising a child were only that easy. Satisfied, I went back inside to finish cooling off.

Downing a glass of cold water at the kitchen table, I was suddenly hit by this intense feeling that I had to get in touch with my parents. Keeping the whole SEC inspection thing from my dad was weighing on me. I was going to put an end to it. He was going to find out about it anyway, and if some disciplinary action was coming my way, then so be it. And more than that, I needed to do something that I wished I'd done the last time I spoke to my mother: tell her I loved her.

When my dad answered, his voice was strained. "What is it? Is it Mom?" I blurted out.

He swallowed. "Your mother is having an adverse reaction to the treatment. She's been very weak the last few hours, and Dr. Schmidt admitted her to the ICU just a little while ago. They're giving her lots of fluids and oxygen. If . . ." His voice broke. "If she doesn't stabilize soon and her blood levels don't improve, they're going to have to give her a transfusion."

Blood transfusion?

The two words unleashed a strong chemical reaction in my body that I immediately recognized. It was the same woozy sensation I typically got about thirty seconds after a needle entered a vein in my arm to draw blood, except there was no needle, just awful news. Clammy hands, light-headedness, and a pit in my stomach. I'm sure that if I could've seen myself in a mirror, my face would've already turned to a pale shade of whitish green. I was hoping I could digest the news about my mother sitting, rather than having to lie down because I was in the kitchen without a sofa or bed nearby.

The hazy cloud filled my head, and I struggled to get out an: "So, what does all that mean?"

I tilted my head between my legs as Dad said, "We're not sure yet. We'll have to see how she responds over the next couple days."

"Can she still get the treatment?" Would she be back to square one or worse . . . left with nothing?

"We don't know that either. Dr. Schmidt said that her reaction might actually be a good sign that the treatment is working and that they might have to just tweak her dosing. But she has to stabilize first. So, there's just a lot of unknowns right now, Martin."

My dizziness subsided as the blood started flowing back to my head. "What can I do? Should Alan, Stephanie, and I come over there?"

"No, there's nothing you can do here," he said. "I'm with her, and we need you there. How are Jessica and Ryan?"

"Dad, they're fine," I said, frustrated that he was changing the subject so quickly.

"Okay, okay, just asking. What about at the office? This correction has been pretty rough."

Shop talk? Now?

"We're doing okay," I said, all plans of coming clean dissolved. I couldn't stress him out any more, given the news about Mom.

Dad cleared his throat. "I'm sorry, but it's really hard for me to stay plugged in and help you right now, Marty."

My heart twisted. The only other time I could recall hearing him so choked up was when he spoke at his own father's funeral. I remember thinking how much pain he must've felt for his voice to break like that.

"Dad, don't worry about it," I told him reassuringly. "We're fine here. Just be with Mom."

Until then, I had convinced myself that my mother would be okay. Yes, I was worried, but despite the woeful five-year survival rates for

Stage III lung cancer, I always expected my mom to survive it. When my dad told me about this new treatment in Germany and described it as "promising," I just assumed it would work. It wouldn't be pleasant, but in the end, she would make it. My parents were too practical to go all the way to Germany for some bogus treatment. But now the seriousness and gravity of her situation hit me hard. After asking Dad to give my love to Mom, I put the phone down and dropped my head into my folded arms.

I was totally lost.

34

JD adjusted his six-foot, svelte frame on the thinly cushioned, contemporary loveseat. After checking in with the receptionist, he took a seat on the petite sofa at the end of the waiting area. He grinned at the only other person sitting in the room, a sixty-something woman seated in a chair to his right. The woman broke from reading *Inner Realm* magazine to catch a quick glimpse of the well-dressed gentleman and smiled back.

The room's spalike, Asian-fusion ambiance helped sooth JD's racing mind. What would he say to Alexa? Should he come clean about his true motives for his visit that day or wait until they became entrenched in a deep relationship before sharing the details of his innocent deception? Within minutes he'd be staring into the beautiful, entrancing eyes of a woman he'd never met but might spend the rest of his life with. Destiny was playing out in real time. He marveled how he had successfully tracked her down, using the shul's recorded livestream to identify her, finding her on the list of mourners, and ultimately discovering her practicing holistic medicine in an inconspicuous office building on the artsy east side of downtown. He was convinced that using the synagogue's resources for a personal quest was in the synagogue's best interest. Having their rabbi in a deeply committed relationship could only be a good thing in the eyes of congregants.

JD filled out the new patient paperwork. He amused himself at the thought of writing "finding soul mate," as the primary reason for the office visit, but settled on "persistent back pain." After all, a couple of months earlier he had a mild lumbar spasm that lasted a couple of days. It bothered him enough to skip his weekly poker game. So, the claim, while a stretch, wasn't technically unfounded.

As the receptionist slid open the opaque glass window to retrieve his completed forms, JD poked his head through the square frame opening, searching for any sign of the doctor. He didn't confirm anything other than the overpowering scent of incense permeating from the inner sanctum of the office.

He settled back into his seat and waited. Minutes later, the receptionist opened the door and called the woman back, leaving JD alone in the waiting area. He checked his phone to pass the time. Other than some general synagogue-related emails, he opened a note from his client service liaison with the Atlanta Falcons organization. He had recently put in a request to upgrade his seats for the upcoming season.

Hi Rabbi Aron,

I tried to process your $6,500 deposit for your season's tickets today and the charge was declined by the credit card company. Please check on this ASAP and let us know if there is an issue so we can complete this transaction. We don't want you to lose your upgraded seats!

Go Falcons!

Kelly Turner—Senior Sales Associate

Declined? JD scratched his head. Could he have possibly exceeded his credit limit? Certainly not. The bank bumped his $20,000 credit limit by another $5,000 just a few months earlier so he wouldn't unexpectedly run into this very issue. But his quick mental math made him nervous. The Falcons' tickets…plus $5,000 to secure the Deer Valley condo, $3,000 on a signed Mickey Mantle baseball bat he picked up on eBay, and his regular bills could've gotten him close. He pulled up the bank's number and entered information to get through the multiple layers of security to gain access to his most recent transactions. A robo-assistant began listing the most recent items, which included some purchases he had forgotten: $2,500 on a custom suit, $700 on dinner at Umi's, and $400 on a gas-fired firepit for his veranda.

"Excuse, Mr. Aron."

JD looked up to see the receptionist opening the sliding window once again. He hung up his call before getting a customer service representative on the line.

"We're ready for you now. Come on back," she said.

JD tucked his phone in his jacket pocket and skipped toward the door leading to the back of the office where Alexa presumably waited for him. Before he reached the door, the receptionist stopped him.

"Oh, Mr. Aron. I checked your insurance, and it appears you're out-of-network. So, you'll have to pay for today's consultation. Would you like to take care of the $200 charge now or on the way out?"

JD went into full-blown panic mode. He envisioned Alexa walking him out and the receptionist informing him in front of her that his credit sucked. He never carried more than $20 of cash on him. Could he get ahold of Marty and have him call in a payment somehow? He didn't know if he could get him, nor did he want to get lectured about how a budget would've prevented the situation, even though he was right.

Was God playing a cruel trick on him or saving him from embarrassment by prompting him to check his email just in the nick of time?

JD turned in such a way that the assistant could get a view of the yarmulke on the back of his head and smiled at the young administrator. "You know, I left my cards back in my office... at the synagogue. Certainly, you can bill me?"

The receptionist smiled back. "I'm sorry, Mr. Aron, but we have a strict policy. Shall I reschedule your appointment?"

•

Bizline News Update: Thursday, July 26, 5:26 p.m. ET

As the armada of US navy ships steadily works its way across the Pacific toward Taiwan, it's become apparent that a military altercation with China is now a higher probability event. The global stock markets have reacted accordingly, resuming their downward trend. Since the market correction began just over a month earlier, the S&P 500 had fallen 16 percent, getting ever closer to a full-blown bear market. The growing prospects of a global military conflict kept buyers on the sidelines, overwhelmed by their selling counterparts in the market.

President Pruitt had flown to his personal estate in North Carolina to meet with the Japanese prime minister and South Korean leaders to discuss the evolving situation and how their respective countries might react should a US conflict with China spill out into the broader Asia Pacific region. Upon his return, Pruitt appeared in the doorway of Airforce One soon after landing at Andrews Airforce Base. He stopped and waved to the crowd of onlookers before descending the mobile stairway with his entourage of staffers and security detail following close behind.

As he walked across the tarmac toward his awaiting limousine, the crowd of reporters and other media shouted questions at him.

"President Pruitt . . . are we going to war with China?" one female reporter in the second row asked with such desperation in her voice that it cut through the garble of all the others, stopping the president in his tracks.

He turned his head toward the reporters and shouted back his familiar refrain, "We'll see! We'll be positioning our forces to intervene if necessary, but we don't like how China's been behaving." He climbed into the back of the heavily fortified presidential limousine.

•

35

My skin hurt under my clothes, and I had that achy feeling like I was in the early stages of coming down with something. I relaxed my grip on the wheel, and breathed in and out, determined to decompress on my ride home from work. I needed an escape and for the world to stop so I could catch my breath. It had been a rough grind.

The remainder of July was more of the same and August wasn't any better. Up days in the market were fleeting. The persistent investor angst over the drawn-out crisis and associated steady drip of persistent losses had piled up. Most of our client accounts were down double-digits from where they stood a few months earlier in mid-June when the correction began. Our firm's assets under management, which surpassed $500 million on the road to $1 billion, now dwindled to $440 million, and we weren't done sliding. While our clients lost less than the market's 16 percent drubbing, my asset tracking chart had the terrifying downward pitch of a black diamond ski slope.

On another call earlier in the day with Mrs. Benoit, who was becoming increasingly rattled by the losses in her account, I did my best to reassure her the decline would prove temporary. And yet now I was starting to seriously doubt that myself. My tone lacked confidence. At one point during the conversation, she inquired when my dad would be returning to the office. I took it as a sign I was losing her trust, if I hadn't already done so. Seeing her and other clients' accounts shrivel on my watch made me sick to my stomach, but I knew that selling and cutting losses was the wrong thing to do and could come back to haunt us later.

At least the Clausky twins hadn't lost all their seed capital, yet. They sent an email, along with a YouTube video link, letting me know that, other than Freddie getting bitten by an aggressive rottweiler in a dog park, their app testing had been going "better than expected."

Curiously, I clicked on the link. The forty-two second clip opened with a shot of one of the boys standing in an empty parking lot. He wore navy blue athletic shorts, a white crewneck undershirt, and a red paisley bandana that concealed his eyes. In front of him were three small orange pylon cones spaced out in an imperfect line. I could've reasonably concluded that I was about to witness some sort of soccer drill, ball handling clinic or sporting feat. But these were the Clauskys. Something else was coming.

As soon as the one filming the scene hollered, "Marco!" The bandana-wearing brother responded, "Polo," and began marching forward slowly and steadily towards the first pylon. He held his phone out directly in front of him, gently moving it side to side like he a divining rod probing for an underground water source. When he got to within a few steps of the orange cone, there was faint buzzing sound.

"Holy crap! Danny…did you hear that?" the walker shouted, clarifying his and the cameraman's identity.

"Woohoo!" Danny yelled back. "It works. It freakin' works. Freddie, go around it and keep heading this way!"

Freddie sidestepped the pylon to his right, then proceeded forward as Danny guided him with another, "Marco."

Once again, a vibrant alarm could be heard as he moved towards the second pylon. They both cheered as Freddie successfully navigated his way around the two remaining cones. Circumventing the final cone, Freddie tore off his bandana and greeted his brother with a huge smile and overzealous high five. The video ended with Danny flipping the camera around and signing off with a thumbs-up and celebratory, "mission accomplished."

I closed the link and returned to the Clauskys' email. It said that based on their successful testing they were sending the beta version of the app out to some "early adopters" and "well-connected people." Well-connected? What influential people could they possibly know, especially those that would risk their reputation on such a nutty idea? All the theatrics, of course, would only delay the inevitable. I had to tell them that their grandmother knew they'd received money but assured them the details I'd shared had been vague.

With regards to the SEC, it had been almost six weeks since Gerald Ingram and his crew left our office. Angela, who was coming by my office to chat daily, was adamantly opposed to using her contacts at the agency to gain any more information about the results of our inspection. With every passing day, my anxiety grew. They had all the power and our firm's destiny in their hands. I pictured Weird Al Ingram sitting around the SEC's office break room with his colleagues discussing what kind of disciplinary action to take against us. Angela, to her merit, was still optimistic we would come through okay despite our noted violations, deficiencies, and longer than usual response time.

I still hadn't let on anything about the inspection to Dad. Nor had I confronted him about his merger discussions during the periodic update calls and email exchanges. My mother's condition was still uncertain. Some good days followed by some bad. She had gone in and out of ICU. According to the doctor, her initial tests regarding the effectiveness of the treatments were inconclusive, given how early on it still was. Her vitals continued to fluctuate as she received further treatments. Without any adverse incidents, they could be returning home by early September, only a month later than originally planned. But that was a lot of ifs.

I needed some music to help me unwind. Out of habit, I hit the first preset button on my steering wheel dash that turned the radio to CNBC. John Conner was advising a caller on his *Crazy Money* financial news show: *"Over two months into this slow-moving crisis and the market's technicals are simply awful. Unfortunately, I see more downside from here. It's treacherous out there, and I want all my listeners to play it safe right now."*

It was too aggravating for me to listen to and was about to flip to the Beatles station when my cell phone rang. It was JD. I wasn't in the mood to listen to him either, but I picked up anyway.

"Hey, JD," I said, clearly sounding downbeat and demoralized.

"What's up, Kaplan?" he said, his deep, powerful voice booming off the cabin walls of my car.

"Not the stock market." I tried to land a joke and elicit some empathy.

"Don't tell me you're not making me money!"

I came close to telling him that if he had bothered to check his last statement, he'd have noticed that not only did I not make him any money, but in addition to the $500,000 he took out for Feldstein last month, he'd lost another 10 percent. Instead, I went with, "Unfortunately, no. It's been a horrendous shitshow."

"Hey, don't worry about it. It'll turn around...and it's actually good news for me."

"Really? And how's that?"

"I've already collected two hundred thousand of the Feldstein sponsorships, so I'll be wiring the money back to my account to reinvest tomorrow. Didn't we sell high a while ago? And now we can buy back low. Lucky me."

"Wow, that's great." That actually *was* good news.

"Yeah, as of now, I've got an assortment of wealthy family dynasties at the synagogue sponsoring. Would love to add the Kaplans to the list. You guys want to come in at the bronze level for $25,000? You'll get a nice write-up in the program, and I'll make sure you get great seats for you and some of your big-hitter clients at the show, buddy."

My parents were very charitable on a personal level, but my dad kept the firm's name out of the public eye when it came to sponsoring high-profile events for reasons I never really knew. But we're going to need some new business to make up for the assets we were losing in the market. Maybe it would be good to get tied into this event after all.

"I tell you what, let me talk to my dad about it," I said. "They're coming back from Germany in a few weeks."

"Awesome. We go to the printers with the invites soon, and I want to have KCM on there with all the other players."

"So enough about me," I said, eager to talk about something not money-related for a minute. "How was your date... or appointment I should say, with Cinderella, Bathsheba, or whatever her name is?"

"Bathsheba, and funny you should ask. Listen to this..." he said, then proceeded to recount how his journey to find Bathsheba led him to the office of this holistic medicine doctor, how he went under the guise of his recurring back problem, and even confessing to me about his credit limit predicament. I bit my tongue, not castigating him with an "I told you so." Instead, I asked, "What did you do…reschedule?"

"Hell no, Kap! Do you *even* have to ask?"

"Sorry…you're right. I should know better by now. So then what happened?"

His tone became sober. "I told her she could hang onto my Rolex until I came back with the funds later in the day."

"Nice move!"

"Thanks, I thought you'd like that."

"The receptionist walks me back to this room that's more like the inside of a Buddhist temple than an exam room with all these candles, incense, and funky aromas in the air. I literally could barely breath in there. Despite all the Zen, my adrenaline is pumping hard, and I start thinking about how fucking nuts I am to have gotten myself into this situation."

"Can't disagree," I chimed in, really enjoying his story, the sheer insanity of which was really starting to lighten my mood.

"You know me. I'm ready to play this thing out and see where it goes. After a few minutes, the door finally cracks open, and Dr. Alexa Roseman walks in…"

"And…is it her? Is it Bathsheba?"

He paused before answering. I couldn't tell if was for dramatic effect or if he wasn't pleased with the end result.

Finally, he slowly uttered, "It wasn't her."

"Shit. Sorry, JD."

"Yeah, Kaplan. It was a dead end. I had this weird feeling we'd be together," he said, not sounding as depressed as I'd expected.

"Honestly, I feel like such a schmuck about the whole thing. Why didn't you try and stop me?"

I suppressed my laughter at his apparent serious question. "Sorry, JD. That sounds awful. So that's it?

"Not totally. While the doctor is sticking a bunch of needles all over my body with this acupuncture technique, which, by the way, *is not* covered by insurance, we start making small talk. She knows I'm a rabbi, and the conversation gets spiritual, you know talking about the soul and crossing over, and I mention my chaplain hospice work. Get this…it turns out she's part of the Chevra Kadisha."

"The what?"

"Chevra Kadisha. It's a Jewish volunteer society where its members sit with the bodies of the deceased while waiting to be buried. It's really an honor to be part of."

"Wow. I've actually heard of that," I said. I did have familiarity with the practice but had never met anyone that did it. At least not that I knew about.

"Pretty cool, right?" JD asked.

"I guess. If you're into that kind of thing."

"So, it turns out she's an interesting woman. And did I mention she kind of has this sensual vibe about her, kind of like a hot librarian minus the glasses."

"You didn't. Sounds like it's worth having a follow-up visit."

"Already got it booked, Kaplan!"

36

The white, dry sand cooled my feet as I buried them just below the surface of the beach. Looking out on the light blue ocean, I sat on a folding chair with the steady breeze of the sea blowing gently in my face. Foamy, white-topped waves broke onto the smooth surface of the beach in a steady rhythm. The waves rolled over onto the shore, coming to within inches of my chair before receding back into the ocean.

It was a relatively tranquil afternoon on the beach, with only a handful of people splashing just off the shoreline. Ryan tried to body surf. He yelled my name and motioned for me to come into the water as he swam farther offshore.

It was hot enough that cooling off in the ocean seemed appealing, so I pulled my feet out of their sandy pockets, removed my hat and shirt, and began to slowly wade into the water. Ryan was now about a hundred feet away from me, bobbing in the water. When I looked to the horizon, I noticed a bigger swell forming in the distance. Ryan was facing the shoreline, and by this point, I was swimming toward him so he couldn't see me. The swell continued to grow and was now a good-size wave. It kept growing, getting larger and larger. By the time it closed in on Ryan, it was a dangerously tall wall of water.

"Ryan, Ryan!" I nervously shouted while pointing to the wave, trying to get his attention, but he couldn't hear me over the wind and ocean's gurgling undertow.

My anxiety surged. I swam as fast as I could toward him, but I wasn't going to make it in time. I looked up and saw the massive wave cresting just as Ryan turned to see it. His knee-jerk reaction was to try to dunk under the wave before it broke over him. Just as he took a deep breath and started to submerge, the massive wall slammed down hard, submerging him under the water. I panicked, lunging toward where he'd gone under. I threw my arms out in front of me and kicked, hoping to feel his body with my outstretched arms and hands. I was there to rescue him.

"What the hell's wrong with you?" I heard as I pulled my head up. "That really hurt," Jessica said.

I turned to see Jessica rubbing her left shoulder. "Sorry, another crazy dream," I said.

"Okay, I've had enough. I'm tired of getting knocked around," she said. "Marty, I'm sorry the stock market sucks right now, but you *need* to stop freaking out. It's not your fault things are going down right now, and your clients will understand that. Now, I'm going to sleep in the guest room until you get your shit together because I'm tired of getting woken up."

As she slid out from underneath the duvet and walk out of our dark bedroom, I almost told her about my awful dream, which involved Ryan, not the stock market. Or did it?

Instead, "sorry" was all I could utter as the door closed behind her.

I hadn't had a decent night's sleep since the start of the correction in June and was getting used to being awakened in the middle of the night by vivid, freaky dreams.

After Jessica left, I got up to use the bathroom, then checked in on Ryan to quell my still racing heart. He was sound asleep, and I was glad one of us in the house felt safe enough to be so content.

Checking the status of the Asian markets in the middle of the night had become routine. It was 2:38 a.m., and Asian markets were dropping once again. The futures markets were indicating it would be a turbulent Friday. I checked my email and saw that I had a late-night message from JD with the subject line: *"Who's laughing now?"*

Kaplan, more sponsorships just came through…up to $450,000!! I'll take care of the remaining $50,000 myself. I'm wiring the rest of the money

back into the account tomorrow. Keep buying and make me some f@#king money, bro!
Shalom
P.S. You're going to love my sermon tomorrow night! Happy Holy Days!

To be honest, I couldn't believe he'd actually raised the money for his event. Some mixture of dreamlike delirium, palpable despondency, and spontaneous inspiration got the better of me, and I immediately emailed him back:

JD, you're the man! Would you mind if KCM split that last $50,000 with you? We'd love to take that bronze sponsorship for this awesome event.
B'Shalom,
Marty

Breaking the event sponsorship commitment to my dad was just another thing on my list of issues. Maybe it would be a great warm-up to telling him about the SEC audit — "If you're not happy about that, just listen to this..."

Since I was still unable to sleep and now alone in the room, I turned on the television looking for a mindless distraction. I started flipping stations when I ironically came across a *Feldstein and Friends* rerun. It was one of my favorite early episodes where Barry buys a rental property with his friends and everything goes awry. Karma?

•

The next morning, an hour into the trading session, the market broke through a key resistance level, which led to an intraday decline that put the S&P 500 officially in bear market territory, meaning it had fallen a whopping 20 percent from its June peak. All those lost opportunities to have sold at higher prices the proceeding couple of months were now a distant memory. I was mentally drained and numb like a punch-drunk boxer that just went ten rounds with a stronger competitor. The frequency of clients' calls, emails, and texts was picking up speed as more and more were becoming aware of the severity their losses.

I now let the phone roll to voicemail. I couldn't bring myself to try to talk one more client off the ledge from selling. I didn't believe myself anymore. Why should they believe me? To make matters worse, it was a Friday and the start of the three-day Labor Day weekend. Nobody would want to buy before the weekend for fear of negative developments over the weekend, making the market susceptible to a deeper sell-off before the close. Once again, I fought off the desire to sell holdings. What was the use anyway? There had already been so much damage. I even plugged my nose and put in some stock buy orders for JD's account to reinvest the money he wired back into his account. At least he was getting back in the market at a lower level than where he sold.

Unsurprisingly, when the closing bell sounded, the market had shed another percent. I was so frustrated by the weak close that I kicked the side of my desk hard enough to crack the wood paneling. It also left me with a sore big toe that throbbed as it pushed up against the tip of my dress shoe. I grimaced at how much discomfort I'd feel sitting in synagogue for the first night of Rosh Hashanah later that day.

37

The bubbly energy in the synagogue's main sanctuary was apparent from the second I walked through the main entryway. It was Erev Rosh Hashanah, the first night of the Jewish New Year, and the beginning of the High Holy Days. Congregants, eager to get their New Year's going, started filling up Congregation Beth Am's magnificent main sanctuary extra early. Since the holidays brought out most of the synagogue's members, parking and getting through security was an arduous and time-consuming task.

My family arrived a full twenty minutes before the service was set to begin. We managed to secure seats in the more comfortable, highly coveted first thirty rows of the sanctuary. Services would last a couple of hours, so comfort was important.

As we waited for Rabbi Borowitz to kick things off, the familiar pre-service chatter echoed off the sanctuary's high majestic walls. I'd been looking forward to the arrival of Friday night, not so much for the start of the New Year, nor the celebratory meal afterward. At that moment, I was just happy that Rosh Hashanah had landed on Labor Day, which meant a three-day weekend. The markets would be closed on Monday, and I wouldn't be tempted to check on them while sitting in prayer services supposedly praying for my soul. More importantly, there would be a blissful, three straight days' break from trading and volatile market gyrations.

It had been a horrendous week and a rough final trading day following the news of President Xin dropping out of the meeting in DC with Pruitt. My head hurt the entire day, and the two Tylenol I popped before we left for services had yet to kick in.

When we took our seats, JD was already perched on the raised bema platform along with some of the synagogue's other clergy and executive leadership. He appeared calm and ready for his big night. He had told me he was slated to have a limited, yet important role, delivering the sermon on opening night. Rabbi Borowitz was saving the highly desirable first day of Rosh Hashanah (the following morning) and Yom Kippur (ten days later) sermons for himself. JD said he found out through some moles on the board that Rabbi Borowitz hadn't wanted him to do anything other than lead a few minor prayers but had been pressured by the board into giving JD a prime-time sermon. The synagogue's board endorsed JD getting some broader exposure to the congregation to see if he could handle the big show. Was he a legitimate contender to eventually fill Borowitz's esteemed shoes? Word had made its way to JD that Borowitz still resented that the executive committee essentially forced him to hire JD, not considering him senior rabbi material.

I sat in a somewhat catatonic state for what felt like hours waiting for services to begin while Ryan played games on his phone. Jessica would have confiscated it had she not been roaming the sanctuary kibitzing with her girlfriends who were scattered in the rows around us.

Soon, Rabbi Borowitz began the service with the familiar refrain, "Please rise and turn to page four for the recitation of the Barechu." We all stood and began chanting the first prayer of the long service along with the rabbi and the cantor. As I chanted, my mind immediately drifted off the page. How pissed will our clients be when they get their August statements? Why didn't I sell down their holdings over the last couple of months before things got this bad? I could almost hear Mrs. Benoit asking me, "Marteen, am I going to be okay?"

As the service progressed, I faded in and out, standing, sitting, and reading responsively as the rabbi directed. I nervously fidgeted and looked around the room, nodding every time I caught the eyes of a familiar face. My anxiety was getting the better of me as I flipped through the prayer book to see how many pages were left before the services would end. I got impatient as the cantor seemed to extend each word he sung, stretching out each note as long as possible. Was he trying to torture me? About forty-five minutes into the service, Ryan said he needed to pee, then went MIA.

Finally, after an hour of my going through the motions, I snapped into the moment as JD got up and moved toward the podium. As Borowitz passed him on the bema, they paused for a brief exchange. I strained to read their lips and imagined Borowitz whispered, "Don't fuck this up," to his young, inexperienced associate on his debut night. Knowing JD, he'd probably have just replied, "Thanks for warming the crowd up for me."

JD slowly approached the lectern, fixed the microphone, and then paused to scan his large flock before him. After waiting an uncomfortably long time for full silence, he finally opened with the customary New Year's greeting of "L'Shana Tova."

"L'Shana Tova," we responded back in unison.

"As a rabbi, I get asked lots of questions from congregants in their search for answers and meaning. They'll ask me, Rabbi Aron, do Jews believe in life after death? Rabbi Aron, do you have to observe all God's commandments to get into heaven? Rabbi Aron, why are my synagogue dues so high?"

The sound of laughter echoed off the sanctuary's high walls. Laughter was a good sign. It was always risky to work humor into sermons, but every good rabbi had to demonstrate the ability to do so. I glanced over at Rabbi Borowitz for his reaction. He was now sitting a good ten feet behind JD on the bema, smiling, along with the other synagogue leaders assembled on the stage.

"Thankfully, rabbinical school does a good job of preparing us rabbis for these challenging, yet common questions. Is there a heaven? Yes. Do you have to observe all God's commandments to get into heaven? No. Why are my dues so high? Ask Executive Director Feldman. He's sitting right over there!"

JD pointed over at Ronnie Feldman who laughed along with the congregation, then said something inaudible as he gave a thumbs-up to the crowd. There was some faint applause.

Nice execution. I allowed myself to let go and get sucked into his sermon. It felt good to focus on something other than the stock market and all my other problems for a change.

"Understandably," JD continued, "what happens to us after our time on earth comes to an end is on the minds of many, as we want assurances that if we do *all* the right things now we will have a glorious afterlife. However, tonight, on the beginning of this New Year, I stand before you, not to talk about how to best prepare and secure your success in the next world. Rather, I'm going to talk about what I believe is an even more pressing challenge for many of us: how to get more joy out of our lives now."

The synagogue was quiet; JD had everyone's full attention. Even Ryan's. I looked over to see if he made it back from his twenty-minute bathroom break. He had snuck back into his seat and appeared to be listening.

"This is usually the part of a well-organized sermon where the rabbi quotes an ancient text to shed some light on the subject," JD went on. "While I'm going to go back to biblical times for some insights, I'm going to make a pit stop in the 1970s first. And instead of a religious scholar, I'm going to quote one of the most venerable singer-songwriters of that era: James Taylor."

JD was a big fan of the '70s classic rockers, even having a nice collection of signed LPs he kept hanging on a wall. But where was he going with this?

"Mr. Taylor found his inspiration for what would become one of his greatest hits while sitting at his home in Martha's Vineyard. One beautiful spring morning, he was looking out the window and playing his guitar when the following words flowed quickly: 'The secret of life is enjoying the passage of time, any fool can do it, there ain't nothing to it.' Enjoying the passage of time? Is that all we must do? Come on, James, if it were only that easy. So much worry, anxiety, and depression in the world. Why do so many people have such a hard time enjoying their lives? Enjoying the present? Why are humans, with all their advanced technology and modern conveniences, such a tough species to please?

"Thankfully, Mr. Taylor doesn't leave us hanging too long as he goes on to provide some deeper insight as to how we can enjoy the passage of time in his aptly titled song 'Secret O' Life' when he sings, 'It's just your point of view, how does it feel for you?' And that, ladies and gentlemen, is it. The key to enjoying one's life is all about your point of view. In other words, your perspective. I'm not talking complicated physics and the theory of relativity here. What I, along with Mr. Taylor, am suggesting is that the amount of joy you experience in your life is all about the perspective you keep. In life, there are plenty of things that are beyond and out of our control. Perspective is not one of them. However, like varying eyewitness accounts to an event, not everyone has the same perspective or perception.

"Let me touch on a couple of real-world examples. Have you ever been on a date where you thought there was an undeniable love connection, but as it turned out, the person you were with wasn't so interested in you after all?"

Here, JD paused for a moment and looked out over the congregation, where many people were nodding, smiling knowingly.

"Of course, that has never happened to me," JD joked, "and probably not you, but I've seen it happen on *The Bachelor* a lot."

Laughter erupted as JD landed another solid one-liner.

"So how can two people on the same date be having two completely different experiences? One falling in love, and the other falling over themselves to get out of there as quickly as possible. In this example, one person's perception of reality is vastly different than the other's.

"Here's another example. This one involving money. Over the past couple of months, the stock market has lost quite a lot of value over this geopolitical flare-up with China. Makes for pretty scary headlines, right?"

Holy shit. I couldn't believe he was treading into my territory. He *was* aware the market had tanked after all.

"To some, particularly those who break out in a cold sweat when the value of their portfolio falls by a percent or two, the current decline in the market might seem to be a bona fide crash. On the other hand, someone else might get more worked up about their favorite character in a TV show getting killed off than the market. In fact, if that person doesn't look at their brokerage statements all that often, they might not even be aware of the decline. And if they *are* aware, they might even view the drop not as something bad, but as something good. Maybe instead of dwelling on how much money they've lost, they view the lower stock prices as an opportunity to invest more money cheaply. Depending on one's perspective of the setback, in this case, a correction in the stock market, one could end up feeling quite depressed or quite happy. Now, while we can't control the market, we can control how we view its inevitable ups and downs over time. Opportunity or tragedy, it's up to you."

Well said. I could've used him on some of my client calls.

"The key to living a happy life is acknowledging that that there will be periodic corrections in life, just like the current one in the stock market. It's how we view, perceive, and respond to those corrections that will define us, and ultimately determine our happiness moving forward. If we are so preoccupied and paralyzed by negative events from the past or terrified by what might happen in the future, it will distract us from leading joyful and productive lives now. How can we be present in the moment with our family, friends, and community when we are so distracted and restless? I guarantee that as I speak to you right now, many of you are thinking about what happened at work this week, what errands you have to get done this weekend, or what happens if we go to war with China."

It felt like JD was talking directly to me. I snuck a peek at Jessica to see if she was listening and saw her watching JD with a rapt expression. She must have sensed my interest because she reached over and tenderly squeezed my hand. Her smooth skin against mine felt reassuring and full of love and affection.

JD continued, "Does that mean we should throw caution to the wind, and live like today is our last day on earth? While it is tempting, and I've definitely had my share of hedonistic living, we all should strive to strike the right balance between learning from our past, enjoying the present, and planning for the future. Let's not be so concerned about making mistakes that we can't get out of bed in the morning or be so obsessed with the future that we can't enjoy the life we're living today.

"I recently saw a news report about a man who spent fifteen years of his life incarcerated for a crime he did not commit. After he was released, he was asked how he got through the horrific ordeal. He said his mother's incredible wisdom helped him. She told him, 'Son, when you're looking out the prison window, don't focus on the bars, look at the blue sky.' In other words, we all have the power to alter our own reality by taking control...control of our own perception.

"I've recently had a personal setback of sorts with something that I was working toward, as we all do from time to time. I was convinced I *needed* something, that I *deserved* something, that I was *entitled* to something. And as some of you may know from experience, I can be fairly persuasive."

JD paused as laughter spread throughout the sanctuary.

"However, this time, despite my best efforts, it just didn't work out for me. Or did it? Sometimes we must accept that the true meaning in a setback will only become apparent later, once we have seen the full picture through the course of time. A friend of mine helped me gain the right perspective when he reminded me that even the best of us don't always get what we think we deserve. Look no further than Moses, who, after spending forty years leading our people to the Promised Land, was not allowed himself to enter. I mean, talk about a personal setback!"

JD raised his voice, speaking with a commanding tone and at twice the volume as when he started.

"Unbelievably, Moses, not only kept his faith in God, but he also kept his perspective. Even though he couldn't enter the Promised Land, he was pleased he got to see it from Mount Abarim."

Jessica told me to "shoosh" when I turned to ask her if that was true.

"I'll now go back even further to 450 to 200 BCE, to the wisdom found in the poetic writings of the Book of Ecclesiastes. Depending on one's perspective, these verses, which reflect on the meaning of life, can be interpreted optimistically or pessimistically. Man's fate, the anonymous author Ecclesiastes suggests, does not depend on righteous or wicked conduct, but is a mystery that remains hidden in God. All attempts to penetrate this mystery and thereby gain the wisdom necessary to secure one's fate are vanity or futile. In light of this senselessness, the author suggests one should enjoy the simple pleasures of daily life, such as eating, drinking, and one's work, which are gifts from the hand of God.

"So, my fellow congregants, as we embark on another year, I challenge you. I challenge you to enjoy your life more. Focus on being more present. Present with your friends, family, and coworkers. Listen to one another. When you hit that inevitable rough patch, setback, or correction, work through it. Do that by keeping the right perspective. Yes, there are things that can and will go wrong, but there's a lot more that can go right if you only adjust and keep the right mindset. And let's not forget to enjoy the simple pleasures that life can offer.

"I'll finish with the same simple words that James Taylor used to conclude his song about finding life's meaning, 'Try not to try too hard, it's just a lovely ride.'

"L'Shana Tova. Happy New Year."

As JD left the podium and headed back toward his seat, a gradual chorus of applause swept through the sanctuary. Clapping during services, especially during High Holy Day, wasn't a common occurrence and reserved for only those situations where congregants were deeply moved. Rabbi Borowitz shook JD's hand and appeared to congratulate him.

I knew JD could deliver a good sermon, but he absolutely crushed it. No doubt, everyone in the sanctuary was suspended in a contemplative state, weighing JD's poignant words in the context of their own lives, at least until Rabbi Borowitz resumed his position at the podium and broke the silence.

"Thank you, Rabbi Aron, for that optimistic and much-needed message," he said. "We now continue with our service on page one hundred and eighty-two."

I settled back into the service, my mind not cluttered by the disastrous market, the pending outcome of the SEC investigation, or the future of the firm.

A few minutes later, my phone buzzed. I should've ignored it. It was a group text from Dad to me and my siblings.

Dad: Mom's had a setback. Back in ICU. Will keep you posted.

What could possibly be the right perspective to view that?

38

After spending Saturday back at the synagogue for Rosh Hashanah prayer services, on Sunday I hunkered down in the house, frantically checking flights to Berlin. Dad was sending cryptic updates on Mom's condition every few hours. Mostly status quo.

My mother's precarious health worried me. Memories of her nightly bedtime tuck-ins in my early years to acting as my twenty-four-hour caretaker when I was recovering from my emergency appendectomy in college gave me comfort.

Given the tenuous circumstances, Jessica and Ryan went to a friend's country club on Labor Day while I stayed behind. Thankfully, by Monday morning, Mom was showing signs of stabilizing, then by early Monday afternoon, Dad sent:

Dad: Great news! Out of ICU.

It was huge relief as Alan, Stephanie, and I were booked to fly to Germany the next morning.

With no resolution to the global crisis at hand, Tuesday morning offered no reprieve from the market selling pressure. I put my tired head down on my desk, not wanting to face the bloody red numbers that chewed up my computer screen on the very first minutes following the long weekend. The phone rang, disturbing my zombielike state. I tilted my head and lifted my eyes just enough to see that the caller ID on my phone read *Benoit*.

I sighed. *Yep, there it is.* She was going to fire me for sure. Dad's oldest client . . . gone. Things had only gone from bad to worse since I told her not to worry.

I almost didn't pick up. But, in a warped way, I was ready to welcome more mental anguish, and what better way to satisfy that desire than to get fired by a sweet old widow? Mrs. Benoit had plenty of reason to fire me. She had called me concerned about her money, and I convinced her not to do anything about it. The thought of letting her down made me feel terrible about myself. Even though I knew I gave her sound advice, things weren't working out like they should. Unfortunately, she probably wouldn't see it that way. She was scared and losing money. It was *my* fault.

I sat upright in my chair, took a breath, and answered.

"Good morning, this is Marty," I said with all the cheer I could muster.

"Hello, Marteen, this is Camille Benoit speaking," she said as if I couldn't immediately recognize her accent.

"Hi, Mrs. Benoit, how are you?" I asked and then immediately regretted it. *How do you think she is you dumbass? She's just lost a bunch of money, and she's about to unload on you.*

"Oh, Marteen, I got my account statement and wanted to talk to you about it."

"I know it's not pretty," I said in what I hoped was a comforting voice. "August was a terrible month." I was at a loss for what else to say. I didn't even want to try. I was ready for her to just drop the guillotine.

My cell buzzed with a text from JD.

Buckle the fuck up! Remember, it's only a correction . . . keep the faith!

I thought back to his sermon and the renewed confidence and serenity, although fleeting, I felt during it. Perspective. That's what she needs right now. Give it to her. I shot off a quick *"Thx buddy!"*

"Marteen, you know I've been very concerned. And the news is terrible."

I had to reassure her, talk her off the edge again. I could be strong and guide her like my dad would, except I had to do it my way.

"Well, investing isn't always easy, Mrs. Benoit. It's frightening out there right now. Honestly, I'm scared, too. But I really believe there *will* be a better time to sell stocks at some point in the future. Now isn't the time for selling. It's really the time for buying," I said with genuine sincerity. Opening up and confiding in her about my own self-doubt felt good. It was a much-needed release. I felt more human letting her know that I was feeling the pressure, too. We were in this together.

Like a Jedi warrior sensing a disturbance in the force, I began to feel the internal mental struggle between fear and sensibility in Mrs. Benoit's mind. There was a long pause on the phone before she finally responded. "Tell me, Marteen, are there some stocks that are a good value?" she asked. "Yes. Things look terrible right now, but that's when the values are the best. We'll likely look back at this time and realize that it was an opportunity."

She paused again, then said, "I trust you, Marteen. Let's buy some stocks in my account. And Simon always likes the ones with good dividends; please look for some of those companies."

I couldn't believe what I was hearing. Our firm's most nervous client was ready to put some money to work; albeit with some special requests from her deceased husband. Could this be some kind of contrarian market signal—the *Benoit Buy Indicator*?

"I do think you have some room to get more aggressive," I said, treading carefully. "And we do like to invest in stocks paying good dividends, and solid growth prospects, so we can get some of those."

I documented my conversation with Ms. Benoit then sent a note to everyone in the office to drop everything and meet in the conference room in ten minutes. It was time for action and time for me to adjust our perception of the situation. We couldn't control the market, and our clients understood that. We could, however, control how we reacted to it.

Trying to destress before the meeting, I stood closing my eyes, taking long, deep breaths. As the Zen overtook me, I opened my eyes and noticed my college diploma hung crooked on the wall. As I pushed up on the bottom right corner to adjust it, I felt the heavy wooden frame and remembered my mom saying how important it would be to see this on my office wall one day. They'd had it framed for me as a graduation gift. After taking a step back and confirming it was now level, I turned my attention to the adjacent wall, where a picture of me with Jessica and Ryan hung. Jessica hired a photographer to come to the house when Ryan was about five. I was shocked by the expense of the photo shoot but went along. Jess got the picture framed for me for a Father's Day gift. We all looked happy. It wouldn't be another couple of years until Ryan would start seriously acting up.

When I got to the conference room, everyone had already gathered. Angela had her notepad ready, and Shelley and Devon sat ready with their laptops open in front of them. Everyone was quiet, and the room brimmed with nervous tension. I took a seat at the end of the table where my dad would normally sit.

I swallowed, then smiled. No one knew what I was going to say—myself included.

"Thanks for gathering on such short notice," I began, addressing all nine of the firm's employees. "I'd like to start by saying that I know it's been a rough few months. On both a personal and professional level, I want to thank everyone here for your support as well as your dedication to this firm during this challenging time."

Angela grinned at me from the other side of the table.

"Now, as we all sit here in this room, stocks probing bear market territory, there is a real possibility that a military conflict between the United States and China could break out at any time. While this is a scary situation, we need to keep in mind that the steep drop in the market already reflects a pretty bleak outcome playing out. Anything less than an all-out war and the market will shoot up. It's times like these that I will remind you of the old investment adage: 'One should never bet on the end of the world because you won't be around to collect the payoff.'" I glanced around the table and saw several heads nodding in agreement. "With that being said, it's time to make lemonade from the lemons. We need to view this sell-off as an opportunity instead of travesty. It's possible things get worse and the markets fall farther, but there is a better chance that cooler heads prevail and things will turn around at some point. I want us to look at every client account this morning and determine which clients have the capacity to increase their stock exposure. Let's do some buying, people!" Unknowingly I raised my voice like I was a three-star general getting his troops ready to mount an assault on a hill held by the enemy.

"All our orders must go through Phil to make sure we execute all trades properly to avoid Angela's wrath." I smirked, and Angela, to her merit, laughed along with everyone else.

Right when I was about to call the meeting to a close, Devon, who was sitting toward the other end of the conference table, jumped in. "Speaking of making lemonade from lemons…"

Everyone turned their heads toward Devon.

He passed a copy of the paper he was holding around the table. "I filtered through our clients' portfolios, looking for those that were holding a position with material losses. We can sell the position, book the tax loss, and buy something similar. I went ahead and listed some similar security options."

I looked down at his spreadsheet, which neatly listed account numbers, security positions, loss amounts, and alternative stocks to purchase.

"Great suggestion, Devon," I said, genuinely impressed.

Tax-loss harvesting made a lot of sense and was another way to add value for our clients.

"Can you get with Shelley and figure out how to work these into our buy orders?"

Devon looked at Shelley, who nodded back her support. He grinned, clearly pleased with himself.

I called the meeting to a close. By the looks on my colleagues' faces, their deflated spirits had been lifted. I returned to my office still feeling wound up and typed up the following note:

Dear (insert client name),

The correction, which began back in mid-June, is now more than two months old. Given the geopolitical nature of this severe correction, it is impossible for us to know how it will end and whether it will lead to a sustained bear market. While times like these are unsettling, history suggests that it is likely a buying opportunity rather than the time to reduce risk. We remain focused on each client's long-term objectives while ensuring we retain ample liquidity to weather the storm. We will be looking to add to equities given the current weakness as we remain optimistic in the future of our country for the years and decades to come.

Sincerely,

Martin Kaplan

I sent the note to Angela for her review. A couple of minutes later, there was a knock on my door. *That was quick.*

Expecting Angela, I was surprised to see Elise holding a small white cardboard box with a big blue bow wrapped around it.

"This was just delivered for you. You have an admirer." She sounded like a seventh-grade girl teasing a boy in class.

I must've given her a perplexed look because she hung around long enough to watch me open the Tiff's Treats box. The freshly baked cookie smell hit me before I looked inside.

"Yum!" Elise said, edging toward me, eager to take a sample.

I opened the card resting on top.

Hope you're having a better day! Love you lots. —Mark.

JK…Love you, Jessica.

I laughed out loud.

"Relax, they're from my wife," I said. "Don't worry. Nothing juicy going on here." I held the box toward her so she could select her cookie.

A moment later, the person I had expected appeared.

Angela.

"Okay, that smells good," Angela said, walking straight into my office.

"Come join us," I said.

Elise nabbed a second cookie and left me and Angela alone.

"Your client note looks good, Marty," she said, taking a bite of a chocolate chip macadamia cookie. "We'll add some minor compliance disclosures and send it off shortly."

I nodded enthusiastically; my mouth full of a peanut butter cookie.

"And that was quite a pep talk you delivered. I especially appreciated that shout-out regarding the trading protocols." She grinned. "And on that note, I have a development to share with you."

I hadn't noticed the large envelope in her hand until she put it on my desk. It was a letter addressed to Leon Kaplan from the Securities and Exchange Commission. This was it. Our verdict. I picked up the letter, waving and weighing it in my hand as if I could tell something about the SEC's findings by the air resistance of the envelope.

"Are clean inspection reports usually this thick?" I asked.

"That looks about average to me," she said. "Hard to tell if there are some serious deficiencies in there or not. We'll have at least thirty days to respond if any response is required on our part, so it can wait if you don't want to open it."

I almost tore it open right there, but the letter wasn't addressed to me. Would Dad care? All of a sudden, immense guilt and regret washed over me. I should have told him. The least I could do was tell him now and go over the results with him, together, in person. "Angela," I said. "Let's leave it on his desk. I'm going to go over everything with him this weekend."

"Okay, good luck with that," she replied.

•

Even with uncertainty from the SEC inspection hanging over my head, I went home in a decent mood. My talk with our employees and the treats from Jessica made me feel better. I hadn't said anything to Jessica about her gift just yet as I was planning on giving her a big hug and a kiss in person. Unfortunately, as soon as I cracked the garage door to the house, I knew that would have to wait. Ryan and Jessica were standing in our kitchen a few feet apart in an apparent standoff.

"Marty, I really need some help here. Ryan just told me to *shut up* for asking him to turn off his phone until he finishes his homework, which he is refusing to do." Jessica was trying her best to remain calm but was obviously exasperated by yet another confrontation with Ryan.

I turned to Ryan, shooting him the most crushing look of disgruntlement I could muster.

"Dad," he grumbled, "I told her I was just finishing something and then I was going to shut it off." He hoped to win me over to his side.

I resisted the urge to snatch the phone right out of Ryan's hands. "Ryan, you heard your mother. Give her the phone and apologize."

I could see the look of defiance on his face slowly slipping away, replaced by uncertainty. Rather than doubling down like he had so many times in the past, he relented.

"Sorry," he said, showing some genuine signs of regret.

"Now let's have your phone," I said.

"But when can I have it back?" he asked before releasing it.

"Your mother and I will talk about it and decide," I said.

He looked at both of us, sensing our unified front. After a moment, he let out a, "Fine." He handed over his phone and headed off to his room.

Jessica gazed at me with appreciation and said, "Thank you."

•

Bizline Market News: Wednesday, September 12, 5:46 p.m. ET

US and Chinese armed forces remain on high alert and poised to strike on command with the world left wondering what act might be the match that ignites the flame of war. Given his shoot-from-the-hip style of diplomacy, a meeting between Pruitt and his Chinese counterpart was a highly anticipated wild card event. Practically anything could've happened.

As one news correspondent had said, "We're one unscripted comment away from being toast, literally."

When news broke that President Yang was backing out of the meeting at the last minute and sending China's longstanding ambassador to the United States instead, expectations for a diplomatic breakthrough plummeted.

Meetings between the Chinese delegation and the United States were originally scheduled to be held throughout the day today with a tentative early dinner scheduled for the two leaders, assuming things had gone reasonably well. But the afternoon session ended earlier than expected after negotiations hit an impasse. Around three, the meetings broke for the remainder of the afternoon. There was no official statement from either side on the status, leaving everyone to reflect on the dire consequences of a failed summit.

Irritated by the lack of progress and the snubbing from President Yang, Pruitt canceled his dinner with the ambassador, but has agreed to hold one last meeting with the senior diplomat in the Oval Office later tonight.

•

39

I was watching a livestream on my computer from my office. Pruitt stood behind the presidential podium in the White House rose garden. The fragile markets, which had broken to new lows after the market's open, were now back to flat on the day. The fact that a news conference had been so hastily put together could have meant either good or bad news.

After a few minutes, the president and the Chinese ambassador walked into the briefing room. Both men appeared tired and serious.

President Pruitt spoke first, reading from a teleprompter. "I want to let everyone know that Ambassador Wei from China and I met late last night and then again this morning," he said. "We finished our discussions just a few minutes ago. We talked at length about a lot of things but specifically about the recent military provocations taken by both sides. I must tell you that our meetings earlier yesterday didn't go so well and that neither of us were in a particularly good mood heading into our meeting last night.

"However, upon the ambassador's arrival at the White House last night, he told me about an unexpected incident involving one of our security agents that had just transpired on their way over to the White House. He said the experience made him reflect harder about our shared fate as a human race and the common obstacles we all face, irrespective of our unique cultures. When the ambassador relayed his encounter with the agent back to President Yang, I received a very nice call directly from President Yang this morning. We acknowledged our shared responsibility to demonstrate restraint and diplomacy while expressing mutual respect. As a result, we had a very productive call and agreed that it would be in our respective best interests to de-escalate tensions."

The president's demeanor then changed, becoming more animated, apparently going off-script. "I want to let the world know that the United States and China remain close partners and that there will be no military conflict between our two great nations. Okay, so everyone can calm down."

By the time Pruitt finished speaking, the market was rocketing higher.

The reporters in the room started shouting questions. "What incident? What happened? Tell us more!"

"Ambassador, would you like to say a few words?" Pruitt asked the distinguished foreign diplomat.

He began speaking slowly and deliberately. "Thank you, Mr. President. As President Pruitt said, we share a common human bond even though we may have occasional conflicts. Last night, I would have experienced a great indignity if not for having special Agent Thompson with me. His actions showed great consideration for my well-being and set the tone for constructive dialogue between our countries. We are pleased to move forward in the spirit of friendship, decency, and mutual respect between our two great nations."

A stocky, red-headed male reporter thrust his microphone toward the podium like a fencer lunging in for a kill. "Mr. Ambassador . . . Mr. Ambassador, can you elaborate and tell us what happened?"

Pruitt smiled. "The ambassador is a classy guy. What he's trying to say . . . at least as far as I understand what happened . . . is that our very fine security agent did a beautiful thing. He stopped the ambassador right before he stepped in a big pile of dog shit, okay?" The president cupped his hands out in front of him as if he were holding an object of considerably large mass.

Dog shit? Wow. Maybe's there's something to the Clauskys' idea. Hopefully, they're watching this.

The market continued to blast higher, finishing the day up more than

3 percent, recording its best one-day gain in years while lifting the markets back out of bear market territory.

I called Mrs. Benoit, figuring she had seen the latest developments, but there was no answer on her home phone. That was odd, because she was mostly at home. I called her cell, and she finally answered.

"Mrs. Benoit, looks like you've got a knack for calling market bottoms," I told her enthusiastically.

"What's that, Marteen? Is everything okay?" she said, clearly unaware of what I meant.

"It looks like we've ended our standoff with China, and the stock market is moving back up."

"Oh, that's wonderful news, Marteen," she said, sounding far more nonchalant than I expected.

"Is everything okay, Mrs. Benoit?" Maybe she didn't understand what I was saying.

"Yes, everything is wonderful, Marteen. I'm taking my sweet new granddaughter, Chloe, for a walk in the zoo right now."

"Oh, that's fantastic. How does she like her quilt?" I asked, trying to make some casual small talk.

"It's wonderful. Thank you for calling, Marteen," she said, practically rushing to get off the phone with me. It was refreshing and comforting to have her brush me off for something more important than talking about her money. It appeared that the international crisis was drawing to a peaceful close, but the markets would still be looking for signs of follow-through from both governments that they were truly committed to a de-escalation of tensions.

•

By Friday afternoon, the market completed a trifecta of three consecutive up days. After the market closed, I checked Pruitt's Twitter feed and saw the following post:

4:42 p.m. ET

Ambassador Wei was saved by CrapMap! US ingenuity Making America Clean Again (MACA)...WINNING!

I was totally floored.

"Holy fucking shit!" I jumped out of my chair.

It was way beyond the realm of comprehension. Danny and Freddie's app had something to do with ending the global crisis, and the President of the United States was now pitching it. I had no idea how, but they had done it. They had really done it!

"Excuse me, but did I mention the new rule in our compliance manual against shouting expletives during office hours?"

I turned to see Angela once again standing in my office doorway.

"Angela, you're not gonna believe this, but you know that ill-advised disbursement I made to the Clausky boys for their venture . . ."

40

We stood, clustered tightly in the airport's international terminal, holding our ground against a steady stream of travel-weary passengers arriving in the United States on a Sunday morning.

Alan checked the flight status as we awaited our parents' arrival.

He stuck his cell in his back pocket. "They should be coming out any minute."

It was hard to fathom that she was in an ICU less than a week earlier and now coming home. A few days earlier, Dad sent word that she bounced back and suddenly found her strength. Amazingly, her medical team cleared her to travel. Dad didn't want to miss the opportunity to bring her home now that the initial treatment cycle was finished, and she was feeling much better.

Stephanie gnawed on her fingernails and stressed over Mom's potentially frail appearance. She was already physically worn and diminished from the effects of her illness and various treatments before she left. There was no telling how much more of a decline she had experienced from the treatments and its effects. Other than a few emailed pictures soon after they left for Europe, it had been months since we had last seen our parents.

Ten minutes later, my parents finally emerged from behind the opaque glass doors into the terminal's arrivals hall. Mom came into view first, and

I almost laughed with relief. She was so full of life, galloping a few steps in front of Dad just like her old self. It was incredible considering that a week earlier she was in the ICU. Her feisty demeanor was more like that of a restless passenger eager to get home than a terminally ill elderly woman returning from a life-saving pilgrimage. We moved quickly toward each other and embraced. My mother's smile grew wider with each gentle squeeze from her three children. Her warm eyes filled with tears of happiness.

"I'm good, I'm good, I'm good," she kept repeating as her slight arms pulled us in close for a group hug. I felt hopeful of what was to come. Dad followed Mom's lead, one by one briefly holding each of his three children in his arms. I was last in line, trying to get a read on his face to see if he showed any signs of regret for keeping the merger discussions from me even though I was guilty of withholding my own information. Nothing. Other than some uncharacteristic facial stubble, he looked me straight in the eyes and appeared relieved to be home.

After loading their luggage, we hopped into my parents' SUV for our half-hour ride back to my parents' house. Dad had texted in advance. *Please bring my car to the airport so I can drive us home.*

He climbed in the car, adjusted the driver's seat and mirrors to his liking, and turned the radio completely off, which was tuned to the pop station we were listening to on the way to the airport.

"Dr. Schmidt is a good man, and Berlin is surprisingly quite nice," he said while weaving in and out of heavy airport traffic like his old self. "You should definitely make a point to visit."

The three of us in the backseat all looked at each other wondering whether we should delve deeper into his obvious change of heart about the country.

"So, they're not all Nazis," Alan said, not about to let the comment go without a remark.

"I'm pleased to report we didn't meet one the entire time," Dad said.

"That's great, but what's going on with the treatments? Are they working?" I asked.

Dad glanced over at Mom who was holding a tissue near her face to soak up her intermittent tears. He answered for her. "As of the last scans from two days ago, her tumors are showing signs of shrinking. She'll have to get more scans next month, some follow-up work, and more testing, but they believe the immunotherapy drug is working."

Their last update confirmed the disease wasn't progressing, but this was the first word the treatment might actually be reversing the disease's course. I was elated. Maybe Mom would be around for Ryan's high school and college graduations, and perhaps even a wedding one day.

"That's amazing news, Mom!" Stephanie exclaimed, leaning forward from the second-row middle seat to rub Mom's shoulders.

"So great to hear that," I chimed in. "Dad, what company makes this wonder drug?"

"I *knew* you were going to ask that!" Alan said, reaching across Stephanie, who was sitting in between us, so he could lightly clock me on the shoulder just like when we were kids.

Dad looked at me in the rearview mirror. "It was developed in a collaboration with the Berlin University Hospital and a private German company, so unfortunately, Marty, no there isn't a public company that we can invest in."

It was my first stock-related conversation with Dad in months. The fact that it ended so quickly left me wanting more, but I knew my sentiment wasn't shared by anyone else in the car.

"I'm very fortunate. We'll see how it goes, but so far, so good," Mom said before changing the subject in her typical unassuming fashion. "So, other than this craziness with China, what have we missed?"

Alan jumped in first. "It's been a pretty quiet summer for us. Family's good. Working on some interesting cases and enjoying the hell out of our pool. You missed a great Fourth of July party." He turned and gave Stephanie a look, clearly a jab for being a no-show.

Stephanie went next, talking about a new project she was involved with at the nonprofit organization where she worked as a social worker. She grew quiet as soon as Alan inquired if she was dating anyone.

"Marty, how are Jessica and Ryan?" Mom asked to relieve Stephanie from the awkward moment.

"They're good," I said, feeling bad about my white lie. Jessica was deeply annoyed with me, and Ryan was still pushing Jessica's buttons on a daily basis.

"Marty's been a little stressed," Alan said.

It was so like Alan to try and stir it up.

Dad made eye contact with me in the mirror again. "Work or something else? We can talk about work later," he said, cutting off the line of conversation.

"It's all fine. A few developments at the office we can get into later," I said, not wanting to get into it in front of everyone. I gave Alan a stern look and shook my head.

"Good. I'm looking forward to catching up. We've got a lot to discuss," Dad said.

What's that supposed to mean?

Had he made a decision about the future of the firm? I tried to put it out of my mind until I could discuss it with him.

A small welcoming party was waiting at my parents' house where Jessica and my sister-in-law had stocked their empty refrigerator and made lunch for everyone. The house was a bit musty since their air-conditioning hadn't been turned down to fully cool the home for most of the summer.

"It's so nice to have the whole family in our own home again," my mother said with a relaxed sigh, sitting down on their living room sofa and running her hand over the soft beige-colored cloth fabric.

It was heartwarming to see Ryan sitting so closely and conversing with his grandparents, undistracted by his phone. I was envious of my parents' discipline-free relationship with him. Ryan had been less combative since I came down on him hard for copping attitude with Jessica. Now, seeing him more relaxed, even enjoying a game of Scrabble with his grandfather without his face buried in a phone, made me optimistic he was turning the corner.

Just as we were about to leave a couple of hours later, my dad asked me if I could come back that evening to debrief on work-related matters before his first day back at the office the following day. I agreed.

Around eight, on the drive back over, I decided that I was going to tell Dad about the SEC inspection. After all, the letter from the agency lay waiting for him on his desk, and it was better he found out from me rather opening a piece of mail. His interest in merging the firm was a different story. I wasn't sure how to bring it up, if that was really what he was up to. I didn't want to betray Angela's confidence. Either way, I needed clarity as to his intentions. What was he doing with the firm? The answer wasn't just for me; Angela put her career on the line to join KCM. She deserved to know.

When I arrived back at their house, my mother was already resting in bed. My father and I retreated to the kitchen so as not to disturb her.

He grabbed an extra-large navel orange from the bowl of assorted fresh fruit sitting on the countertop. "So much for some uneventful time away from the office. I leave town, and the market drops twenty percent, the world almost implodes, and the Clausky boys, of all people, help save the day." He peeled the orange as he spoke. "You never know what can happen. Life is exciting, fragile, and unpredictable. I learned a lot about that this summer. We had a few scary moments."

"The news about Mom is so great," I said. "Hopefully, she'll continue to do well."

Dad held out half the peeled orange, and I took it, pausing before putting a wedge in my mouth. "Now tell me about what's going on at the office," he said.

I spoke calmly and slowly. "There were definitely some interesting developments while you were out." I wondered what to get into first: my blowup and reconciliation with Angela, the SEC inspection, learning about the merger, or my commitment to JD to sponsor his charity event? "On the market front, it looks like it's going to continue to rebound from here," I said. "As of Friday's close, most of our clients' accounts have already bounced back. We did some buying last week, near the bottom, so that's helped. Even for Mrs. Benoit!"

"I'm sure our clients will be pleased that you didn't flinch and sell at the wrong time. It's a really hard thing to do. Even the best of us get unnerved at times," he said.

It was comforting to hear him say that, and his words gave me the boost I needed. I cleared my throat. "We did have some extra excitement at the firm other than the market correction and the Clausky boys while you were away."

"Are you referring to the SEC audit?" he said, not skipping a beat.

"Uh . . ." *What the hell?* "Yes, that's exactly what I'm referring to. How did you know?"

"I went by the office for a couple of hours this afternoon. Read Mr. Ingram's findings summary letter. It's a big envelope, so hard to miss."

I rounded my shoulders sheepishly. "Sorry I didn't tell you about that earlier, but I didn't want you to worry while you were away. I thought Angela and I could handle it."

"Marty, you know an SEC inspection is a *very* big deal."

I couldn't tell if it was a statement of fact or his expression of his disappointment in me.

So is betraying your son.

I bit my lip. I'd listen to him lecture me about the SEC and how he should've been told about it. When he was finished, I'd apologize some more then express my own disappointment with him undermining me with his merger discussions.

Dad reached down and grabbed his heavily worn, black vinyl briefcase that was sitting at his feet under the kitchen table. He plopped it on the kitchen table, popped the two clasps with his thumbs, and pulled out a large white envelope before shutting the case. It was *the* SEC letter. I mentally braced myself for my world to fall apart.

I looked down at the envelope, avoiding eye contact and thinking about the verdict that lay inside.

Dad took a moment as if he were going over in his head what he was about to say so the words came out just the way he wanted. "The thing is, Marty, I'm glad you didn't tell me about this while it was going on."

What?

"There really isn't much I could've done, and it would've been an unnecessary distraction to me. Your mother really needed me, not the work version of me...and I needed her. You made the right call."

I was taken aback. It was out-of-character for him to express his innermost thoughts like that to me.

"Thanks, Dad." I lifted my head and looked into his eyes for any hint of what was coming next.

"So...what did the letter say?" I asked, holding my breath, nodding to the envelope that was resting under the palm of his hand.

"There *were* some noted deficiencies," he said.

My heart sank.

"Any disciplinary action or anything that will go on the firm's or particular employee's disclosure record?"

He stared at me, letting me squirm. Did he know I was the *particular* employee of interest? "I don't suspect they're going to shut us down, and no one is facing disclosable disciplinary action, but we *will* have to answer more procedural questions and demonstrate that we've taken the necessary steps to strengthen our firm's policies and protocols."

"Okay, that's a huge relief," I said, my entire body relaxing.

Dad smiled. "I bet."

"Dad, Angela did a great job. Thankfully, she discovered some compliance issues before the SEC even showed up, including a couple of my own. There was one related to the Clauskys' trust account I was particularly worried about. I thought there was a chance the SEC was going to take some harsher action."

"Glad you brought that up. The report did address that," he said.

Did I speak too soon?

"The good news is that they *did* confirm that our internal audit and monitoring efforts successfully identified the violation and that we took appropriate corrective action to remedy the situation. They assessed that no client was harmed as a result, but that we needed to strengthen our cash disbursement protocols. Marty, you dodged a bullet on that one."

Thank God.

"I know that compliance hasn't exactly been your passion, but it's a crucial aspect of what we do. It's all about maintaining our clients' trust. I'm very pleased you and Angela worked through this so well together."

It was both ironic and incredibly comforting to hear him comment on me and Angela working together considering what we had gone through. I was also incredibly relieved that Dad wasn't harsher on me. He knew me well enough to know I was hard on myself, but given what happened with Alan, I naturally thought this would reaffirm why he was reluctant to commit to another child. Would it impact his thoughts on succession planning? It was time for me to find out. I steadied myself, ready to confront him about his intentions.

He began talking again before I could get off another word. "Marty, you did a great job managing the firm through some pretty challenging circumstances. The global crisis, the steep correction, the SEC, your mother's illness. Tough summer."

He didn't even know about my problems with Jess and Ryan.

Dad then paused, giving me a curious look. He flipped back open his briefcase and took out another envelope. "I was planning on doing this later this year, but next week I'm going to be officially transitioning the role of president of the firm over to you. You deserve it. I've prepared this draft proposal for an ownership transition plan. I'd like you to read it over and get back to me with your thoughts. And while you're at it, go ahead and review this SEC letter. You and Angela have some follow-up work to do." He slid over both envelopes.

"What? Really?" I was at a loss at what to say. A minute earlier, I didn't know if I was going to escape our meeting with my career intact. Now, I was slated to be KCM's president and an owner of the firm?

Dad continued speaking, giving me time to digest the news. "Before your mom and I left for Europe, we didn't know what was going to happen with her health. We're very grateful and fortunate that the treatment appears to be working, but we don't know how much more she'll improve or how long she'll be feeling better. Hopefully, it's a long time, but I'm not going to take her improved health for granted. I'm going to spend time with her. Take more time off. We want to do some more traveling. You've shown that you can take care of the firm and our clients without my daily oversight and involvement."

"Seriously?"

"Now, don't get too excited, I'm not retiring just yet and still holding on to my chairman title, at least for the time being," he said, chuckling.

My mind raced trying to understand. Could he really step away from the work he loved so much?

Clients come first.

Alan's failure.

Angela.

Mom!

He'd brought Angela in to help me so he could step aside when the time was right. And Mom made this the right time. Then everything started to click. Merging had only ever been a backup plan in the event that I wasn't ready. It was just another case of putting the clients' needs first. I couldn't blame him for that, and neither would Angela. There was no need to even bring it up.

We finished our conversation, and he walked me out of the house. I was so thrown off by the events I held in my emotions in check.

"I love you, Marty," Dad said before giving me a sustained full-on hug on the brick-paved driveway.

"Love you too," I reflexively responded, almost choking up.

I couldn't remember the last time, if ever, that we had an exchange like that. Maybe my bar mitzvah? He must've done some real soul searching while he was away. Mom's illness really shook him up. I was deeply touched by his opening up and expressing his feelings toward me. Could I do the same to Jessica and Ryan?

I opened my car door and jumped in. Before closing the door, Dad called out, "Hey, Money Man…see you tomorrow morning."

"Not you too," I groaned.

"It's got a nice ring to it," he said. "I think this Ingram character with the SEC even liked it."

Great.

I glanced over at the envelopes I had tossed onto the passenger's seat, then turned back toward Dad. "Oh, I almost forgot. Do you and Mom like the show *Feldstein and Friends?*"

"Your mom loves it. We watched some old episodes while in Berlin. Why?"

"Great! Remind me to tell you about it tomorrow," I said before shutting the car door and driving off.

I was pumped, eager to get home so I could read through Dad's proposals and comb through the SEC report. I tried calling Jessica from the car so I could share the great news. I called her cell because it was already after ten. With Ryan back in school, he *should've* already been in bed, and I didn't want the home phone to wake him.

Her phone just rang. I called again. Same thing, no answer. I started to worry, fearing she and Ryan were in the midst of yet another blowup, and I wasn't there to intervene. My good mood started to deflate. I had been hopeful and optimistic that Ryan was turning the corner since I confiscated his phone earlier in the week for disrespecting Jessica. Ryan had shown some early signs of being more cooperative at home, even taking his dishes off the table after dinner without prodding. In fact, he had shown enough improvement in his attitude that Jess and I agreed to give him back his phone on Saturday, believing that maybe he learned a lesson. I was furious with myself for having let Ryan dupe me. We had clearly made the wrong decision to reward him so soon. The tension at home had to stop. The status quo with Ryan was simply no longer acceptable. As I exited the highway, I ran through the various kinds of punishment we could deliver that would finally have an impact and cause him to change his behavior. I was at a complete loss.

After several failed attempts to reach Jess's cell phone, I finally tried our home number while stopped at a light. Five rings later, Jessica finally answered. I prepared myself to hear what he had done wrong this time.

"Hi, are you on your way home?" she asked, sounding rushed and out of breath.

"Yes, I'll be there in a few minutes. What's going on?"

In the background, I could hear Ryan shouting, "Mom, come on, Mom, come on . . ."

"I gotta go," she said.

"Wait, what's happened now? What's going on?"

"Marty, I've got to get back to Ryan. We're in the middle of a close game of ping-pong. See you soon, bye," she said before hanging up on me.

"Thank you, Lord!" I shouted.

I sighed, turned up the radio, and smiled.

41

"I'm still having a hard time believing it," I said to Danny and Freddie as they sat next to each other at the conference table. The boys' khaki pants and blazers from their earlier summer office visit reverted to their usual jeans and hoodies.

Danny leaned back in his chair, his bony, hairless arms confidently folded across his chest. "Pretty awesome, right?"

I shut the door behind me and took a seat across from them. "You guys should've seen my face when I read the president's tweet. I about passed out from shock. How in the world did the app end up on that security agent's phone?"

Danny smiled. "That's the really wild part. Freddie had the great idea to use our marketing money to pay Sasha Touché to promote the app."

"Sasha who?" I asked.

"Touché," Freddie said with his usual bluntness. "She's a pretty hot internet personality."

"She's a social influencer," Danny further explained. "Anyway, one of her four million followers is Lindsey Thompson."

I shook my head in confusion. "Sorry, guys, I'm not following."

"Lindsey is Secret Service Agent Thompson's daughter," Freddie said, telling me the story as if they were an old married couple that finished each other's sentences. "She put our app on her dad's phone because he walks the family's goldendoodle, Maggie, every night. She didn't want him to step in any crap while on his walk."

"Seriously?" I said, dumbfounded.

"True story," Danny chimed back in.

"Tell Money Man about the alarm," Freddie giddily blurted out.

"Why don't you tell him?" Danny snapped back, apparently annoyed he'd have to hear about it again, whatever *it* was.

Freddie smirked. "So, it was getting dark outside when the ambassador greeted Agent Thompson at the front door of the embassy. As they were walking toward the limo, the ambassador hears this big fart come from Thompson."

I gave them a confused look. "What?"

Danny interjected, "He didn't really rip one. It was the app's alarm going off...was supposed to be a buzzer sound, but Lindsey had the app set to the fart noise by accident."

"We had the developers put that sound effect on an early beta version as a joke...it was my idea," Freddie proclaimed.

"Okay, now that's really weird, but pretty amusing." I laughed out loud.

Freddie took back over. "So, the ambassador stopped to look back at Thompson right before he was about to step in a pile of dog shit on the road. Thompson pointed the hazard out just in the nick of time...and the rest is history."

"That's what they call the network effect," Danny said, sliding a piece of paper to me. It was a letter from Google's director of strategic operations, expressing an interest in acquiring the crap app and requesting an initial meeting.

"This came in the mail yesterday. Would you mind calling him and seeing what this is about?" Danny asked. "We'd like you to represent us in negotiations."

"*If* we even want to sell," Freddie added.

I was speechless. The irony of the situation was more than apparent. I had no intention to approve the money for their venture, but figured they'd learn a thing or two about the real world when they failed. But now I was the one getting schooled.

"Wow, guys. This is just incredible." I scanned the letter. "You literally saved the world, and now it looks like you're going to get a nice fat payoff as well." The preliminary numbers mentioned in the proposal were staggering.

"We couldn't have done it without you. Thanks for all your help," Danny said.

"Yeah, thanks for believing in us, Money Man," Freddie echoed.

If they only knew.

On the way back to my office, I was still baffled by their farfetched success story. Did their creation really stumble into altering the course of history? Were they really about to sell it for a ton of money? I was envious. Not so much of their success, but the way they did it. No fear of failure, not worrying about the risks or potential loss of capital. They just did it. I relished my small role in the whole thing.

Back in my office, I woke my large desk monitor to see my screen was full of green. Trading closed a half hour earlier, and virtually all our positions were up nicely on the day. I took the impressive gains in stride. The latest news briefing summed up the action.

•

Bizline News Update: Wednesday, September 26, 4:30 p.m. ET

S&P 500 notches new record high along with other major world indexes. Global economy continues to expand. President Pruitt announces economic summit with China planned for early next year.

•

I snatched the report tracking our firm's assets under management off the printer. Not surprisingly, we hit a new record high that day along with the market—$516 million. I stared at the chart, letting my eyes roll up, down, then back up the roller coaster black and white line that depicted the correction's impact on our clients' nest eggs. On paper, the dramatic drop that began in June and fully recovered by October didn't capture the story and raw emotions of the episode. If one hadn't paid attention, you might never have known about the carnage over that stretch. A few months earlier, the world was seemingly coming to an end. And now, everything was going well again. Was it worth all the stress and anxiety? With our assets at a new record high there was something to be said for tuning out the noise in life.

I scanned the list of clients and their account values under the chart. JD, Mrs. Benoit, Mitch Satir, the Gillmans, and virtually all of our clients had more money in their accounts now than they did at the start of the year. Even Evan Lanter, who I thought was being poached by Bill Fredrington, was happy. Not only did he express his satisfaction with our management, he referred a good friend of his to me during a recent lunch meeting. Things were, indeed, back on track. Even so, I knew that it was only a matter of time until the next trouble spot. As head of the firm, I needed to keep the right perspective and keep my emotions in check to get through it.

I crumpled the page into a tight ball and took aim at the trash can. With my arm cocked and ready to release, I thought of our clients and the confidential account values and names that were listed on that sheet. I put the wadded-up paper down on my desk and did my best to iron out the crinkles with the side of my hand, before sliding it into the shredder beside my desk. The machine chewed and chopped the page into countless tiny pieces as the steady, monotone, humming sound soothed my ears. I'd never felt so sanguine about the future.

42

Jessica and I took our seats ten rows back from center stage. The martini I downed while we hung out in the VIP reception room before the show was starting to kick in. The lights dimmed and JD walked out onto the stage. The audience, largely made up of Beth Am congregants and their guests, welcomed him with a mixture of rowdy applause and cheers.

"Thank you so much. Before we bring out the man everyone came to see, I want to give special thanks to everyone that helped make this incredible evening possible," JD began as he addressed the audience that filled The Tabernacle in downtown Atlanta. Unsurprisingly, he appeared as comfortable on the stage of a concert hall in front of a couple thousand people as he did on the bema of the synagogue. It was JD's idea to have the show at the performance hall rather than at the temple to give it a special gala-like feel. Plus, the bigger venue had allowed him to sell more tickets.

"I'd especially like to acknowledge our financial sponsors for tonight's amazing event. Without their generosity and their support for those less fortunate, this wouldn't have been possible: Bryer Steel, the Linteen Group, Standerman Automotive, the Candler family, Edgar Trading, Zellen Jewelers, and Kaplan Capital Management."

As JD mentioned our firm, I looked over my shoulder at my parents, who were in the row behind me. My dad returned my gaze with a grin and a wink of approval. Mrs. Benoit was sitting next to my mother, looking more radiant than I had ever seen her. My parents and I really wanted to have her as our guest given her long tenure as a client and close bond to our family. I made a point to tell her before the show in the VIP lounge how amazing she looked in her black evening dress. She told me she was wearing the diamond earrings her husband Simon had given her on the occasion of their twenty-fifth wedding anniversary. She was delighted to be out.

Sitting in that auditorium, I had nothing on my mind other than being there with my friends and family. I took in a couple of long, deep breaths and exhaled. I was ready to let go and enjoy myself.

"Now, I'm going to get off the stage so we can all hear the man you all came to see. Let's give a very warm welcome to the one and only... Mr. Barry Feldstein," JD said as he exited stage left and Feldstein walked out from the right to rapturous applause. He was sporting his signature dark suit, white shirt, and blue tie. There was nothing but a microphone stand and a wooden stool with a tall plastic bottle of water on it waiting for him at center stage.

Feldstein smiled at the crowd, picked up the mic, and began. "Thank you, thank you so much. Good evening. It's great to be back here in Atlanta performing at The Tabernacle...and I must say, what an authentic venue for this event. We're in this historic place of worship, we've got a rabbi in the house, an audience filled with congregants, and a Middle-Eastern-looking valet guy at the door who just peeled off in my car. It's a rental, so I'm not too concerned."

The audience broke into laughter.

"I suppose I'll still have to tip him...even though, the sign *clearly said*...complimentary valet...two words that would set my dad off like nobody's business...complimentary valet. Growing up, my dad drilled a lot of his virtuous principles like...the Feldsteins *do not* valet our cars... into my head. Being the child of immigrants, my dad couldn't bring himself to pay someone to simply spare him the inconvenience of walking a few steps. He was so adamant and dogmatic like he was following a God-given commandment. Wait a minute—maybe that's it? Where's Rabbi Aron?"

Feldstein turned his head to the side of the stage where JD walked off moments earlier.

"Rabbi, does the Torah say anything about self-parking, perhaps a commandment sandwiched somewhere between coveting your neighbor's wife and listening to false prophets? And God spoke unto the children of Israel, with a shout-out to Larry and Judy Feldstein, *Thou shalt not valet.*" Feldstein chanted the commandment slowly with a deep God-like voice.

The crowd was really getting going at this point.

"I'm serious, nothing would irritate my dad more than being pressured to valet park his car. I can still see it like it was yesterday. The family, all six of us crammed into the Oldsmobile, heading out for dinner."

Feldstein stood erect, shrugging his shoulders and arms in tightly like he was packed into sardine can.

"As soon as we'd enter a restaurant parking lot, you could see Dad physically entering a state of hyperawareness, scouring the lot for any signs of a parking attendant. Over the years, he developed a finely tuned, *valet-dar* that was set off if men in black vests, clip-on ties, carrying large wads of one-dollar bills breached a twenty-foot perimeter of the car. Red pylon cones cordoning off parking spots instantly put him on a Defcon One alert, requiring aggressive countermeasures."

I laughed, thinking about how the Clauskys might want to tweak their app to alert Feldstein's dad.

"I can still see the puzzled faces of those poor valet guys, perched at the front of the restaurant, waiting for my dad to open his door, step out, and politely hand him the keys. Instead, Dad would shake his head like he was turning down a panhandler on the street corner, then roll the car a few feet forward before letting my mother and three sisters out. Dad and I would literally drive around the neighborhood until we could find a spot."

Feldstein walked up to the front of the stage. As he looked down at the crowd, it felt like he was talking directly to us as he continued with his bit. "But the sign said it's *complimentary, it's free*, I'd plead with him. Can we go back to the restaurant? Please...I'm starving. Just give him your keys."

Feldstein pointed to someone in the audience behind me. "I bet this gentleman down here has heard that before from one of his kids. You know what I'm talking about, right?"

I glanced back and realized he was talking with my dad.

"Sir, how many laps would you go before giving in?" he asked.

"Ten!" Dad enthusiastically shouted back.

I'm sure Dad was thinking about how well he'd get along with Feldstein's father.

"Ten...that's the best you got. My dad would drive around that block a hundred times if he had to. He was a man deeply stuck to his principles. 'If it's so free, then why am I paying?' he'd say. 'Dad, it's a tip, it's optional,' I'd tell him. Which leads to another one of Dad's core principles and why I'll be taking care of the valet tonight...only a *schmuck* doesn't tip."

•

I, along with everyone else, laughed a lot over the next hour during Feldstein's set. Afterward, Jessica and I stayed around for while talking with my parents and then JD and his new girlfriend, Alexa. The two held hands as we all compared notes on the funniest parts of Feldstein's performance. Being that it was the first time I had met her, I was struck by the fact that she wasn't like what I would've imagined. Attractive, but not over the top good-looking. Talkative, but not bursting with charisma. She had more of a thoughtful, natural, warmth, and charm to her.

JD pulled me aside as Jessica and Alexa chatted.

"She seems very cool," I said, preempting any question about what I thought of her.

"Very!" he said. "She laughed her ass off the entire show, which says a lot."

The fact that he didn't say a word about her looks or lewd comments about her sexual appetite said a lot about him, and how this relationship was impacting him.

"Gotta hand it to you for pulling this off!" I told him, changing the subject.

He put his arm around my shoulders. "Kap, it's a good day! Glad you were part of it!"

Driving home, I was at ease and satisfied. I wanted to hold on to that feeling. I looked over at Jessica, and a wave of emotion washed over me. I was lucky to have her and Ryan in my life. I vowed not to take them for granted. I would do my best to be a more emotionally present husband and father.

"Love you," I said, taking my right hand off the wheel to give Jessica's hand a tight squeeze.

She looked back at me lovingly.

43

Two hard taps on the door interrupted JD's concentration. He was reviewing his bank statements online, which was a recent undertaking, and was pleased with his credit card and checking account balances. He glanced down at his watch, confirming the time. He hadn't given the half-hour 4:30 p.m. appointment on Thursday, October 4, much thought since Susan added it to his calendar earlier in the week. All the entry said was "Areto—Prospective New Congregant." Promoting the synagogue to potential new congregants was one of JD's favorite parts of the job, and he was damn good at it. His introductory meetings, which usually followed a meet and greet with Rabbi Borowitz, involved getting some personal background, detailing the shul's extensive programming, and gently pushing the initial membership discount offer.

JD closed the banking app, slid his blazer over his French-cuffed shirt, and opened his office door.

Rabbi Borowitz's heavy frame practically filled the doorway. "Good afternoon, Rabbi Aron, are you ready for your meeting with Ms. Areto?"

"Absolutely, I was just finishing the draft of my sermon for Saturday," JD said to his senior clergyman.

Rabbi Borowitz stepped aside, revealing a woman that was standing behind him and to his right. As she came into full view, JD was struck by a massive adrenaline rush. He could barely refrain from blurting out a name that he hadn't uttered in months.

Bathsheba!

"Rabbi Aron, I'd like you to meet Monique Areto," Borowitz said.

Monique! Fitting.

JD reflexively shook her hand, drilling the name Monique Areto into his head so he would never forget it. Her skin was as soft as he imagined, but her shake was firm and businesslike. At point-blank range, her penetrating green eyes made him hyperaware. He tried to decipher as much about her as he could from their initial exchange, but her spellbinding glare disoriented him.

"Monique recently moved here from Chicago and is thinking about joining the synagogue. I told her you'd be a *much* better person than I to talk to about what the younger generation does in this city for fun and, equally important, what Beth Am's social programming has to offer," Borowitz said before taking a couple of steps backward to excuse himself. "I'll leave you two to talk."

It had been a couple of months since JD gave up his search for her. Now there she was, not more than two feet right in front of him. Monique Areto. Holy shit!

JD escorted her to a chair in front of his desk, his heart palpitating at twice its normal rate. He couldn't help but admire her shapely figure as she elegantly settled into the seat. She looked as good as he remembered. And still no ring.

JD took the matching brown leather chair beside her rather than sit directly facing her across his large wooden desk.

Her self-confidence radiated off his office walls. Her commanding presence and smooth, controlled mannerisms led JD to size her up as a successful professional.

She clutched her hands together across her knee. "I was actually at services here a few months ago," she said with a matter-of-fact tone.

"No kidding," JD said, playing it cool. "And when was that?" JD thought back to that memorable Friday night and his subsequent slow-motion video analysis that set him off on his fanatical quest to find her.

"It was back in June. I was in Atlanta for work and needed to say mourner's kaddish for my late father. I had a plane to catch. Otherwise, I would've hung around and introduced myself."

Yahrzeit...I knew it!

He congratulated himself for picking up on that clue. It also explained why she wasn't on Susan's list since it didn't include non-member guests.

JD nodded along with Monique's story, clinging to every word, looking for subtle keys to her inner soul.

"Tell me, Monique, how did you find Beth Am?" JD asked, looking to flush out any connections they might have.

"I googled the nearest synagogue to the hotel I was staying at," she said.

JD thought about how the Google search would fit into his inevitable retelling of the story of how they met to his friends. Random or preordained?

"Sorry about your father...did he pass recently?" he asked, putting together pieces of her character profile to build a mosaic like an experienced FBI investigator.

"No, he's been gone fifteen years. Sudden heart attack."

No need to console, just build the relationship and get more information.

"It's nice you still say mourner's kaddish for him every year," JD said.

Her cool stare was borderline hypnotic. JD struggled to stay on track. Was she deconstructing him as much as he was her? He couldn't process her essence and the meaning of her reemergence in his life.

"Honestly, it's really important to my mother that I do it. I'm not too observant. She also wants me to join a synagogue now that I've moved here. I've watched some of Beth Am's streaming services as part of my due diligence...I'm impressed...*especially* with you, Rabbi Aron."

Ironic.

JD picked up on her shifting demeanor, taking on a flirtatious tone. Had *she* been stalking *him*?

He gleamed his movie star smile. "Thank you, I aim to please," he said, catching himself slipping into his naturally playful mode. Since he began dating Alexa, he was determined not to engage in salacious, suggestive conversation with other women. He was enjoying his first meaningful, monogamous relationship since his divorce, both he and Alexa recently agreeing not to date other people. But, Bathsheba was back! Just when he had put her behind him and moved on. Why now, God?

JD doubled down on his efforts to keep the conversation flowing on a professional level, at least until he could properly digest the significance of her reappearance. "Monique, what kind of work do you do?"

She slowly uncrossed her toned, slender legs, then recrossed them in the other direction, further ensnaring JD into her seductive trap.

She lifted her hands and pressed the palms together under her chin, as if in a praying position. "I'm an attorney."

Bet she's a dragon slayer in the courtroom.

"Really, what kind?"

"Intellectual property."

He was impressed, but it wasn't the answer JD expected.

Monique paused. Then offered, "I specialize in business litigation."

Bingo!

"Sounds like rewarding work," he said.

JD bobbed his head, growing self-conscious that she'd find his conversation trite as he squelched his natural urge to take things in a more provocative direction. "You must be busy," he spat out.

"Yeah, it's very demanding at times. Since transferring to my firm's Atlanta office over the summer, I've been totally swamped. But, I just finished a big case and I'm ready and *available* to explore my new community."

Stressing *available* was a thinly veiled message to JD that she was trolling for a date. He didn't bite. Not yet.

"And did you win…the case?"

She leaned forward toward JD and spoke softly. "Rabbi Aron…I always win."

Her self-assurance about knocked him out of his chair. A feisty, powerful tigress! And he was her prey. Was he compatible with someone that aggressive, smart, and powerful? Perhaps. But she was throwing him off-balance. He was the one that usually controlled the tempo of the pursuit.

Composure, JD, composure.

JD struggled for direction. Succumbing to Monique's advances would almost certainly derail his ongoing relationship with Alexa. Was he willing to risk that? He desperately wanted closure with Bathsheba, not left wondering, "What if?" He panned his eyes across his office, grasping at anything that could help guide him before looking up in search of divine intervention. In that moment, he found his answer.

44

I threw on some clothes and headed out the door. It was a dreary and misty early October morning. Thankfully traffic was light for a Tuesday. Sunny Side Up was fairly quiet when I arrived. I walked past the vacant hostess stand and through the maze of tables to get to JD who was already sitting in a booth in the back corner of the diner. We hadn't seen each other since the night of the big Feldstein show a month earlier.

"What's up, Kap? Good to see you buddy," he said as we shook hands.

I slid onto the cushiony red vinyl bench across from him just as a graying older waiter with thick black-rimmed glasses and a stubbly face approached our table. We ordered a couple of toasted sesame bagels with cream cheese and some orange juice.

"So…you still basking in the glory of your big night?" I asked.

"Absolutely. Check this out." JD pulled out his phone and swiped through photos of him and Feldstein taken backstage before the show. "This one is my favorite." He held up a shot of the two of them standing side by side, arms across each other's shoulder like they were close friends.

"You need to frame that on your office wall!" I said. "It was an amazing night, JD. Really, job well done. I would imagine the powers that be at synagogue were pleased?"

"The board was really happy. Even Borowitz had a good time and told me he loved it. And more importantly, we ended up raising a few hundred thousand for our community service fund. And thanks again for your support. I need to call your dad and thank him as well for your firm's sponsorship."

"I'm sure he'd enjoy hearing from you. They're in Palm Desert on vacation right now so you'll have to wait until he's back."

I settled into the booth, and JD and I chatted amicably for a few minutes, talking about one another's families and enjoying the morning. Then, JD reached into his briefcase and pulled out a large white envelope.

"Now," he said, passing it to me, "as your reward for being such a great friend and financial advisor, I've got a present for you."

I cocked my head warily at the "Kaplan" written in large letters across the front.

"Go ahead, open it," he said, grinning.

I sighed and tore the envelope open. Inside was a single white piece of paper with "Annual Budget" at the top. As I scanned the spreadsheet, I saw a detailed breakdown of JD's estimated income and expenses for the coming year.

"Wow, is this what I think it is?" I asked in disbelief.

"Yep, it's a budget, baby!" he replied.

As hard as it was to admit, I almost started to cry, knowing that I had a positive impact on him. I couldn't tell if he saw that his gesture hit an emotional nerve or not.

I quickly composed myself and started scanning the budget. "Let's see here. Travel, ten thousand dollars . . . seems a bit light, don't you think? You could drop that in one night in Vegas."

"Maybe, but I'm going to try to tone some things down a bit this coming year. And, besides, I have separate line items for gambling and hookers." He smirked. "Just kidding, Kaplan, that's all included in the ten thousand dollars."

We both laughed.

"Hey, I'm really glad you're taking your financial future more seriously, JD," I told him.

"That I am. I actually put a lot of thought into this. You know, you're right, if I don't pay better attention, I'll go broke. And as you know, I don't want to have any more uncomfortable, mortifying moments. Getting turned down for an important purchase is *way* too embarrassing."

"I understand. Although that situation in the doctor's office ended up working out all right in the end. And your timing on putting the money back in the market was incredible. Speaking of the doctor's office, how're things going with Alexa?" I said, whispering her name softly.

JD flipped the budget over on the table and leaned toward me. "On that note, I've been meaning to tell you something."

"What's up?"

"Remember Bathsheba?"

"Of course. Your mystery queen."

"Well, I found her. Or, should I say, she found me."

JD recounted how this beautiful woman named Monique Areto suddenly appeared from behind Rabbi Borowitz at his office doorway the week earlier.

"I could tell right away it was her, and from the second I shook her hand, it was clear she was this shrewd, strong woman. Kaplan, believe me, she's used to getting what she wants. She told me about how she had just won this huge legal case and hadn't had any fun for months…translation—she was ready to unleash."

"Whoa. That's insane. Sounds like you met your match."

"No kidding. So basically, *she* was asking *me* out," JD said.

"What'd you do?"

"I sat there staring at her asking myself why God sent her to me. Was it destiny? Was it a test? I prayed for answers, and suddenly, it all became clear. I thought about Alexa and how well things were going with her. I've told you we have this real spiritual connection. Here's the part that really makes me believe God has a plan for all of us, Kaplan. If it wasn't for my pursuit of Bathsheba, I wouldn't have gotten together with Alexa. Seeing her in services that Friday night was the spark that started this chain reaction. If that doesn't blow your mind, I don't know what will," JD said, pointing both his index fingers at the top of his head.

This guy's got issues.

I bit into my sesame seed bagel. "That's an interesting thought. Now, get back to the story…what happened next?"

JD took a swig of his pulpy, bitter orange juice and grimaced. "Kaplan...in the end, I thought the best course of action was to treat this goddess no differently than any other single woman that was interested in joining the synagogue."

"So, you *did* have sex with her?"

"Hah! Very funny. No, I politely gave her the name of the president of the sisterhood and recommended she attend some of their wonderful programs. Of course, I thanked her for coming in and offered her the new member's first year discount."

"Wow, I didn't know you had that kind of restraint," I said.

"Honestly, I didn't know either. Crazy story, right? In the meantime, things are going great with Alexa. She's really cool and loves football. I'm optimistic." He had a twinkle in his eye.

"You've really grown, JD. Proud of you!"

JD turned the budget paper back over and handed it over to me. "Now, do me a favor. Review this budget and let's get back together and discuss."

"Will do, but we should probably do that over a beer."

"Now, don't think this means I don't need you to keep making me a lot of fucking money. In the meantime . . ." JD raised his glass of orange juice.

We clinked our glasses over the center of the table.

JD downed the last of his OJ and looked at his watch. "Shit, I better finish up and get going, got a sermon to write for this weekend."

"What's the topic?"

"Not sure yet. You got any good life lessons I can use?"

I reflected for a moment. "Well...over the last several months, I've learned a lot about not losing a connection with things that matter most in life...family...friends...personal relationships. You know, trying to be less distracted and more present. Meditation has helped." I pictured that struggling beetle overturned on its back that I had the presence of mind to assist after my early morning jog months earlier. Since then, I occasionally closed my eyes and visualized the tiny bug turning over and crawling back into the flower bed. The exercise helped me stay centered and grounded. "How can you expect to flip a beetle back over if you can't even see it needs your help?" I suggested.

JD looked back at me contemplatively. "Meditation? Good for you!" He paused. "A beetle on its back. Hmm. That's not bad, maybe I can use that."

"Really?"

"Nah. Who's gonna relate to that? You stick to finance and I'll write the sermons, Kap, it's all good!"

ACKNOWLEDGEMENTS

This story is fiction. I am not Marty Kaplan, nor are the other characters based on my family, friends, colleagues, or clients. With that being said, the truth is that some figures are totally imagined while others are the collective amalgamation and manifestation of colorful individuals I've come across over the course of my personal and professional life. Thank you all for your inadvertent input!

This book took me several years to complete and I deeply appreciate the support of many that encouraged and helped me with this project along the way. Thank you to David, Roslyn, Gerald, Jimmy, Jason, Monica, Brian, Steven, Micah, Paul, and Michael for being my beta readers and providing really insightful, candid feedback. Thanks to Lori and Rachel for their thoughtful and constructive editorial suggestions as well as their feedback and tips aimed at improving my writing (still a work in progress). And to Steph for handling the interior formatting and Bailey for an awesome cover design!

Special thanks to my wife Linda and sons, Jordan and Koby, for allowing me to drift off into my world of writing isolation on many evenings and weekends so I could accomplish my goal of writing my first novel. Through this incredible experience, I, for one, hope to see the beetle more often in my own life.

ABOUT THE AUTHOR

Steven Sheldon has been a practicing wealth manager in Houston for almost twenty years. While he's written extensively on the subject of personal finance, *See the Beetle* is his first novel. He's a graduate of The University of Texas and has a master's degree from Tulane University's business school. He lives in Houston, Texas with his wife, and has two sons.

For more information go to www.seethebeetle.com.